SHAKESPEARIAN FANTASIAS

"I have just completed my *Shakespearian Fantasias*.
This is the best work that I have ever done,
and the most original."

> Esther Singleton
> Letter to Bernard R. Ward
> May 6, 1929

SHAKESPEARIAN FANTASIAS

Adventures in the Fourth Dimension

By
Esther Singleton

Introduction and Annotations
by James A. Warren

Published by
VERITAS PUBLICATIONS
Cary, North Carolina

This edition published by

Veritas Publications
Bringing Hidden Truths to Light

Copyright © 2019
by James A. Warren

First edition

Privately printed, in the United States of America.

Copyright, 1929
by Esther Singleton

[Note: The original copyright was not renewed.]

Foreword

F A N T A S I A , a musical term from the Italian, means a free working-up of a theme, a fanciful air, not restricted to the laws of composition. Like the kindred words, fantastic and fantastical, F A N T A S I A describes something that exists only in the imagination, or fancy, having the nature of a phantom, apparent and not real, whimsical, odd, capricious, grotesque.

The above makes obvious the reason why I have chosen the word F A N T A S I A for these dream-stories, where visions come and go; where the pink and purple heather of autumn blooms beside the flowers of spring and midsummer; and where time, as we understand it in our waking hours, has no existence.

E. S.

New York
53 East 87th Street
4 October, 1929

Editor's Introduction

Esther Singleton had a wide-ranging curiosity—and the ability to write interesting books about the subjects that most interested her: more than sixty all told, on subjects ranging from music, art, architecture, cathedrals, furniture, history, travel . . . to Shakespeare.

Her interest in these subjects wasn't surface level only; she sought to master a subject—to understand its ins and outs—before writing about it. When approaching historical subjects, she wanted to understand not just what happened, but *how* and *why* events unfolded the way they did. Those who knew her commented on her phenomenal memory, her ability to have at the tip of her tongue not only relevant facts on an endless stream of topics, but also long stretches of Shakespeare's plays. They noted her insistence on researching a subject thoroughly before beginning to write about it; then, once things were clear in her head, writing very quickly.

It is these qualities—curiosity and the desire to understand her subjects fully—that led to her receptivity, in the final decade of her life, to the question of who wrote "Shakespeare's" works, and, eventually, to her conclusion that they came from the pen of Edward de Vere, 17th Earl of Oxford.

She had a life-long interest in Shakespeare and read his works continuously, yet wrote only two books on the subject. The first, *The Shakespeare Garden*, published in 1922, is a well-known account of gardens in Shakespeare's day and how their shady walks, pleached alleys and flower-wreathed arbors lent themselves to *re*-creation—to renewing the body

Editor's Introduction

and refreshing the mind and spirit.

The Shakespeare Garden did not, though, directly discuss the plays and the events and characters in them. Nor did any of her other books—not, that is, until the final year or two of her life, when she wrote *Shakespearian Fantasias: Adventures in the Fourth Dimension. Fantasias* was published at the end of 1929, only eight months before Singleton's death. This delightful book is unknown to most readers today because it has been out of print for so many decades and because very few copies exist in libraries or are available from antiquarian booksellers.

In contrast to *The Shakespeare Garden, Shakespearian Fantasias* was not Singleton's usual non-fictional treatment of a subject. It was, in fact, her one and only novel—a novel she described just as she was finishing it as "the best work that I have ever done, and the most original."[1]

So what was it about this book that made it the "most original" and "best work" of Singleton's life? I believe the inspiration for it came from two sources. One was her love of Shakespeare's plays "that," she wrote, "I know so well, that I have read and reread since childhood until they have become bone of my bone and flesh of my flesh."[2]

But it was the second source of inspiration that was decisive—that turned her to fiction for the first time in her life—because that was the only way she could convey the amazement and satisfaction she felt upon concluding that the works known to us as Shakespeare's had been written by Edward de Vere.

Let's examine those two factors in that order.

Drawing on the term fantasia, which implies a world of imagination, fancy or whimsy, Singleton presents us with

---

[1] Letter to Bernard R. Ward, May 6, 1929. Reprinted in Appendix 4.
[2] See Appendix 1.

Editor's Introduction

eleven fantasies or dreams, in which the narrator, a woman from the 20th century, mysteriously finds herself transplanted into the world of many of Shakespeare's plays. Here's a list of the principal setting for each fantasia, and the character or characters that served as her, and our, guide or guides through each of them:

Fantasia 1: Datchet Mead
    Setting: *The Merry Wives of Windsor*
    Guide: Mistress Anne Page

Fantasia 2: In Illyria
    Setting: *Twelfth Night*
    Guide: Lady Olivia, Maria, Viola

Fantasia 3: An Afternoon with Autolycus
    Setting: *The Winter's Tale*
    Guide: Autolycus

Fantasia 4: Under the Greenwood Tree
    Setting: *As You Like It*
    Guides: Jacques, the Duke

Fantasia 5: Lady Sylvia
    Setting: *The Two Gentlemen of Verona*
    Guide: Sir Valentine

Fantasia 6: By Spangled Starlight Sheen
    Setting: *A Midsummer Night's Dream*
    Guides: Puck, Helena

Fantasia 7: The Merry Mad-Cap Lord
    Setting: *Love's Labour's Lost*
    Guide: Berowne

Fantasia 8: In Such a Night
    Setting: *The Merchant of Venice*
    Guides: Lorenzo, Antonio

Fantasia 9: They
    Setting: *Macbeth*
    Guide: Khama (one of the Weird Sisters)

Editor's Introduction

Fantasia 10: Saucy Beatrice
   Setting: *Much Ado About Nothing*
   Guide: Beatrice

Fantasia 11: Cock-A-Doodle-Doo
   Settings: *The Tempest, Hamlet, Two Gentlemen of Verona, Cymbeline, Romeo and Juliet, Henry V, Julius Caesar, Macbeth, A Midsummer Night's Dream*
   Guide: Ariel's Cock of the Dawn

The narrator, whose name we never learn, meets many of Shakespeare's most interesting characters, some of whom confide in her reasons for their actions not fully spelled out in the plays. Maria in *Twelfth Night*, for instance, explains that she thought up the trick on Malvolio in order to attract the attentions of Sir Toby Belch, with the goal of marrying him.

One reviewer compared *Shakespearian Fantasias* to Charles and Mary Lamb's *Tales from Shakespeare*, which gave young and not-so-young readers an accessible introduction to Shakespeare's works, which are, after all, not easy reads for first-time readers given the changes in the English language over the past 400 years. Like the Lambs' book, Singleton's helps modern readers acquire an appreciation and understanding of the plays by imaginatively recounting stories from them. Her love of Shakespeare and her creative interweavings of a woman from the present day with many of Shakespeare's characters in their native settings make these fantasias a delight to read, to sink into, to use as escapes, for a time, from daily concerns. They charm readers, and will perhaps seduce them into reading the original plays in full.

Singleton's second source of inspiration, and the principal reason why I became interested in resurrecting *Shakespearian Fantasias* by preparing this new annotated

Editor's Introduction

edition, is the prominence it gives to Edward de Vere, tying him to authorship of "Shakespeare's" plays and poems. The more open references to him are more general in nature, such as those to viols and other musical instruments that de Vere brought back from Italy (page 14), or the descriptions of the subtle and delicious scent of Italian perfume known as "Lord Oxford's perfume" that was all the rage among court ladies and gallants after de Vere returned from Italy. (138, 202)

The less obvious references include the insertion of the Earl of Oxford in the guise of three of Shakespeare's characters into three of the fantasias: as Jacques in "Under the Greenwood Tree," as Berowne in "The Merry Mad-Cap Lord," and as Benedick in "Saucy Beatrice." These characters display characteristics de Vere had in real life, and Singleton's narrator, who encounters all of them, describes them in terms that were actually used to describe de Vere, as in this description of Berowne:

> Lord Berowne was "the most goodly fashioned man I ever saw; from head to foot in form, rare and most absolute." He fascinated me. (140)

Even more interesting, these characters recite poems actually written by Edward de Vere. Jacques, for instance, recites de Vere's *What is Desire?* in the Forest of Arden (*If women could be fair and yet not fond . . .*), and Beatrice recites a shortened version of another of his poems, which she attributes to Benedick (*Is he god in peace or war? . . .*). (83, 202)

She has Berowne, in explaining the nature of Euphuism, make statements that could only have been truthfully made by de Vere.

> "And what is Euphuism?" I asked.
> "Oh, Euphuism," Berowne replied, "is a new literary movement – I am surprised you do not know this when all

Editor's Introduction

Europe is affected by it – to enrich language by graceful rhetoric and choice of words of new fashion. The name came from a book called *Euphues, the Anatomie of Wit*, written by my fellow-worker, John Lyly, and printed a few years ago."

"Do you remember the date?" I asked.

"Oh, yes," Berowne replied, "Euphues appeared in 1579. I am supposed to be Philautus. In the next year, Lyly published *Euphues and his England*, which he dedicated to *me;* and he wrote here: 'whoso compareth the honor of your Lordship's noble house with the fidelity of your ancestors may well say which no other can truly gainsay, *Vero nihil verius.*'" (146)

Singleton also provides her thoughts on why Shakespeare's works have been so enduring and so endearing for more than 400 years. Her 20th century narrator—hearing Jaques lamenting that he "met a fool 'n the forest," the Duke describing how "Sweet are the uses of adversity" and Amiens describing how the winter wind is "not so unkind as man's ingratitude"—tells the Duke that "The world hasn't changed in these many hundred years . . . that song might easily have been written today." She then muses to herself about how timeless are so many of Shakespeare's works:

> I realized that a great deal of what we call modern today, with so much superficial assurance and pretentious arrogance, is not progress nor will it be permanent, being but a fleeting phase that our shell-shocked world is passing through before it can right itself again – if it ever will – whereas everlasting is the culture expressed by this forgiving, and kindly, and gracious Duke and by the tender-hearted, although cynical and melancholy, Jaques, lover of beasts and birds and hater of intrigues and shams, cruelty and deceit. Here, in the forest of Arden, I have found the Eternal Verities and all the Humanities; and that is the reason I should like to dwell here. (90)

Editor's Introduction

J. Thomas Looney and "Shakespeare" Identified

In September, 1922, when Singleton published *The Shakespeare Garden*, with its description of "the small and simple garden such as [Shakespeare] had himself at Stratford-on-Avon and such as he walked through when he visited Ann Hathaway in her cottage at Shottery," she believed that William Shakspere of Stratford-upon-Avon was the author of Shakespeare's plays and poems. In October, 1929, when she published *Shakespearian Fantasias*, with its many references to Edward de Vere, she believed that de Vere was the author of Shakespeare's works.

So what happened during that seven year period to change her belief about who the author really was? The answer, Singleton explained in a Statement she wrote, "Was Edward de Vere Shakespeare?" is that between writing the first book and the second she read J. Thomas Looney's *"Shakespeare" Identified in Edward de Vere The Seventeenth Earl of Oxford*, which convinced her that de Vere, not the man from Stratford, was Shakespeare. As she wrote in the Statement, "I now pronounce myself a believer in the theory that Edward de Vere, Earl of Oxford, was the author of the great Shakespearean plays."

But knowing of Singleton's belief in de Vere's authorship raises a second set of questions. Why all these coy references to de Vere in *Fantasias*? Why does she not make a simple declaration in that book of her new belief? Why all the coded language and references that only Oxfordians would even notice, rather than a clear statement that de Vere was the creator of the characters in her fantasias?

The answer is again found in Singleton's Statement, where she describes her deep aversion throughout most of her life even to considering the question of whether anyone other than William Shakspere of Stratford-upon-Avon was the author. Realizing that many other people still have that same

Editor's Introduction

reluctance to question their deeply held belief in Shakspere, she begins her Statement by imploring her readers not to reject out of hand her or her belief in de Vere: "You who read this, I beg you not to condemn me and the theory but to read further on." She then describes the mental process, painful and almost against her will, that she went through as she became convinced of de Vere's authorship. And even more important, she describes how elated she felt at finding that obscure passages in the plays, reread with knowledge of de Vere's authorship and of the details of his life, had become "so clear, so plain, so reasonable, and so delightful."

Singleton withheld the Statement from publication during her lifetime. It was first published in 1940, ten years after her death. Because no summary of Singleton's declaration can do justice to the power of her own words, which have been so successful in opening the minds of people I have shared them with to the idea of de Vere as Shakespeare, I have included it as an appendix to this book. Other appendices bring together appreciations of Singleton and her works by people who knew her and wrote about her during her lifetime or shortly thereafter.

Shakespearian Fantasias was reportedly among the prize acquisitions of Henry Clay Folger, founder of the Folger Shakespeare Library. He was so fascinated by the book that he not only purchased twenty copies to present to friends, but was also negotiating to purchase the original manuscript when Singleton died. He himself died only a few months later. Her family later donated the manuscript to the Library, and it is now a part of the Folger Library's collection.

Editorial Considerations

Shakespearian Fantasias, written by an American author but published privately, has mostly American spelling but mostly early 20th century British punctuation. So what is an

Editor's Introduction

American editor, preparing the book for a mostly American 21st century readership, to do?

Some decisions were easy: modernize the text by removing the blank space between words and punctuation marks, by removing punctuation marks before dashes, by changing "to-day" to "today," "to-night" to "tonight," and "to-morrow" to "tomorrow," and by italicizing titles rather than leaving them inside quotation marks.

A bit trickier was deciding what to do about other aspects of British punctuation, which places colons and semi-colons after quotation marks, but periods/full stops before. I decided to leave them as they were in the original. I made the opposite decision regarding British spellings of words such as "Travellers" and "marvellous," changing them to the modern American English spellings of "Travelers" and "marvelous."

Harder still was deciding how best to standardize the book's formatting. In the original edition, quotations were sometimes indented a quarter inch, sometimes half an inch; sometimes there was a half space between the main text and indented lines, sometimes a full space. Quotations were sometimes proceeded by a colon, sometimes by no punctuation at all.

Hardest of all was deciding what to do about Singleton's singularly odd, yet consistently odd, grammar, which includes what Americans would call a run-on sentence, as in these examples:

> "No, I don't know all," I replied, "I don't know about *you*! Please tell me, if I may be permitted to make such a request."
>
> "How did *you* get here?" she retorted, "that is more extraordinary. Now *I* am always here."

Should I replace the commas after "replied" and

xi

Editor's Introduction

"retorted" with periods/full stops and capitalize "that" in the second example, or leave things as they are? After much deliberation I left those passages as Singleton wrote them because they capture the phrasings of real-life speech regardless of whether American grammarians would approve.

An easier decision, but still an important one, was whether to identify the sources of literary quotations in footnotes or endnotes. In all cases, I made decisions on the basis of what would be least distractive for modern readers so that their attention could remain focused on the text and the wonderful images it conjures up.

Given Singleton's pride in *Shakespearian Fantasias*, it is with a great deal of pleasure that I am able to bring this delightful book back into print after a gap of almost ninety years. I hope you enjoy it.

Contents

Foreword [by Esther Singleton]   i
Introduction [by Editor]   iii

FANTASIA ONE
    Datchet Mead   3
FANTASIA TWO
    In Illyria   31
FANTASIA THREE
    An Afternoon with Autolycus   51
FANTASIA FOUR
    Under the Greenwood Tree   71
FANTASIA FIVE
    Lady Sylvia   93
FANTASIA SIX
    By Spangled Starlight Sheen   109
FANTASIA SEVEN
    The Merry Mad-Cap Lord   129
FANTASIA EIGHT
    In Such a Night   149
FANTASIA NINE
    They   171
FANTASIA TEN
    Saucy Beatrice   190
FANTASIA ELEVEN
    Cock-A-Doodle-Doo   209

Appendices

Appendix 1
Esther Singleton: "Was Edward de Vere Shakespeare?"   243
Shakespeare Fellowship Newsletter (American), Vol. 1/4 (June/July 1940): 9-10. [Published posthumously; see Editor's Introduction for more information.]

Appendix 2
Esther Singleton: "A Great Courtier"   247
[Review of *The Seventeenth Earl of Oxford* by Bernard M. Ward], *Saturday Review*, July 21, 1928, p. 1049-51.

Appendix 3
Eva Turner Clark: "Introduction"   251
to *The Shakespeare Garden*, 2nd edition (1931) by Esther Singleton. New York: W. F. Payson.

Appendix 4
<u>Other Writings about Esther Singleton</u>

Col. Bernard R. Ward, "An Introduction to Shakespeare,"   255
Shakespeare Pictorial, February 1930, p. 20.

Col. Bernard R. Ward, "A Poetical Alice in Wonderland,"
Shakespeare Pictorial, March 1930, p. 16.

Claire McGlinchee, "Esther Singleton" [Letter],
New York Times, August 31, 1930, p. X7.

Col. Bernard R. Ward, "Miss Esther Singleton,"
Shakespeare Pictorial, September 1930, p. 16.

Shakespeare Fellowship Quarterly, "The Oxford-
Shakespeare Book that Charmed Mr. Folger: Esther Singleton's *Shakespearian Fantasias*," Vol. VII/1 (Jan. 1946): 14.

SHAKESPEARIAN FANTASIAS

Datchet Mead

I STOOD on the Terrace of Windsor Castle in the soft depths of the purplish blue mist — mist like the velvet bloom on plum or grape — which was the most striking feature in the view I had had of this majestic building about an hour ago from the window of the little toy-like train that carried me from London. Gliding rapidly and almost noiselessly over the rails that seemed like glass through the loveliest of sylvan scenery, I had been watching impatiently for Windsor Castle long before it was due. When the noble pile flashed across the little square window of my carriage — there it was and *perfect*. The outline was exactly as I had known it from pictures, with the massive Round Tower conspicuously dominating the long silhouette of wall and with the smaller towers dark against the sky. There was one charm, however, which I had not anticipated and that was the amethystine mist which is always one of the beauties of English scenery. This atmospheric drapery softened all the outlines, threw a glamorous twilight hue over the old walls, and transported Windsor Castle into the land of fairy enchantment.

Although I could not see this bluish haze after I had climbed Castle Hill and was standing on the ramparts, I knew that it was there and that it completely surrounded me and completely enveloped me and that I was actually

Shakespearian Fantasias

breathing this beauty as I was actually breathing the romance of the place. I liked to think that anyone on the train succeeding mine from London who happened to look out of the window at the moment Windsor Castle first appears could (if his eyes were strong enough) have seen me imbedded in this deep, blue mist.

I stood, as I said, on the Terrace with the massive gray walls of the Round Tower behind me and a scarlet-coated British Grenadier with huge bearskin busby walking up and down, giving the one note of bright color to the scene.

Leaning over the wall, I looked about me, enthralled with the beauty of the view. In the far distance I noted Richmond Park and Hampstead Heath, also Burnham Wood, and, nearer, wooded hills and tree-shaded roads. Windsor Forest, with its patriarchal oaks and its rolling glades of emerald velvet, spread out its miles of beauty below the bluff and the serpentine river looped around parks and purled gently through meadows that belong to Spenser and to Shakespeare. Beyond these verdant meadows, so serene and lovely in the silver-gilt sunshine of England, I saw the façade and spires of Eton and realized that I was standing in the very spot where Gray wrote his *Ode on a Distant Prospect of Eton College.*

Everything was so beautiful here and so redolent of song and story that it seemed strange to me to be looking over that expanse of grove, of lawn, and of mead from Windsor's height; and I had the peculiar feeling that the real scene upon which I was gazing was less real than the pictures with which I had been familiar all my life.

My gaze turned from Eton and lingered upon the red roofs of the quaint little town of Windsor nestling below

Datchet Mead

Castle Hill and then it followed the "silver-winding Thames."

I thought of how this peaceful stream had slipped along for many miles from those quiet reaches near Oxford where Alice rowed in the old Sheep's boat[3] among the reeds and rushes and water-lilies, twisting and turning through green meadows spangled with flowers and shaded by willows, past Iffley and Abingdon and Henley and Marlow and Maidenhead, on, on, on to Windsor; and, below Windsor, to Runnymede; and was travelling on, on, on, to London. I looked down on Runnymede and the tiny green islet of Magna Charta, where King John signed that famous document in 1215 — a soft, little islet appearing like a velvet pin-cushion — and then, as I looked back again towards Frogmore, my eyes suddenly lighted on Datchet Mead, where the Merry Wives of Windsor sent Falstaff in the buck-basket to be dumped; and I wondered why it was that Falstaff and Mrs. Page and Mrs. Ford should be so much more real to me than King John and his Barons and even more real than the scarlet-coated sentry, who paced up and down the Terrace, or who, after tightening his white belt and straightening himself up to his full height, posed like a wooden statue in the purple shadows of the great doorway.

"Datchet Mead! Datchet Mead! And the Merry Wives of Windsor!" I exclaimed excitedly.

"Would you like me to show you around Windsor?" a very sweet voice asked me.

---

[3] Alice and the Sheep are fictional characters in Lewis Carroll's *Through the Looking-Glass*.

Shakespearian Fantasias

Turning, I saw an extremely pretty young girl with lovely brown hair, a fresh English complexion, and merry eyes. She was simply, but rather elegantly, dressed in the costume of a young Tudor lady of wealth.

"I should be delighted," I quickly responded.

"I can show you places and people that travelers *never, never* see. I imagine that you are a traveler and that this is your first visit to Windsor, because you have been dreaming so long over the parapet. Just now I heard you scream out so wildly, 'Datchet Mead! Datchet Mead! And the Merry Wives of Windsor!' *That* brought me to your side. I am Mistress Anne Page and sometimes I am called 'sweet Anne Page.'"

"I don't wonder at that," I ventured to say, not knowing how she might accept the compliment which her beauty and her pretty, graceful manners compelled me to express; "but, oh! Mistress Anne Page, how did you get here?"

"How did *you* get here?" she retorted, "that is more extraordinary. Now *I* am always here. People never see me, although I see them."

"I came in the train from London," I replied, "and only arrived about an hour or so ago."

"Oh, I don't mean *that*," she answered, "I mean how did you manage to come into our century and into our Shakespearian World?"

"I haven't the slightest idea," I said.

"Well, it really doesn't matter," she sweetly responded, "you *are* here anyway and I am going to show you around. I am sure my father and mother will desire your acquaintance. Come with me; we have a venison

Datchet Mead

pasty to dinner — Justice Shallow sent us the venison as a present — and wine — and very good Canary it is, too — and pippins and cheese. We have company today. Justice Shallow, his cousin, Master Slender, and Sir Hugh Evans, the Welsh parson — I'm afraid you won't be able to understand anything he says though. He says 'Peds of Roses' and 'Pabylon' and 'Fery well' and he is solemn and serious. My father intends me to marry that silly fool, Slender; and oh! how I hate his 'little wee face with a little yellow beard' — a 'Cain-colored beard' — and his 'stuttering gait.'"

"And *are* you going to marry him?" I asked.

"No, indeed, I am *not*," she exclaimed; and here Mistress Anne gave a series of silvery peals of laughter. Then she began again:

"Master Slender — oh, you must see him — is my father's choice; and such a fool he is, too! All he can talk about is his *Book of Riddles* and Alice Shortcake and dogs and bear-baiting and bears; and he pretends that he has taken the famous bear Sackerson by the chain. I don't believe it. I am awfully afraid of bears; and I believe he is, too. Master Slender is very rich and

> O what a world of vile ill-favor'd faults
> Look handsome in three hundred pounds a year.[4]

"But I don't need Abraham Slender's money. I have a little fortune of my own coming to me when I shall be seventeen — seven hundred pounds and some gold and silver left me by my grandfather; and, besides, my father is going to give me what Sir Hugh Evans calls 'a petter

---

[4] *The Merry Wives of Windsor* (Act III, Scene 4).

penny'; and he often says about me that 'seven hundred pounds and possibilities is goot gifts.'"

Mistress Anne paused for a moment and then continued: "Do you know what Master Slender said when Justice Shallow asked him if he could love me?"

"Well, that would be an easy question for any man to answer," I interrupted.

"Now this was his reply," Mistress Anne went on without taking any notice of my second compliment. "'I will marry her, sir, at your request; but if there be no great love in the beginning, yet Heaven may decrease it upon better acquaintance when we are married and have more occasion to know one another — I hope upon familiarity will grow more contempt; but if you say *marry her*, I will marry her, that I am freely dissolved and dissolutely.'"

Here Mistress Anne laughed again and most merrily, her eyes dancing with humor.

Then she began afresh: "My mother desires me to marry Dr. Caius. Dr. Caius is a French physician. My father always introduces him as 'Master Doctor Caius, the renowned French physician.' He certainly 'abuses the King's English.' He says 'shallenge' and 'troat' for throat and 'little-a-while' and 'mine host of de Jarterre' — he means the Garter Inn, you know — and *'diable! diable!'* and he says to everybody he meets 'By gar, I vill myself have Anne Page'; and, worse still, he says to everybody 'Ay, by gar, de maid is love-a-me; my nursh-a-Quickly tell me so mush'"; and again, after mimicking the French doctor's pronunciation and manner, Anne Page burst forth with her merry laugh that sounded like a peal of little silver bells.

Datchet Mead

"And are you going to marry Dr. Caius?" I questioned.

Anne Page with an expression of petulant disgust on her pretty face exclaimed:

> "Alas! I had rather be set quick i' the earth
> And bowled to death with turnips."[5]

Then, changing her mood, she invitingly said:

"Come along; dinner will soon be ready and I must be getting home. My father always has me serve the wine."

By this time we had walked quite a distance and passed by quaint little houses and tiny shops until we reached a more imposing building, in the front of which a sign hung out over the street bearing the words "The Garter Inn."

"Peep in the window," commanded Anne Page; "there is the Host of the Garter Inn — 'mine host de Jarterre'; that mountain of a man is old Falstaff; that's his page, Robin — and a very saucy boy he is, by the way — and those red-nosed wights are Bardolph, Nym, and Pistol, Falstaff's disgraceful companions."

"I recognize them all," I said.

"You *do?*" she exclaimed wonderingly.

But she went on explaining: "Now Falstaff doesn't live in Windsor: he is only here on a visit — nobody knows why. Some say — you see he is Sir John Falstaff and can go to Court — and so some say Queen Elizabeth told Shakespeare that she wanted to see Falstaff again — and in love — and others say Falstaff and his three companions came here for a lark and to pick pockets. Well; I'm glad they came for one thing. The other night

---

[5] *The Merry Wives of Windsor* (III.4).

Shakespearian Fantasias

Bardolph, Nym, and Pistol seized Master Slender, carried him to the tavern, made him drunk, and afterwards picked his pocket.

"Falstaff has written two letters — exactly alike — one to my mother and the other to Mistress Ford; and he is now trying to get Pistol, or Nym, to deliver them; but they have refused. Now you see he is handing the letters to Robin. Mistress Ford and my mother are called 'The Merry Wives of Windsor' because they are always playing tricks. I think I have inherited some of my mother's ingenuity, for I have contrived a little plan with Fenton — oh, I haven't mentioned Fenton to you, have I? Well; you will find it all out later. So never mind just now. This is the house of Master Doctor Caius that we are coming to. Mistress Quickly is his servant, his 'nursh' he calls her; and, oh dear! what good care she takes of him! She makes nice seacoal fires and brews hot possets for him at night, and she washes, wrings, brews, bakes, scours, dresses meat and drink, makes the beds, is up early and down late, and tries to calm the crazy Frenchman when he gets too excited. There's Mistress Quickly at the casement window now, looking for Dr. Caius. It is time for him to come home to dinner."

"Oh yes, I recognize Mistress Quickly, too," I interpolated.

"You *do?*" said Anne Page again. "How strange! But," she added in a somewhat injured tone, "you didn't know *me.*"

"That's easy to account for," I replied. "You see Mistress Quickly and Falstaff and Nym and Pistol and even Robin are Shakespearian and of the Sixteenth

Datchet Mead

Century; but *you*, sweet Anne Page, belong to all times and periods. We even meet you — although very rarely — in the Twentieth Century. You are the lovely young girl whom we characterize as 'sweet sixteen.' I did not associate you exclusively with Shakespeare when I first saw you, although he has so charmingly perpetuated you."

"Yes, I'm glad I am going to live forever," Anne Page said proudly and confidently; and then, turning a searching glance upon me and through me, asked: "What do you mean by the Twentieth Century?" and then: "Which one of Shakespeare's Plays do you belong to?"

It was fortunate for me that we came to a turning in the street which brought us into a narrow lane so that I did not have to answer, for Anne Page, calling my attention to a half-timbered house with low roof and many gables, said: "That's my home!"

It gave me a queer, eerie feeling to be introduced by Anne Page to her father and her mother, who, in their turn, presented Sir Hugh Evans, Justice Shallow, the latter's nephew, Master Abraham Slender, and, last of all, little William Page, Anne's brother, who almost stared me out of countenance. Everyone was cordial and curious regarding me, and they, all and each, asked me many questions about my clothes and my speech. I also found it hard to understand their pronunciation.

I was much impressed with the handsome Tudor silver on which the dinner was served. There was a gorgeous silver-gilt standing-salt in the centre of the table and all the plates, or "trenchers," were of heavy silver; *but there were no forks!* The famous "venison pasty," of which

Shakespearian Fantasias

Anne Page had spoken, appeared with a great top-crust of rich pastry, the baking-dish standing on an enormous silver platter. I was not a little shocked to see, when we had finished this course, each of our "trenchers" scraped with a special knife into a large silver dish which they called a "voyder." Canary and sack were served to us by sweet Anne Page. For dessert we had custards and sillabub and a beautiful and very artistic sugary confection, which Mrs. Page called a "subtletie" and which she had made herself in honor of the venison pasty.

We finished with pippins and cheese.

"Let us have some music," Mr. Page suggested, rising from the table and walking into the adjoining room, to which we all followed him.

"Do you like music?" he asked, turning to me.

"Oh, indeed I do," I replied. "I am particularly devoted to Wagner. In fact, I am a far more perfect Wagnerite than Bernard Shaw."

"What *is* a Wagnerite?" inquired Mr. Page, "and *who* is Bernard Shaw?"

"Oh, I forgot," I apologized. "It seems so strange to me that I know *your* century so well and that you have no knowledge of *mine*."

"I don't understand you," Mr. Page remarked with a puzzled look on his face. "What do you mean by *your* century? We are all living in the last years of the Sixteenth Century, are we not? And when you say Twentieth Century, why not say the Thirtieth, or the Fortieth, Century? It would be just as sensible. How can you look so far ahead? You must have been talking lately with Dr. Dee, our noted astrologer; but even Dr. Dee has never

Datchet Mead

projected such fantastic ideas as you have expressed occasionally during dinner. How did you get here, anyway? Anne says she found you on Windsor Terrace, talking very strangely to yourself and muttering that Shakespeare's characters were actually real — more real than the people of your own *time* — whatever *that* may mean. Why, *of course*, we are real. How could you ever doubt it? And, *of course*, Windsor belongs to *us*. But let's to the music! Do you play or sing? Of course, you do one or the other. All Elizabethans do."

"I am glad you class me as an Elizabethan," I delightedly ventured.

"Why not?" responded Mr. Page. "You certainly are one of us — although you do not wear our clothes — or you could never have reached us. To which one of the Plays do you belong?"

"That's exactly what your daughter asked me when we first met," I replied. "I — I — I'm afraid — "

"Oh, well, never mind," my host cheerfully came to my rescue, "you are one of us anyway, although your English is very difficult to understand and your pronunciation *most* peculiar. But let's clap into a song of some kind."

Then opening the doors of a huge oaken cupboard that ran across the entire upper part of the room — "a boarded chest" he called it — Mr. Page revealed to my delighted view, a set of six viols: a big double bass; a bass viol, which Mr. Page called a viol de gamboys, reminding me at the same time that Sir Andrew Aguecheek boasted that he could play it; and four smaller viols, graduated in size. The smallest of these Mr. Page took up very tenderly, remarking: "This is a new instrument called the violino,

Shakespearian Fantasias

or the violin, and it is made by Andreas Amati, in Cremona. It has, you see, lovely, graceful curves and the varnish is a beautiful amber color — don't you think so? Amati says the violin is going to have a great future and that it may possibly revolutionize music. I don't know anything about its future, but it certainly is a beautiful little instrument and it has a sweet, clear, and very penetrating tone. And how beautifully the scrolls are cut! We tune it in a new way — in *fifths*."

I hardly dared mention to Mr. Page that it was the only instrument in his collection with which I was familiar and that I once had an Amati myself. However, he continued: "The other viols are all by Gasparo di Salò. Edward de Vere, Earl of Oxford,[6] picked them all out for me when he was in Italy a few years ago. Now here are the lutes," and Mr. Page pointed out the long-necked boxes near by. "I think I'll select this one."

The instrument that Mr. Page chose for the impromptu concert was a lovely instrument. Its body was rounded like a melon and built up of strips of pine and cedar with exquisite purflings and ornaments of ivory, ebony, and silver. A beautifully carved and inlaid rose adorned the belly and the long neck was fretted semitone by semitone and furnished with twelve pairs of strings. On some shelves near the panelling of the room I caught sight of several manuscript books of music and two or three printed books, such as Anthony Munday's *Banquet of Dainty Conceits*, William Byrd's *Psalms, Sonnets and*

---

[6] Edward de Vere, 17th Earl of Oxford, spent almost a year in Italy as part of a trip to the continent that lasted almost a year and a half in 1575-1576.

Datchet Mead

Songs, and John Wilbye's *First Set of English Madrigals*. I was about to pick up the latter when Mr. Page asked me if I would play something.

Very fortunately I was spared the embarrassment of confessing that I could neither tune nor play the lute, for the pompous Welshman, Sir Hugh Evans, came forward saying "*I* will sing"; and taking up the long-necked lute, which he tuned not too well, he began:

> "To shallow rivers, to whose falls
> Melodious birds sing madrigals;
> There will we make our peds of roses,
> And a thousand fragrant poises.
>   To shallow..."[7]

"Oh, Sir Hugh, you are all wrong; you haven't even started properly," laughed Anne Page, taking the lute from his hands.

"Oh, sweet Anne Page!" Master Slender exclaimed ecstatically with clasped hands in a most affected attitude; and little, old, withered Justice Shallow sighed audibly: "Would I were young for *your* sake, Mistress Anne!"

While Anne Page was tuning the lute afresh, an extremely handsome young man, of noble mien and courtly manner and dressed in the top of the Tudor style, approached the open window. Leaning his arms upon the sill in a nonchalant pose of extreme grace, he gazed deeply, devotedly, and devoutly upon the pretty singer,

---

[7] *The Merry Wives of Windsor* (III.1). Sir Hugh Evans is misquoting the poem "The Passionate Shepherd to His Love." Attributed to Philip Marlowe, it was first published in *England's Helicon* in 1599, six years after his death.

Shakespearian Fantasias

who, after a few well-chosen chords, began to sing with a fresh, clear quality of voice that suggested English meadows shining with the morning dew.

"Her voice reminds me of Melba!" I whispered to Mrs. Page.

"What is *Melba?*" Mrs. Page whispered back.

"Oh, I forgot!" I murmured.

I now noticed that Anne's large and lustrous eyes looked directly at the visitor as she sang the following:

> "Live with me and be my love,
> And we will all the pleasures prove
> That hills and valleys, dales and fields
> And all the craggy mountains yields.
>
> "There will we sit upon the rocks,
> And see the shepherds feed their flocks,
> By shallow rivers, by whose falls
> Melodious birds sing madrigals.
>
> "There will I make thee a bed of roses,
> With a thousand fragrant posies,
> A cap of flowers and a kirtle
> Embroider'd all with leaves of myrtle.
>
> "A belt of straw and ivy buds,
> With coral clasps and amber studs;
> And if these pleasures may thee move
> Then live with me and be my love."

Anne Page paused here; and, as her long, white fingers picked out a few more well-chosen chords, she gave the young man another glance, which he perfectly interpreted, for his lovely young tenor voice rang out with

LOVE'S ANSWER,

for which Anne Page continued her same accompani-

Datchet Mead

ment, adding here to her enchanting smile:

> "If that the world and love were young,
> And truth in every shepherd's tongue,
> These pretty pleasures might me move
> To live with thee and be thy love."[8]

Then, jumping lightly in through the casement window, young Fenton (for I soon learned that it was he) took Anne's lute; and, fastening his ardent gaze upon her, sang words and notes that came from his heart to his lips:

> "O mistress mine, where are you roaming?
> O stay and hear, your true love's coming
>   That can sing both high and low:
> Trip no further, pretty sweeting;
> Journeys end in lover's meeting,
>   Every wise man's son doth know.
>
> "What is love? 'tis not hereafter;
> Present mirth hath present laughter;
>   What's to come is still unsure:
> In delay there lies no plenty;
> Then come kiss me, sweet-and-twenty,
>   Youth's a stuff will not endure."[9]

This song was sung with such beauty, fervor, and sincerity that everyone was spellbound; but on its conclusion Mr. Page approached the newcome-guest — very rudely, I thought — with:

> "Why, how now! what does Master Fenton here?

---

[8] A stanza from "The Nymph's Reply to the Shepherd," a poem written in response to Marlowe's "The Passionate Shepherd to His Love." It appeared in *England's Helicon* directly after Marlowe's poem, and was attributed to Ignoto.

[9] A song from Shakespeare's *Twelfth Night* (II.3).

Shakespearian Fantasias

> You wrong me, sir, thus still to haunt my house:
> I told you, sir, my daughter is disposed of."[10]

"Nay, Master Page, be not impatient," Fenton replied — very graciously, I thought; but Mistress Page, taking the cue from her husband, added with asperity:

"Good Master Fenton, come not near my child."

"She is no match for you," Mr. Page cried angrily.

"Sir, will you hear me?" pleaded Fenton.

"No, good Master Fenton," Mr. Page answered very crossly and followed Justice Shallow out of the room.

Then, turning to Anne's mother, Fenton very gracefully made another appeal:

> "Good Mistress Page, for that I love your daughter
> In such a righteous fashion as I do,
> Perforce, against all checks, rebukes and manners,
> I must advance the colors of my love,
> And not retire. Let me have *your* good will."[11]

"Good mother," interposed Anne, with a contemptuous, fiery glance towards Slender and a scornful toss of her pretty head, "do not marry me to yond fool."

"I mean it not," answered Mistress Page, "I seek you a better husband."

Considering himself insulted, Master Slender strutted out of the back door and took his way into the orchard, where Justice Shallow and Mr. Page were already seated under the trees.

Mistress Page, touched by the sentiment that had been so beautifully voiced by Fenton and by the lovelight

---

[10] *The Merry Wives of Windsor* (III.5).
[11] *The Merry Wives of Windsor* (III.4).

Datchet Mead

that was shining so brightly in Anne's lovely blue eyes, said:

> "Come, trouble not yourself, good Master Fenton,
> I will not be your friend, nor enemy:
> My daughter will I question how she loves you,
> And as I find her, so am I *affected*;
> Till then, farewell, sir."[12]

Anne started to leave with her mother, but turned back. Fenton, advancing to greet her, encircled her slender waist with his arm and exclaimed sadly:

> "I see I cannot get thy father's love;
> Therefore, no more turn me to him, sweet Nan."[13]

"Alas, how then?" Anne sobbed upon his shoulder. And Fenton replied:

> "He doth object I am too great of birth;
> And that my state being gall'd with my expense,
> I seek to heal it only by his wealth.
> Besides these, other bars he lays before me,
> My riots past, my wild societies;
> And tells me 'tis a thing impossible
> I should love thee but as a property."[14]

"Maybe he tells you true?" Anne queried archly.

> "No; heaven so speed me in my time to come!
> Albeit, I will confess, thy father's wealth
> Was the first motive that I woo'd thee, Anne:
> Yet, wooing thee, I found thee of more value
> Than stamps in gold, or sums in sealèd bags;
> And 'tis the very riches of thyself

---

[12] *The Merry Wives of Windsor* (III.4).
[13] Same.
[14] Same.

Shakespearian Fantasias

> That now I aim at."[15]

"Gentle Master Fenton," Anne murmured tenderly,

> "Yet seek my father's love; still seek it, sir:
> If opportunity and humblest suit
> Cannot attain it, why then – Hark you hither."[16]

As the handsome young lovers retired to converse apart, I was reminded of what sweet Anne Page intimated to me on the Terrace of Windsor Castle — that she had a definite plan concerning Fenton: and, having inherited no little of her mother's ingenuity and wit, was almost certain that she could carry it through to a successful issue.

I now walked out of the house and wandered down the leafy lane and through the tiny streets of Windsor, hardly heeding where I was going — and caring less — feeling myself a shadow among the *living* Shakespearians, who inhabit Windsor untouched by the disintegrating forces of the Twentieth Century and removed from its furious and insane speed.

"Oh, I've found you at last!" I heard the sweet voice of Anne Page exclaim, as she touched me lightly on the arm, "Where *have* you been these last two days? We have been looking *everywhere* for you. We have all found you very interesting and very sympathetic, although very, *very* strange; and we wondered where you disappeared so suddenly. Yes," she repeated, "we have been looking for you *everywhere* — in Frogmore and Eton and Windsor,

---

[15] *The Merry Wives of Windsor* (III.4).
[16] Same.

Datchet Mead

Stoke, and Datchet Ferry — *everywhere.* Just a minute ago I bethought me of hunting for you in the place where I first met you; and, thank goodness, here you are! Much has happened in the last two days. Oh, it has been most exciting and —"

"Two days!" I interrupted. "What in the world are you talking about, Mistress Anne Page? Why, I've been standing here only a few minutes!"

"Well; I don't know anything about *that*," Anne replied, "but I do know you have been gone *two* whole days and a good piece of this one as well. Oh, what fun we have had!" and Anne Page laughed long and merrily.

"Tell me about it," I begged, "about all I have missed."

"You know," began Anne, "that Sir John Falstaff sent letters to my mother and to Mistress Ford. Mistress Ford brought her letter to my mother to read and my mother showed her its fellow. On comparing these letters, they were found to be word for word. First, my mother and Mistress Ford were angry; and then they were amused; and, finally, they decided to play Sir John a trick. So Mistress Ford sent Sir John word by Mistress Quickly that she would be at home the next day between ten and eleven and my mother sent word that her husband was seldom from home, but she hoped there *would* come a time and begged Sir John to lend her his page, Robin, to be a come-and-go between them.

"Then Mistress Ford and my mother laid their plans. My mother took Robin into her confidence, promising him a new doublet and hose if he would act his part. Well, Sir John came swelling and puffing along to Mistress Ford's house and Mistress Ford received him and let him

Shakespearian Fantasias

make love to her, pretending to be greatly pleased.[17] All of a sudden Robin rushed into the room with the news that Mistress Page was at the door sweating and blowing and looking wildly and would need speak with Mistress Ford. Falstaff went behind the arras 'to ensconce himself' and my mother entered, making a great ado and saying that Mr. Ford was coming with half Windsor at his heels and, if by any chance Mistress Ford had a friend here to convey him out as soon as possible.

"'What shall I do?' Mistress Ford exclaimed, pretending to be dismayed. 'There *is* a gentleman, *my dear friend*; and I fear not mine own shame so much as his peril. I had rather than a thousand pounds he were out of the house.'

"Then my mother grew more excited and begged Mistress Ford to bethink of some conveyance. Then she called out:

"'Look! here is a basket' (Mistress Ford and my mother had placed the basket there on purpose); 'if he be of any *reasonable* stature, he may creep in here; and throw foul linen upon him, as if it were going to bucking; or, it is whiting time, send him by your two men to Dachet Mead.'

"'He's too big to go in there,' Mistress Ford objected. 'What *shall* I do?'

"Then Falstaff came out from behind the tapestry crying 'Let me see it! Let me see it!' and he crept into the basket and the Merry Wives of Windsor covered him up

---

[17] "Make love *to* her," as in speak romantically to her, should not be confused with "make love *with* her" a phrase that sounds similar but has a very different meaning.

Datchet Mead

with the foul linen and in great excitement called the men-servants, John and Robert, and ordered them to take up the basket and carry it to the laundress in Datchet Mead.

"Now the fun began. Just as John and Robert were staggering with the heavy basket through the door here came Mr. Ford, my father, Dr. Caius, and Sir Hugh Evans. Mr. Ford, on asking the servants where they were going, was perfectly satisfied with their answer: 'To the laundress, forsooth.'

"Then Mr. Ford ran into the house, upstairs and downstairs, turning everything upside down in his search 'to unkennel the fox,' as he kept on screaming out. My mother and Mistress Ford laughed themselves into stitches over the fun and over the crazy jealousy of Mr. Ford."

What happened at Datchet Mead?" I asked.

"Oh yes, Datchet Mead," replied Anne Page. "Falstaff was dumped into the river and when he clambered out with his stomach full of Thames water and his clothes all dripping wet, he found his way to the Garter Inn, where he made Bardolph fetch him a quart of sack."

"Is that all?" I asked.

"Oh, dear, no," laughed Anne Page. "Next day here came Mistress Quickly with another message from Mistress Ford — an apology to Falstaff: her 'men mistook her order,' she said, 'and she hoped that Sir John would come again that she might make amends, between eight and nine, as her husband was going a-birding with Mr. Page, who had promised him a fine hawk for the bush.' So, Sir John made a second visit, and just as he arrived my

23

mother rushed in to cry danger, for Mr. Ford was coming. Sir John refused to go into the basket again and 'be drowned like a litter of blind puppies'; and as there was no place to hide, the Merry Wives persuaded him to disguise himself, for they told him he certainly would be killed if he went out of the house in his own semblance. Mistress Ford now remembered that her maid's aunt, the fat woman of Brentford, had a gown upstairs and so they brought it down and dressed Sir John in it, with her thrummed hat and her muffler. Oh, it was *too* funny," laughed Anne. "For a ruse the servants were again ordered to carry out the basket of foul linen: and this time Mr. Ford, my father, Dr. Caius, Justice Shallow, and Sir Hugh Evans examined the basket very carefully, turning out all the clothes. In the excitement Sir John escaped, but he got a severe beating from Mr. Ford, who thought he was old Mother Prat, whom he hates. Sir Hugh was really scared. The old woman of Brentford is thought to be a witch and Sir Hugh muttered, 'I like not when a 'oman has a great peard. I spy a great peard under her muffler.' Mr. Ford was too crazy to notice it. Oh, Falstaff was such a ridiculous sight!"

"What happened next?" I then inquired, as Anne ended her narrative with a great outburst of merry laughter.

"Oh, yes!" she replied, "everything was all cleared up. My mother and Mistress Ford told the whole story and Mr. Ford begged Mistress Ford's pardon and Sir Hugh said over and over again: "Tis one of the pest discretions of a 'oman as ever I did look upon.'"

"'All's well that ends well!'" I remarked sententiously.

Datchet Mead

"Oh, but it isn't ended *yet*," Anne Page retorted, "there is another and still better kind of fooling to come; and this time my father and Mr. Ford are in the game. The plans are all laid for tonight. Of course, the whole idea originated with the Merry Wives of Windsor. You perhaps know," Anne Page continued, "that Windsor Forest is a fairy place. The old tale goes that Herne, the hunter (sometime a keeper here in Windsor Forest), walks around a certain oak-tree at still midnight, with great ragg'd horns and then he blasts the tree and takes the cattle and makes milchkine yield blood and shakes a chain in a most hideous and dreadful manner. So, you see, many people are afraid to walk at deep of night by this Herne's Oak. Now it is arranged that I and my little brother, William, and some others of our age and growth, are to be dressed like urchins, ouphes, and fairies, and, with lighted waxen tapers on our heads and rattles in our hands, are suddenly to appear while Falstaff, disguised as Herne, the hunter, is making love to my mother and Mistress Ford under Herne's Oak. We are to pinch and burn the unclean knight and ask him why he thus disturbs our sacred hour of fairy revels? We are all to wear vizards and I am to be Queen of the Fairies, so my mother says, in a *green* dress; but *I* have a different idea. My father has told Slender to carry me off as I am to be dressed in *white*; and my mother has told Dr. Caius to carry off the *green* fairy; but *I* have a different idea," repeated Anne. "I must go now to prepare for this evening's jollity. It is getting late."

"Yes," I replied, "these long English twilights are very misleading —

Shakespearian Fantasias

> Light thickens; and the crow
> Makes wing to the rooky wood:
> Good things of day begin to droop and drowse;
> While night's black agents to their prey do rouse."[18]

"I wish you'd tell that to Falstaff," said Anne, "we want him to be thoroughly frightened."

And with that last remark Anne disappeared down the Terrace.

It did not seem long to me before I heard the Windsor bell strike twelve and very soon again the hour of one. And then in a few moments sweet Anne Page returned to my side, this time bringing Fenton, gallantly attired, her pretty face aglow with dimples, smiles, and blushes.

"It is all over," Anne announced in her ringing, silvery voice, "with surprises for everybody. We danced around Herne's Oak and we burned and pinched and poked sir John, singing all the time:

> 'Pinch him and burn him and turn him about,
> Till candles and starlight and moonshine be out.'[19]

"At last all we fairies ran away and Falstaff took off his horns, and while my mother, Mistress Page and the rest were teasing Falstaff and laughing everything into friendly good humor Fenton and I came on the scene — unnoticed by everybody — just as my father was saying:

"Yet, be cheerful, knight: thou shalt eat a posset tonight at my home, where I will desire thee to laugh at my wife that now laughs at thee. Tell her, Master Slender

---

[18] *Macbeth* (III.2).
[19] *The Merry Wives of Windsor* (V.5). The following dialogue is also from the same play and scene.

Datchet Mead

hath married her daughter.' Then my mother laughed: 'If Anne Page be my daughter, she is by this Dr. Caius's wife.'

"I looked at Fenton and we nearly laughed aloud. At this moment, here came Master Slender screaming: 'Who, ho! ho! Father Page'; and then he cried, 'I came yonder at Eton to marry Mistress Anne Page and she's a great lubberly boy! If it had not been i' the church, I would have swinged him!'

"'Why, this is your own folly,' my father answered. 'Did not I tell you how you should know my daughter by her garments?'

"'I went to her in *white*,' Master Slender whined, 'and cried *mum* and she cried *budget*, as Anne and I had appointed; and yet it was not Anne, but a post-master's boy.' Then my mother, with a confident smile, said to my father: 'Good George, be not angry: I knew of your purpose; turned my daughter into *green*; and indeed she is now with the doctor at the Deanery and there married.'

"Just as she finished speaking here came Dr. Caius rushing into the Forest, waving his arms wildly and ejaculating: 'Vere is Mistress Page? By gar, I am cozened; I ha' married *un garçon*, a boy; *un paisan*, by gar, a boy; it is not Anne Page: by gar, I am cozened.'

"'Did you not take the one in *green*?' asked my astonished mother.

"'Ay, by gar,' replied Dr. Caius, 'and 'tis a boy; by gar, I'll raise all Windsor'; and Dr Caius rushed away as quickly as he had come, waiving his arms and chattering French.

"'This is strange,' Mr. Ford now remarked. 'Who hath got the right Anne?'

Shakespearian Fantasias

"Then we came forward.

"'Pardon good father! good my mother pardon,' I begged; and Fenton added:

> 'Hear the truth of it.
> You would have married her most shamefully,
> Where there was no proportion held in love.
> The truth is, she and I, long since contracted,
> Are now so sure that nothing can dissolve us.
> The offense is holy that she hath committed.'[20]

"Then Mr. Ford spoke again:

> 'Stand not amazed: here is no remedy.
> In love, the heavens themselves do guide the state;
> Money buys lands and wives are sold by fate.'[21]

"Now you wouldn't have thought Mr. Ford, after all his unreasoning jealousy, would have been so nice, would you?"

"No, I certainly would not," I replied, "Mr. Ford spoke very handsomely, I think."

"Sir John now gave expression to a jeering jest," Anne continued, "and then my father turned to my husband (Anne pronounced the unaccustomed word with a charming mixture of pride and shyness), and said:

> 'Fenton, heaven give thee joy!
> What cannot be eschewed must be embraced';[22]

and my mother added: 'Master Fenton, Heaven give you many, many, merry days.'

"Then, slipping her arm into the arm of my father, said

---

[20] *The Merry Wives of Windsor* (V.5).
[21] Same.
[22] Same; lines are combined and paraphrased.

Datchet Mead

to him:

> 'Good husband, let us every one go home,
> And laugh this sport o'er by a country fire:
> Sir John and all.'[23]

"And then my father and mother told us to go and find you, for they desire you to be one of our wedding-party. Will you go with us?"

"With the greatest pleasure," I replied.

"Come on then," said Fenton; and Anne (a potential Merry Wife of Windsor), imitating Sir Hugh's Welsh speech, laughed out: "Trib, trib, fairies, trib, trib"; and then we three ran joyously down the sloping streets and leafy lanes of Windsor to the home of "Sweet Anne Page."

---

[23] *The Merry Wives of Windsor* (V.5).

In Illyria

I HAVE not the slightest idea how I got there but one summer morning not long ago I found myself strolling about in a most delightful Elizabethan garden — "a curious knotted garden" — in the highest state of cultivation, radiant in color and redolent of scent. As I gradually recovered from the first sensations of bewilderment, the details became apparent and I began to perceive that the gorgeous assemblies of blooming flowers that gave forth such lavish perfume were arranged in formal beds, or "knots," that occupied the large squares produced by the intersection of broad paths of finely powdered yellow sand.

After I had discovered the symmetrical, yet very simple, plan of the garden, I saw that it was surrounded on three sides by a pleachèd alley, or pergola, completely covered with blooming roses and honeysuckle. The fourth side ended in a terrace with heavy balustrade and flights of steps leading into the garden. Beyond this terrace there rose a long and low manor-house of dull red brick with mullioned windows, tiled roof, and clusters of tall chimneys, some of them spiral and ornamented with zigzag patterns of black bricks. The house, thickly covered with dark ivy and climbing roses, harmonized perfectly with the lines of the garden.

While I was wondering into whose domain I had

strayed — although I felt perfectly certain that I was in Essex or Kent — I noticed over the little gate that led into the pleachèd arbor opposite the terrace in large letters the name "Illyria."

"And what should *I* do in Illyria?" I exclaimed, remembering the words uttered by a certain charming young lady when she found herself shipwrecked on the coast of Illyria.

"Ah, what indeed *are* you doing in Illyria, and how did you get into my garden?" a cold, haughty, and extremely aristocratic voice asked me.

To my amazement, before me stood a young Elizabethan lady of commanding presence and great elegance.

Her stiff and wide-spreading farthingale and pointed bodice of white satin and black velvet and her black velvet slippers with diamond buckles showed that the wearer was in mourning costume, while her tall, standing ruff of handsome Venetian lace and her long ropes of Oriental pearls proclaimed that she was possessed of wealth. Beneath the white veil, so gracefully wrapped around her head and hiding her face, I discovered features of unusual beauty.

"I cannot imagine how you got in here," the lady continued, "thus invading my privacy. Since my dear brother's death I go nowhere and this garden is the only place where I take my recreation (she pronounced this *re-creation*). I have given Malvolio the strictest orders to admit no one."

"Malvolio!" I shouted, "Malvolio! Then *you* are the Lady Olivia!"

In Illyria

"*You* know Malvolio? The Lady Olivia replied, so greatly astonished that she threw back her veil to have a better look at me. "This is passing strange!"

"Oh yes, I know Malvolio," I laughingly acquiesced, "although I have never seen him; and I know your ladyship also."

As I looked upon her large gray eyes and her fresh red and white complexion, I added: "and you are very much lovelier and very much younger than I had pictured."

"Indeed!" the Lady Olivia acknowledged coldly. "I suppose because I am mistress of this house and have the care of a large estate people forget that I am not yet sweet-and-twenty. And then my sorrow for my father and beloved brother, both lost during the past twelvemonth, and the management of my household make me seem much older than I am." Then in a warmer tone of voice she said, rather graciously: "I am glad that you do not think of me as a demure personage of middle age. I am about the same age as the latest emissary from the Duke Orsino, a very fascinating young man with whom I have fallen very deeply in love. I do not understand why I am telling you this, because I am a very reserved person; but you seem to draw it out of me. I have nobody to confide in now (and the beautiful gray eyes filled with tears). Malvolio is only my steward; Maria is too flippant; my clown makes a jest of everything; and my kinsman, Sir Toby, is always roystering. So, you see, I am utterly alone. I cannot love my neighbor, the Duke Orsino; and I have told him so again and again. The gentle youth, whom he has lately sent to plead his cause, has won my heart completely. The Duke, however, has a charming mind and

33

Shakespearian Fantasias

is possessed of extraordinary culture and delicate taste. He also has much sentiment and is full of graceful sayings. One of these is:

> 'Away before me to sweet beds of flowers;
> Love-thoughts lie rich when canopied with bowers.'[24]

"This suits my mood, so let me show you my garden, now that you *are* here. I have many fine things, including some very rare outlandish flowers. Would you like to see them?"

"Oh, please show them to me," I delightedly replied, "this is, indeed, an honor and a privilege."

"Come on then. Now do notice my box-trees and hedges," the stately young lady remarked as she led the way down the widest forthright. Pausing beside a large bed, she explained: "Here are my very choice carnations, pinks, picotees, and gilliflowers, 'the fairest flowers o' the season' *I* think they are. They all came from Master Ralph Tuggie's garden in Westminster. Master Tuggie, as you probably know, makes a specialty of carnations, gilliflowers, and pinks. This one, for instance, is the Red or Clove Gilliflower (we also call it Sops-in-Wine, because we sometimes use it to add a spicy flavor to wine); this one is the Yellow, or Orange Tawny Gilliflower; this is the Gray Hulo; this, the Blue Hulo; and this, the Red Hulo; this is the Lustie Gallant; this, the Fair Maid of Kent (Ruffling Robin some people call it); this is Master Tuggie's Rose Gilliflower; this is Mastser Tuggie's Princess; this is the Oxford Carnation; this, Master Bradshaw's Dainty Lady;

---

[24] *Twelfth Night* (I.1).

In Illyria

this, the Striped Savage; this, the Feathered Tawny; this, Grandpère; and this is my favorite of all, the Great Harwich. What a gallant, great flower it is, rising up with such beauty and stateliness. Is it not worthy of a prime place in the garden? Look at its two long whitish crooked threads, like horns, growing out of the centre. And what a scent! Neither too quick, nor too dull! Slow in growing, but very magnificent in bearing." Then, withdrawing her hand, which had lightly held the blossom, Olivia added: "I must not touch it. This grand old English carnation dislikes to be handled, which indeed showeth a kind of stateliness — don't you think so?"

"I do," I replied, "I do, indeed!"

"Ah! you should taste the conserve I make of the Clove Gilliflower with sugar. It is exceedingly cordial and doth comfort the heart, being eaten now and then. Here are my pinks, double and single, feathered and jagged," the Lady Olivia said, pausing at the next bed. "I grow, as you see, single red Sweet Johns, single white Sweet Johns, double Sweet Johns, single red Sweet Williams, double red Sweet Williams, speckled Sweet Williams, or London Pride, and London Tufts."

Never in my life had I seen such gorgeous carnations and pinks, nor had I smelled such rivers of spice floating upon the air.

"Do you like marigolds?" was the Lady Olivia's next question.

"Do I like them? I *adore* them," I answered:

"And winking marybuds begin

Shakespearian Fantasias

> To ope their golden eyes![25]

"Do I like them?

> The marigold that goes to bed with the sun
> And with him rises weeping.[26]

"Rather!"

"I love the marigold, too," my companion responded, "the Gold-Flower, the Sun's Bride, the Sun's Spouse, always turned towards the Royal Star; in the night time closed and shut as if pensive for him, but at the noontide of day fully spread abroad as if it, with spread arms, longed, or diligently attended, to embrace her Bridegroom. Now here are my lovely blue larkspurs, lark-heels, larkstoes, and monkshoods, and also the yellow lark-heels — *Nasturtium Indicum* — lately brought by explorers from the West Indies. This is a very interesting outlandish flower. Talking of outlandish flowers — flowers from foreign countries –" she explained as she noted my bewildered look — "here is the new Crown Imperial. It comes from Persia and has only been in England for a few years. It was brought here in 1576. Gerard has it in his garden and I got a plant from him. I think the Crown Imperial, for his stately beautifulness, deserveth the first place in a Garden of Delight."

A few steps more brought us to another bed.

"Look at my lilies!" the Lady Olivia ran on. "I have lilies of all kinds. See my beautiful white lilies and my martagons, or Turk's Caps — red, scarlet, yellow, spotted — are they not deserving of place and commendation?

---

[25] *Cymbeline* (II.3).
[26] *The Winter's Tale* (IV.4).

In Illyria

And here are my irises, or flower-de-luces, in which I take great pride. Here is the Great Turkey; this is the Great Dalmation; this is the Yellow of Tripoli; this, the Purple or Murrey; this, the Peach-colored; and this, the White with Yellow Falls. Here is the Double Purple and this is the Purple Dwarf. I have all the known roses," she added, "you see how the eglantine and the musk roses climb everywhere; and my yellow roses are famous; and perhaps you have noticed how I mingle the delicious honeysuckle with the roses. Do you not get the perfume on the air which comes and goes, as Lord Bacon says, 'like the warbling of music'?"

"I do," I answered. "I never realized before that the perfume of flowers was like melody and that the studied combinations of these perfumes produced chords of scent, like harmonies in music."

"Oh," she answered, "you should hear what Duke Orsino says with regard to this. He compares music to perfume — just the reverse of your remark. One day, so Cesario told me, while lying on a divan and listening to some lovely music, he called out:

> 'That Strain again! It had a dying fall.
> O, it came o'er my ear like the sweet south,
> That breathes upon a bank of violets,
> Stealing and giving odor.'[27]

"Yes," she added, "it is important to know what be the flowers that do best perfume the air. And, of dear! you should come into this garden when the morning dew is fresh on everything."

---

[27] *Twelfth Night* (I.1).

Shakespearian Fantasias

"'Morning roses newly washed with dew!'" I sang out.

"But you have not noticed my pansies," Olivia remarked, "my little Three-Faces-under-a-Hood, my Johnny-Jump-Ups or Love-in-Idleness; and I must call your attention also to my rosemary. You see I let the cheerful rosemary run all over the garden walls because my bees love it and because it is a plant sacred to friendship." Breaking off a little spray, she handed it to me with the words: "*That's* for remembrance."

"Thank you," I responded, "I shall always remember this enchanting Garden of Delight."

The Lady Olivia had suddenly turned from me and I saw her bouncing farthingale ascent the steps of the terrace. Very soon she disappeared through the doorway of her mansion. I was impelled to follow: but the Countess was too quick for me; for when I reached the house she was nowhere to be seen.

However I entered — although perhaps I should not have done so without an invitation — but I could not resist the pleasure of seeing an Elizabethan house. The door being wide open, I passed in and entered a great hall. While I was busily examining the heavy oaken rafters, the panelling, the great chimney-piece so ornately carved, the painted coats-of-arms on the windowpanes, and the long, narrow oaken table in the centre of the room, a young lady, dressed in a simple yet very picturesque Tudor costume, came tripping in. She held out her hand in a charming manner and, her pretty face aglow with smiles and with merry dimples dancing in her rosy cheeks, remarked: "You are very welcome."

"Thank you!" I replied, "but how did you know that I

In Illyria

was here?"

"Oh, my Lady told me that you had followed her; and it is her will that I should take on me the hostess-ship of the house. You are very welcome."

"Aren't you Maria?" I burst out enthusiastically.

"My name is Mary," she replied.

"That may be," I answered, "but you are, nevertheless, delightful, delicious, clever, brilliant, and charming Maria of *Twelfth Night* fame. I cannot be mistaken! Are you not she?"

"Yes," she admitted, "I am that merry person."

"I shall desire you of more acquaintance, good Mistress Mary, or good Mistress Maria, whichever you please," I replied. "I have long wished to see you, but I never imagined that such a pleasure would be possible."

"I am glad to hear that," laughed Maria, "for you see I am so completely overshadowed by the Lady Olivia and Viola that nobody ever thinks much about me. Consequently, I have rarely been properly interpreted to the world."

"I cry you mercy!" I exclaimed. 'You are mistaken. You are one of the most delightful personages in Illyria."

"And what should *you* do in Illyria?" Maria questioned, looking at me with deep wonder in her eyes.

"To meet the people I have so long enjoyed in my Shakespearian dreams," I answered.

"I know nothing about *that*," was the reply. "You will find this a queer household. I'm afraid you will think us all tainted in our wits."

"Oh, please don't let that worry you," I interposed quickly. "I know you *all*."

Shakespearian Fantasias

"That's passing strange," Maria observed. "I have never seen *you* before. How *could* you know us? And you knew *me* right away! And my Lady says you know Malvolio — you told her so — and she thinks that explains how you got into the garden. Malvolio disobeyed her orders and opened the gate for you. My Lady hath summoned Malvolio to show why this occurred."

"Poor Malvolio, he is always getting into trouble!" I exclaimed.

"Poor Malvolio indeed!" Maria sniffed contemptuously. "Malvolio is sick of self-love. He's an arrant coxcomb, and he's an overweening rogue. Because he's my Lady's steward, he thinks he can be round with Sir Toby, my Lady's kinsman. Malvolio thinks, too, because he is virtuous there shall be no more cakes and ale. Sometimes he's a very Puritan and then again he's not. Malvolio is not anything constantly but a time-pleaser. He is an affectioned ass, so crammed, as he thinks, with excellences, that all who look on him love him. But if I do not gull him into a nayword and make him a common recreation, do not think I have wit enough to lie straight in my bed. I know I can do it."

"I am sure of it," I interrupted. "Maria you remind me of Mistress Ford and Mistress Page. I have just come from Windsor and the pranks of the 'Merry Wives.' Your ingenuity in devising clever tricks and carrying them to success makes me think also of Anne Page."

"Well that's not to be wondered at," explained Maria. "Mistress Page is my aunt and sweet Anne Page my cousin; and as we are of the same Shakespearian blood, it is not strange that we have the same talents and the same merry disposition. Clever how Anne managed to run away with and marry Fenton, wasn't it?"

"Very," I agreed. "I *loved* her for it."

"Well," and Maria's red lips parted in a knowing smile; and as she looked at me her eyes twinkled like stars, "you will have to love me, too; for I am going to marry Sir Toby Belch! There; what do you think of *that*?"

"I would endorse anything you please to do, clever Maria," was my comment. "When did Sir Toby ask you? I don't remember."

"Oh, Sir Toby hasn't asked me yet," laughed Maria. "Sir Toby hasn't the slightest idea that he is going to marry me. Sir Toby is very wild and roystering, yet for all that he is delightful, full of fun and high spirits, has the best heart in the world, and is a gentleman born and bred. Sir Toby says he will live and die a bachelor; but *I* know better. Sir Toby is not going to spend the rest of his life caterwauling all night in this hall with Sir Andrew Aguecheek."

"How are you going to manage it?" I ventured.

"It is very simple," Maria replied. "You must know that Sir Toby detests Malvolio, who is always reprimanding him; and if Malvolio is not trying to get my Lady to bid him turn Sir Toby out of doors, never trust me! Just now my Lady's taking great exception to Sir Toby's late hours; and besides his quaffing and drinking, is greatly annoyed of a foolish knight, Sir Andrew Aguecheek, whom Sir Toby has brought here to be her wooer. My Lady is much out of the quiet since the Youth of the Count was here to woo her; and therefore I have planned a device. I intend to write a letter in the hand of

Shakespearian Fantasias

the Countess Olivia so that Malvolio shall think her in love with him. Moreover, the letter shall desire that he appear in yellow stockings — a color she abhors; and cross-gartered — a fashion she detests; and also that he shall smile upon her continuously, which cannot but turn him into a notable contempt. Perhaps you will stay in Illyria long enough to see this trout caught with tickling?"

"I hope so," I replied, "but where does Sir Toby come in?"

"And if I do not catch Sir Toby in this net, let me be boiled to death with melancholy," said Maria. "I am sure when I thrust this greatness upon Malvolio, sir Toby will ask me if I will set my foot on his neck, call me a noble gull-catcher, and say, 'I could marry the wench for this device and ask no other dowry with her but such another jest.' Sir Toby's limned, I warrant you."

"Then Malvolio's not the only gull you are planning to catch," I remarked:

> "If I prove so, then loving goes by haps,
> Some Cupid kills with arrows, some with traps."[28]

Whether Maria heard me or not, I do not know, for she had suddenly vanished and I was transported in some mysterious way back to the garden; and there I was standing by the great bed of carnations and gilliflowers, trying to remember which was the Fair Maid of Kent, which the Lustie Gallant, and which Master Tuggie's Rose Gilliflower.

Looking towards the gate I saw approaching a slender and graceful Youth, whom I at once identified as the

---

[28] *Much Ado About Nothing* (III.1).

In Illyria

Duke's messenger, and a figure in motley, who of course, was Olivia's Clown. They were in close conversation; and I heard the Clown giving out the following piece of wit and wisdom:

> "A sentence is but a cheveril glove to a good wit. How quickly the wrong side may be turned outward!"[29]

"Art not thou the Lady Olivia's Fool?" the Youth inquired.

"No, sir," the Clown mockingly retorted, "the Lady Olivia will keep no fool till she be married. I am, indeed, not her Fool, but her corrupter of words."

"I saw thee late at the Count Orsino's," the Youth observed.

"Foolery, sir, does walk about the orb like the sun: it shines everywhere, I think I saw your wisdom there."

"Nay, and thou pass upon me I'll no more with thee," the Youth answered. "Hold, there's expenses for thee. Is thy Lady within?"

The Clown, replying in the affirmative, ran off to apprise his mistress of her coming visitor.

The Youth then espied me and came nearer with the greeting: "Good morrow; have you seen the honorable lady of the house?"

"I have," I answered, "and she is a most sweet lady."

"Yes; she is fair, a nonpareil of beauty. My lord and master loves her with adorations, with fertile tears, with groans that thunder love, and sighs of fire. I have been sent to unfold the passion of his love; and I must do my best to woo this lady —

---

[29] *Much Ado About Nothing* (III.1).

Shakespearian Fantasias

> Yet a barful strife,
> Who e'er I woo, myself would be his wife."[30]

"Poor, dear Viola!" I sympathized.

"Oh, you know me!" she whispered in alarm, and looked around fearfully to assure herself that nobody overheard.

"I do," I admitted, "and your history, too. I know you are dressed like your brother Sebastian and I know that when you told Orsino yesterday that your father had a daughter loved a man as you might, were you a woman, love his lordship; that she let concealment like a worm i' the bud steal o'er the crimson damask of her cheek; that she pined in thought and with a green and yellow melancholy sat like patience on a monument smiling at grief; *that* daughter of your father was yourself, Viola. If men were not so stupid when they are in love, Orsino would have discovered this. You certainly gave him a chance to do so. You acknowledged all your love."

Viola smiled. "Yes," she confessed, "I do love Orsino. He is charming, noble, virtuous, of great estate, of fresh and stainless youth, free, learned, and valiant, and in dimension and the shape of nature a gracious person. Orsino is a noble Duke in nature as in name."

"Olivia is in love with you. Do you know that?" I asked.

"Poor lady, she were better love a dream," Viola answered. "My master loves her dearly. And I, poor monster, fond as much on him

> As she, mistaken, seems to dote on me.
> What will become of this?

---

[30] *Twelfth Night* (I.4).

In Illyria

> O time, thou must untangle this, not I;
> It is too hard a knot for me to untie."[31]

And Viola, sighing deeply, went up the steps of the terrace and entered the house.

I now heard three male voices singing the catch, "Farewell, dear heart, since I must needs be gone"; and from the pleachèd arbor of roses and honeysuckles here came Sir Toby Belch, Sir Andrew Aguecheek, and Fabian, who were, indeed, making the welkin ring with their lusty voices.

I was about to accost Sir Toby when he exclaimed:

"Here comes the little villain"; and, walking briskly towards Maria, who was running down the path, called to her: "How now, my nettle of India?"

Maria, however, took no notice of Sir Toby's complimentary salutation, but cried excitedly: "Get ye all three into the box-hedge. Malvolio's coming down the forthright. He has been yonder in the sun practising behavior to his own shadow this half hour. Observe him, for the love of mockery, for I know this letter will make a contemplative idiot of him."

I was certain that the letter Maria had dropped on the path for Malvolio to pick up was the one of which she had spoken to me; and I followed Maria, who, like the others, found a hiding-place in the thick green hedge through which they could peep.

No sooner had I done this when here came Malvolio strutting down the walk like a turkey-cock. As he mused out loud on his brilliant future when he should be

---

[31] *Twelfth Night* (II.2).

Shakespearian Fantasias

married to the Lady Olivia and become Count Malvolio, how he would reprimand his new kinsman Sir Toby, the latter's humorous and indignant exclamations amused me greatly; and when the conceited Malvolio picked up the letter and examined it to make sure it was the Lady Olivia's handwriting, Sir Toby prayed aloud: "May the spirit of humors intimate reading aloud to him." It was, indeed, mirth provoking to watch Malvolio's face as he read each line and to see his antics. When he had finished reading the letter, his comments were most amusing; and we were all delighted to hear his determination to wear yellow stockings and cross-garters and to smile continuously upon the Lady Olivia.

As Malvolio strutted away, the others came from their hiding-places, and, surrounding Maria, paid her many compliments. Then, led by the laughing Maria, the merry group went up the terrace steps and into the house, with the idea of getting more fun out of Malvolio's actions.

I now roamed about the garden admiring all the brilliant and beautiful blossoms and enjoying their delicious perfume, wondering as I did so how it was that I had penetrated to this charming place. Yet how natural it seemed for me to be strolling up and down the forthrights and the smaller paths. How familiar it all appeared! I was, indeed, at home here!

I longed to see the Lady Olivia again; and I, therefore, kept my eyes fastened on the steps of the terrace, hoping that she might return for more *re-creation* of health and spirits. But it was all very quiet and still among the gilliflowers, irises, and roses; and the silence was only broken at intervals by the twitter of a bird or the drowsy

In Illyria

hum of a bee. The folding petals of some of the flowers and the soft flutter of a tawny night-moth informed me that twilight was approaching. The petals of the flowers began to take on darker shades and some of them exhaled a luscious nocturnal perfume. The entire garden assumed a new aspect as the violet mist descended like a veil of delicate gauze.

As I was watching the first faint glimmer of the Evening Star above the tall box-hedge the Clown came bounding down the terrace steps, singing:

> "Hey Robin, jolly Robin,
> Tell me how thy lady does?"[32]

Then, spying me, he laughingly said:

"A holiday! A holiday for me! The Lady Olivia hath got a husband! So she hath, in sooth, a new servant now to wear her motley."

"The Lady Olivia married!" I exclaimed.

"Oh yes," the Clown answered. "Why, where have you been these last few days?"

"Just here, in the Lady Olivia's garden," I replied, "but I have only been here a few hours."

"Oh no, you are mistaken," the Clown answered, "several days have gone by and a great deal has happened. The Lady Olivia hath married Sebastian, whom we all mistook for Cesario when he arrived here. Sebastian, however, proved to be Cesario's twin-brother and Cesario proved to be Sebastian's twin-sister, Viola, who, shipwrecked on our coast of Illyria several months ago, took service with the Duke Orsino as a page under

---

[32] *Twelfth Night* (IV.2).

Shakespearian Fantasias

the name of Cesario. When the two appeared on the scene together we were all astonished, for no apple cleft in two was more like than these two creatures. Sebastian fell in love on the spot with my mistress, who promptly married him; and the Duke Orsino suddenly remembered Cesario's words of devotion. You should have heard the earnestness of his voice when, looking at Cesario very tenderly, he said:

> 'Boy, thou has said to me a thousand times
> Thou never shouldn't love woman like to me.'[33]

"And how did Viola look?" I asked.

"Beautiful," said the Clown, "and she answered: 'and all these sayings will I over-swear.' The Duke, who had been mooning over the Lady Olivia for so long, awoke to a real passion and there was a new love-light in his eyes when he stepped closer to Cesario with

> 'And since you called me master for so long,
> Here is my hand. You shall from this time be
> Your master's mistress.'[34]

"And then he expressed great eagerness and curiosity to see Viola in her woman's dress."

"How lovely all that sounds!" I exclaimed.

"Doesn't it?" acquiesced the Clown; "but there is more to come. We are going to have a wedding in our house! The Lady Olivia embraced Cesario — Viola, I should say — called her sister, and begged the Duke to let the wedding take place in her house and at her proper cost."

"And what did the Duke say?" I asked.

---

[33] *Twelfth Night* (V.1).
[34] Same.

In Illyria

"Oh, the Duke graciously accepted the invitation, of course, I hope you will come to the wedding."

"I hope the Lady Olivia won't forget to ask me," I said, very earnestly. "If she does, I'll get Maria to slip me in."

"Oh, Maria!" exclaimed the Clown. "I nearly forgot to tell you. Maria is married, too."

"To Sir Toby Belch, of course," I said.

"Why, how on earth did you guess?" exclaimed the Clown; and, without waiting for me to reply, continued: "Sir Toby was so delighted with the letter than Maria writ to Malvolio he hath married her in recompense."

"What does the Lady Olivia say about *this* match?" I inquired.

"Oh, the Lady Olivia is delighted," replied the Clown, "she loves her kinsman and she loves Maria; and, in good sooth, it bodes peace and love and quiet life for her house. Maria will keep Sir Toby in bounds, yet we shall have our stoups of wine and our cakes and ale, no matter what Malvolio says; and, moreover, Malvolio can never turn Sir Toby from our roof."

Lights from candles now appearing from various windows of the house caused the Clown to say: "It is now supper-time and they will want me to make some merry jests anent these three pairs of mating-birds, and so

'Farewell, dear heart, for I must needs be gone.'"[35]

The Clown then leaped up the terrace steps, singing gaily as he went:

"When that I was and a little tiny boy,
  With hey, ho, the wind and the rain,

---

[35] *Twelfth Night* (II.3).

Shakespearian Fantasias

> A foolish thing was but a toy,
>   For the rain it raineth every day."[36]

Left alone, I looked towards the house and thought of the prediction that Maria had made to me in the great hall; and I knew — what the others did not know — that Maria's merry device upon Malvolio was planned for the sole purpose of pleasuring and of capturing Sir Toby Belch. I also felt certain that Maria's little foot was firmly planted on Sir Toby's neck forever and that Sir Toby would always be willing to follow his

> little devil of wit to the gates of Tartar.[37]

---

[36] *Twelfth Night* (V.1).
[37] Paraphrase of lines from *Twelfth Night* (II.5).

An Afternoon with Autolycus

IT IS very quiet and very lovely here on this typical English road — which has been a highway ever since the days of the ancient Romans — and I have paused to rest on a stile that enables the wayfarer to step across the fence into the adjoining meadow. The road is a pale golden yellow, firm and hard. On both sides of this road are wide, deep, and carefully tended ditches (of the kind the White Knight was always falling into from his horse for poor little Alice to extricate)[38] and beyond the ditches are fences, so overgrown with brambles and briars that they are practically hedges, absolutely impassable; and these fences enclose long stretches of emerald meadows on which placid cows are grazing. Scarlet poppies, yellow kingcups, and trailing bell-flowers brighten the ditches; and if I look carefully enough I can discover an occasional little daisy with her stiff and pink-tipped ruff peeping up above the grass. This grass, which grows close to the ground (almost like a carpet of moss), is sparkling with raindrops from a recent shower. Every now and then from some distant tree a little bird calls out as plainly as can be for "A little bit of bread and *No* chee-ee-ee-se!"

Farther away the gentle river — more like a stream than a river — laves the slender rushes so lightly that

---

[38] The White Knight and Alice are fictional characters in Lewis Carroll's *Through the Looking-Glass*.

Shakespearian Fantasias

only the rushes can hear what it says. Tall trees are throwing black shadows of themselves upon the bright green meadow grass that spreads from the edge of the river right up to the crumbling walls of a monastic building that was dedicated with pomp and grandeur many hundred years ago.

This ruin is now roofless and its jewelled glass perished long ago; but the fine tracery of decorative trefoils and quatrefoils stands out with peculiar beauty and distinctness against the pale blue summer sky. Noble trees at its side seem to offer protection from the warm July sun; and ancient ivy, with roots as thick as the trunks of these trees and great heart-shaped and very dark-green leaves picked out with ivory-white veins, climbs over and around the gray walls, most lovingly and most tenderly to enfold the remnants of this building in a rich and graceful garment that ripples every now and then in the gentle breeze.

The landscape is so mellow and its sylvan beauty so finished, so softened, and so perfected by centuries of thoughtful care that it may be compared to the expression of exquisite art — to a Chinese carving, to a Persian miniature, to a Beethoven Symphony, or to a Chopin Nocturne. The scene is unspeakably precious, intensely sophisticated, delightfully civilized! Every individual object — river, trees, grass, flowers, brambles, briars, birds, and crumbling ruins — connect with a remote Past, so continuous that there has not been the slightest break in the line. The birds I hear chirping and singing are descendants of those birds that sang to Robin Hood and his Merry Men and the ancestors of the flowers that are

An Afternoon with Autolycus

blooming so radiantly before my eyes live in the verse of Spenser, Shakespeare, Herrick, and Milton. As I saturate myself in all this loveliness certain familiar lines and lyrics seem to issue from the very birds and flowers themselves. From bough and branch trills and melodious roulades resolve themselves into Bottom's song:

> The ousel-cock* so black of hue,
> With orange-tawny bill,
> The throstle with his note so true,
> The wren with little quill.
>
> The finch, the sparrow, and the lark,
> The plain-song cuckoo gray,
> Whose note full many a man doth mark
> And dares not answer nay.[39]

And the blossoms all around me seem to sing very softly as they wave in the breeze:

> When daisies pied, and violets blue,
>   And lady-smocks all silver white,
> And cuckoo-buds of yellow hue,
> Do paint the meadows with delight.[40]

As I listen to the voices of these birds and flowers I realize that such scenes as this have inspired the greatest English poets; and it seems to me that all this sylvan beauty must be but a dream of mine: it *cannot* be real. It does not belong to the Twentieth Century. If *I* am real, then this must surely be a vision; if, on the other hand, this scene actually exists, then *I* must be an unreality. Which is it?

---

* The blackbird. [Singleton's note]
[39] *A Midsummer Night's Dream* (III.1).
[40] *Love's Labour's Lost* (V.2).

Shakespearian Fantasias

This moment of speculative musing is interrupted by a sharp call to life. I hear the voice of a young man — a clear, sweet tenor — singing, as he comes down the road towards me:

> "Jog on, jog on, the foot-path way,
>   And merrily hent the stile-a;
> A merry heart goes all the day,
>   Your sad tires in a mile-a."[41]

His quick and long strides soon brought the young man close to me and I saw that he had the figure of a Mediaeval tumbler, *jongleur*, or acrobat, and that all his motions were quick, graceful, and extraordinarily flexible. His costume was peculiar, belonging to the late Sixteenth Century; but his hose was full of tears and holes, his doublet was in rags and tatters with several missing buttons, his linen collar was far from clean, and he had

> more feet than shoes for his toes looked through the over-leather.[42]

Approaching me, he made a long, low bow, nearly sweeping the ground with his hat — a bow that was a ridiculous mimicry of the style of a courtier, revealing intimate acquaintance with the manners of the dashing young nobles of Elizabethan times. I immediately placed the newcomer as serving-man to some lord, or as comedian in a London company of actors. Whatever he may have been he now was an out-and-out vagabond, rogue, and rascal. As I acknowledged his salutation I quickly read his face and noted the small, bright, and

---

[41] *The Winter's Tale* (IV.2).
[42] Paraphrase of lines from *The Taming of the Shrew* (Induction.2).

An Afternoon with Autolycus

restless eyes betraying a character that was dishonest and dishonorable and a mind adept in trickery. Yet for all that there was something arrestingly magnetic and attractive about the scoundrel and he had for me a certain diabolical fascination. In fact, he was possessed of personality — and a great deal of it. His humorous wink, his agreeable smile, his interesting gestures, his swinging gait, his long, slender hands, and his ringing, cheery voice all compelled me to gaze upon him, to watch his every action, and to await impatiently whatever he might be pleased to say. And in sooth, I had to wait a long time because this arch vagabond stood for several minutes staring at me with astonishment. Evidently I was a mystery too difficult for him to comprehend.

A humorous shake of his head, a mocking smile, and a deep sigh of resigned despair said better than any words could have done that he gave up the puzzle; and with another ridiculous and obsequious bow he introduced himself as follows:

> "My father named me Autolycus, who, being, as I am, littered under Mercury, was likewise a snapper-up of unconsidered trifles. With die and drab I purchased this caparison; and my revenue is the silly-cheat."[43]

Then, with a very pleasing smile, he threw himself nonchalantly upon the ground, and, to a lovely old English tune, sang lustily:

> "When daffodils begin to peer —
>   With, hey! the doxy over the dale —
> Why, then comes in the sweet o' the year;

---

[43] *The Winter's Tale* (IV.3).

Shakespearian Fantasias

> For the red blood reigns in the winter's pale.
>
> "The white sheet bleaching on the hedge —
>   With, hey! the sweet birds, O, how they sing! —
> Doth set my pugging tooth on edge;
>   For a quart of ale is a dish for a king.
>
> "The lark that tirra-lirra chants —
>   With, hey! with hey! the thrush and the jay —
> Are summer songs for me and my aunts,
>   While we lie tumbling in the hay."[44]

Then looking straight at me, he told the truth:

> "I have served Prince Florizel, and in my time, wore three-pile;[45] but now I am out of service";[46]

and then, to hide the regret he had betrayed, Autolycus broke out again in song with

> "But shall I go mourn for that, my dear?
>   The pale moon shines by night:
> And when I wander here and there,
>   I then do most go right."[47]

"Autolycus," I said, "I am very glad to see you! I have known you for many years."

"You have known *me*?" he queried. "Known *me*? Why, I have never seen *you* before. Your clothes are passing strange and it is with great difficulty that I can understand your English. Yet you seem to understand me! And when I was singing you looked as if you were well acquainted with my songs."

"I adore your ballads, Autolycus," I answered, "and I

---

[44] *The Winter's Tale* (IV.2).
[45] Velvet. [Singleton's note]
[46] *The Winter's Tale* (IV.3).
[47] Same.

An Afternoon with Autolycus

wish you would sing them all to me, one after the other."

But instead of complying with my request, Autolycus called out: "A prize! a prize!" for his sharp eyes had discovered a young Clownish Shepherd coming down the road; so, giving me a knowing wink, he whispered:

> "If the springe hold, the cock's mine";[48]

and, with an agile, cat-like motion, Autolycus fell grovelling upon the ground.

At first the Clown did not see Autolycus, for his wits were dull and he was talking to himself: "Let me see; let me see," he muttered,

> "what am I to buy for our sheep-shearing feast? *Three pound of sugar; five pound of currants; rice* — what will this sister of mine do with rice? But my father hath made her mistress of the feast, and she lays it on. She hath made me four-and-twenty nosegays for the shearers — three-man, song-men all, and very good ones; but they are most of them means and bases; but one Puritan amongst them, and he sings psalms to hornpipes. I must have saffron to color the warden-pies; *mace — dates —* none; that's out of my note; *nutmegs, seven; a race or two of ginger* — but that I may beg; *four pound of prunes, and as many of raisins o' the sun.*"[49]

"O that ever I was born!" groans Autolycus.

"I' the name of me!" the astonished Clown exclaims, having almost stepped upon the prostrate sufferer.

"O help me! help me," beseeches Autolycus. "Pluck but off these rags; and then, death, death!"

Then, as the sympathetic Clown tires to aid Autolycus,

---

[48] *The Winter's Tale* (IV.3).
[49] Same. The following dialogue between Autolycus and the Clown is adapted from the same play and scene.

the latter explains his condition: "I am robbed, sir, and beaten; my money and apparel ta'en from me, and these detestable things put upon me."

The Clown now lends a helping hand, whereupon Autolycus cries out:

"O, good sir, tenderly, O!"

"Alas! poor soul!" pities the Clown.

"O, good sir, softly, good sir: I fear, sir, my shoulder blade is out."

"How now, cans't stand?" the Clown inquires solicitously.

"Softly, dear sir," replies Autolycus, deftly picking his pocket, "good sir, softly"; and, winking at me, adds: "You ha' done me a charitable office."

"Dost lack any money?" the young Shepherd inquires. "I have a little money for thee."

"No, good sweet sir; no, I beseech you, sir. I have a kinsman not past three quarters of a mile hence, unto whom I was going; I shall there have money, or anything I want. Offer me no money I pray you; *that* kills my heart."

"What manner of fellow was he that robbed you?" asks the Clown.

"A fellow, sir, that I have known to go about with troll-my-dames," explains Autolycus. "I knew him once a servant of the prince: I cannot tell, good sir, for which of his virtues it was, but he was certainly whipped out of the court. I know this man well," Autolycus adds, "he hath been since an ape-bearer, a process-server, a bailiff; then he composed a motion of the Prodigal son, and married a tinker's wife within a mile where my land and living lies; and, having flown over many knavish professions, he

An Afternoon with Autolycus

settled only in rogue: some call him Autolycus."

"Out upon him!" ejaculated the horrified Clown, "prig, for my life, prig: he haunts wakes, fairs, and bear-baitings."

"Very true, sir," Autolycus acquiesces, "he, sir, he; that's the rogue that put me into this apparel."

"Not a more cowardly rogue in all Bohemia," the Clown answers; "if you had looked big and spit at him, he'd have run." Then the Clown asks: "how do you now?" and, learning that Autolycus can stand and walk, offers to bring him on the way to his kinsman.

"No, good-faced sir; no, sweet sir," Autolycus protests, whereupon the Clown said: "Then fare thee well: I must go buy spices for our sheep-shearing." And as the Clown departs, Autolycus, looking at his retreating figure, says: "I'll be with you at your sheep-shearing, too"; and, turning, invites me to go with him.

Of course, I had no business to be amused by the behavior of such a rascal and thief, who took such mean advantage of the kindly, simple-minded Shepherd boy; but, as I said before, there was something so magnetic about Autolycus that I could not help but be entertained; and although I knew I ought not to go prancing down the road with such a disgraceful companion, I could not resist Autolycus's invitation; and while it was hard for me to keep step with his long and swinging stride, I did my best. Autolycus, evidently pleased and flattered by my companionship, gaily sang, as we tramped along:

> "Jog on, jog on the footpath way,
> And merrily hent the stile-a;
> A merry heart goes all the day,

Shakespearian Fantasias

Your sad tires in a mile-a."[50]

The winding road climbed up a hill, from which I saw in the distance a few reddish-purple roofs against the light blue sky. On, on we go, the reddish-purple roofed houses growing more distinct and massing beautifully. As we came nearer, great variety and charm of lines were revealed and luscious tints of red, purple, yellow, and brown. Most of the cottages were thatched and the many soft and iridescent colors under these roofs were repeated in the shadows on the ground. Other cottages were of white with red-tiled roofs and others were of red brick; but in all cases the roofs were low and supplied with large chimneys.

And the flowers!

Flowers, flowers everywhere!

Some of the cottages are fairly smothered with blossoms and creepers and every cottage has a garden brilliant with bright blossoms. Roses twine themselves over the tiny doorways and walls and shake perfume from crimson, yellow or saffron petals when touched by the breeze. Pears and peaches are slowly ripening on the walls and bees and butterflies are humming and darting hither and thither.

As we leave this little cluster of cottages, Autolycus points to a larger cottage in the distance standing in quite extensive grounds, with a much larger and more elaborate garden, and tells me it is the home of the Old Shepherd, where the sheep-shearing is to take place. The shepherd, Autolycus informs me, "is a man that from very

---

[50] *The Winter's Tale* (IV.2).

An Afternoon with Autolycus

nothing and beyond the imagination of his neighbors is grown into an unspeakable estate and has a very beautiful daughter named Perdita. One day when Prince Florizel was out a-birding his falcon flew over the Shepherd's grounds. Prince Florizel pursued it and saw Perdita; and they no sooner met but they looked, no sooner looked but they loved. Prince Florizel is seldom now from the Shepherd's house, where he is known as Doricles. No one, not even Perdita, has any idea that he is the son of the King of Bohemia. Now," concluded Autolycus, "you go along and find a good hiding-place where you can see and hear everything. I will be there anon. I will appear as a pedlar; and I am sure you will know me despite my false beard."

"Anon, anon, Autolycus," I answer.

The grass is so soft that my footsteps cannot be heard as I steal quietly up to the Shepherd's Cottage. Fortunately the windows are all open and I can see within the room, which is large. Florizel and Perdita are talking earnestly. Yes, Perdita is very beautiful, and, with the garland of flowers on her head, she well deserves the name of Flora, by which her lover calls her. Perdita, aware that Doricles is not the simple swain he pretends to be but is the son of someone of high degree, is apprehensive that his father may chance to pass this way, even as his son did; and what would he say to his son marrying a shepherdess? The power of the King, too, might be invoked to prevent this union! Florizel tries to comfort her with promises of his undying loyalty, begging her to be merry and to welcome the coming guests, as if this were indeed their nuptial day.

Shakespearian Fantasias

At this moment the old Shepherd enters with two elderly men, the Clown, his son, who was robbed by Autolycus, and two Shepherdesses, Mopsa and Dorcas, healthy, bouncing, red-cheeked country lasses, presenting a strong contrast to Perdita's delicate beauty. The Old Shepherd chides Perdita for her lack of hospitality and wishes she were like his old wife, who, on these occasions was pantler, butler, cook, dame, and servant, her face red with labor, and who ran about welcoming and serving everybody and taking a sip, too, with every guest.

"*You* are mistress of the feast," he adds, "bid us welcome to your sheep-shearing."

Perdita, then, with a charming grace, greets the two elderly strangers and commands Dorcas to hand her the flowers. Selecting from the basket two little sprays, Perdita offers them with a high-bred manner, hard to reconcile with the rustic surroundings, and with the words: "Reverend sirs,

> For you there's rosemary and rue; these keep
> Seeming and savour all the winter long:
> Grace and remembrance be to you both,
> And welcome to our shearing!"[51]

"Shepherdess," Polixenes, charmed in spite of himself, replies, "Shepherdess, a fair one you are! — well you fit our ages with flowers of winter."

Then I hear a delightful discussion about flowers, for Perdita's garden is the most famous in this neighborhood. She speaks of hot lavendar, mints, savory, and marjoram;

---

[51] *The Winter's Tale* (IV.4).

An Afternoon with Autolycus

of "the marigold that goes to bed with the sun and with him rises weeping"; of "daffodils that come before the swallow dares" and that dance with beauty in the winds of March; or "violets dim but sweeter than the lids of Juno's eyes or Cytherea's breath"; of "pale primroses that die unmarried ere they can behold bright Phoebus in his strength"; of "bold oxlips and the crown imperial"; and of "lilies of all kinds, the flower-de-luce being one."

Perdita is so lovely as she distributes her flowers among the guests, and she speaks so beautifully about them, that Polixenes observes to his companion, Camillo:

> "This is the prettiest low-born lass that ever
> Ran on the green sward: nothing she does or seems
> But smacks of something greater than herself,
> Too noble for this place."[52]

"Good sooth," replies Camillo, "she is

> The Queen of curds and cream."[53]

The Clown bids the musicians strike up and takes Mopsa for a partner. Other Shepherds and Shepherdesses come forward and Florizel and Perdita lead off in the dance. Perdita is so graceful that Florizel murmurs to her:

> "When you dance I wish you were
> A wave o' the sea that might ever do
> Nothing but that."[54]

"She dances featly," observes the critical King Polixenes; and, turning to the Shepherd, asks: "What fair

---

[52] *The Winter's Tale* (IV.3). The rest of this fantasia is adapted from the same play and scene.
[53] Same.
[54] Same.

Shakespearian Fantasias

swain is he that dances with your daughter?"

All the Shepherd can tell Polixenes is that he calls himself Doricles.

Looking behind me, I see Autolycus, disguised as a pedlar, wearing the false beard of which he spoke, and carrying a large pack. He gives me one of his mischievous winks and lays his finger on his lips to command my silence. Then with stealthy strides he approaches the house and knocks at the door.

The Servant who opens it shuts it quickly and runs back to speak to the Old Shepherd:

> "O master, if you did but hear the pedlar at the door, you would never dance again after a tabor and pipe; no, the bag-pipe could not move you. He sings several tunes faster than you'll tell money: he utters them as he had eaten ballads and all men's ears grew to his tunes."[55]

The Clown says he could never have come at a more opportune time. "I love a ballad but even too well," he cries, "if it be a doleful matter merrily set down, or a very pleasant thing indeed and sung lamentably."

The Servant chimes in with:

> "He hath songs for man or woman of all sizes; no milliner can so fit his customers with gloves. He hath ribands of all the colors i' the rainbow; points more than all the lawyers in Bohemia can learnedly handle, though they come to him by the gross; inkles, caddisses, cambrics, lawns: why, he sings 'em over as they were gods or goddesses. He hath the prettiest love-songs for maids."[56]

"Pr'ythee, bring him in," orders the Clown, "and let

---

[55] *The Winter's Tale* (IV.3).
[56] Same.

An Afternoon with Autolycus

him approach singing."

Oh! with what a swaggering manner Autolycus entered, gaily chanting:

> "Lawn as white as driven snow:
> Cypress black as e'er was crow;
> Gloves as sweet as damask-roses;
> Masks for faces and for noses;
> Bugle-bracelet, necklace amber,
> Perfume for a lady's chamber;
> Golden quoifs and stomachers,
> For my lads to give their dears;
> Pins and poking-sticks of steel,
> What maids lack from head to heel:
> Come, buy of me, come; come buy, come buy;
> But, lads, or else your lasses cry:
> Come, buy."[57]

And how these country lasses, bright of eye and rosy of cheek with their rustic swains crowded around the pedlar; and how Autolycus temptingly held up a bright ribbon, a pair of sweet-scented gloves, a piece of lace, a glass brooch, a pomander, a flask of perfume, an amber necklace, or a poking-stick to flute their ruffles! And every ballad that he showed was immediately purchased. Mopsa called for "a Merry Ballad," whereupon Autolycus handed her "a passing merry one" that "goes to the tune of two Maids wooing a Man," adding that it is in great request.

"Dorcas and I can sing it, if thou'lt bear a part," Mopsa suggests. "'Tis in three parts."

"We had the tune a month ago," Dorcas observes.

"I can bear my part," Autolycus confidently remarks.

---

[57] *The Winter's Tale* (IV.3).

Shakespearian Fantasias

"You must know 'tis my occupation"; and then Autolycus, Mopsa, and Dorcas sing, Autolycus beginning:

> A. Get you hence, for I must go;
> Where, it fits not you to know.
> D. Whither? M. O, Whither? D. Whither?
> M. It becomes thy oath full well,
> That to me thy secrets tell:
> D. Me, too, let me go thither.
>
> M. Or thou go'st to the grange or mill:
> D. If to either, thou dost ill.
> A. Neither. D. What, neither? A. Neither.
> D. Thou hast sworn my love to be;
> M. Thou hast sworn it more to me;
> Then, whither go'st? — say, whither?[58]

How delightful to my ears this singing of an Elizabethan part-song! How clear each voice; how prompt the attack; how firm the rhythm!

The Clown commands Autolycus to carry his pack out-of-doors, so that Mopsa and Dorcas can have first choice of his enticing wares. "Follow me, girls," the Clown calls; and they trip out, all the rest following. And indeed who could resist Autolycus, who now sings:

> "Will you buy any tape,
> Or lace for your cape,
> My dainty duck, my dear-a?
> Any silk, any thread,
> Any toys for your head,
> Of the new'st and fin'st, fin'st ware-a?
> Come to the pedlar,
> Money's a meddler,
> That doth utter all men's ware-a."[59]

---

[58] *The Winter's Tale* (IV.3).
[59] Same.

An Afternoon with Autolycus

I watched the little procession moving onward to an open space beneath the trees in the distance and hear the chatter of the voices, the merry peals of laughter, and the ringing tones of Autolycus proclaiming the beauties of this or that article, which he dangled before the eyes of the little group. Occasionally, too, I heard Autolycus sing one of his ballads. Presently I saw the Old Shepherd join the throng in a state of great agitation at which the merry crowd scattered.

Autolycus then walked rapidly up to me and laughingly boasted:

> "Ha, Ha! what a fool Honesty is! and Trust, his sworn brother, a very simple gentleman! I have sold all my trumpery; not a counterfeit stone, not a riband, glass, pomander, brooch, table-book, ballad, knife, tape, glove, shoe-tie, bracelet, horn-ring, to keep my pack from fasting; they throng who should buy first, as if my trinkets had been hallowed and brought a benediction to the buyer. I picked and cut most of their purses and had not the old man come and raised such a whoobub against his daughter and the King's son, and scared my choughs from the chaff, I had not left a purse alive in the whole army."[60]

"What do you mean about the old man?" I asked.

"Why," Autolycus answered, "I am surprised you did not see what happened while I was selling my wares. Polixenes threw off his disguise; cursed his son for stooping to a shepherdess; and threatened Perdita with a terrible death if she ever opened the latches of the house to Florizel again. Then the King went off in a furious temper. The Old Shepherd also denounced Florizel and Perdita; and, crying 'Undone! Undone!' ran out to where I

---

[60] *The Winter's Tale* (IV.3).

Shakespearian Fantasias

was singing a ballad about a fish that appeared on the coast on Wednesday the fourscore of April, forty thousand fathom above water; and all the lads and lasses ran away."

Camillo, Florizel, and Perdita now appeared and Camillo suggested that Florizel should exchange garments with Autolycus, giving Autolycus money, so they might escape and take ship for Sicilia. No sooner had they gone than Autolycus removed his false beard and began to tell me how well equipped he was for the business: "To have an open ear," he said,

> "a quick eye, and a nimble hand, is necessary for a cut-purse; a good nose is requisite also to smell out work for the other senses. I see this is the time that the unjust man doth thrive. The Prince himself is about a piece of iniquity, stealing away from his father";[61]

and then he added "and if I thought it were a piece of honesty to acquaint the King withal, I would not do it: I hold it the more knavery to conceal it; and therein I am constant to my profession!" Then he excitedly exclaimed: "Aside! Aside! Here is more matter for a hot brain"; for his quick eye had noticed the Old Shepherd and the Clown approaching. They were talking about the finding of Perdita as a babe and the strange bundle with her. The Clown was advising his father to go and tell the King that Perdita was not his daughter, but "a changeling."

Stepping forward, Autolycus, supposed by the clown to be a courtier from his new apparel, demanded to know what the fardel contained. Then he terrified them by his fantastic prediction of the punishment both would

---

[61] *The Winter's Tale* (IV.3).

An Afternoon with Autolycus

receive for the attempt to marry Perdita to the King's son. Yes, for gold, Autolycus will use his influence; and the Shepherd decides to leave his son in pawn with Autolycus while he goes to the house for the money. Instead of directing them to the King's palace, Autolycus directs them to the ship on which Florizel and Perdita are about to embark. Autolycus bids the Clown "Walk toward the sea-side; go on the right hand, I will trust you. I will but look upon the hedge and follow you."

The reason that Autolycus wants to look upon the hedge is because I am sitting there on the stile that leads over the hedge into the green meadows, in the very spot where I first saw Autolycus, among the scarlet poppies, yellow kingcups, and the trailing bell-flowers.

Autolycus, looking at me very earnestly, remarked: "If I had a mind to be honest, Fortune would not suffer me; she drops booties in my mouth. I am courted now with a double occasion — gold, and a means to do the Prince my master good; which who knows how that may turn back to my advancement?"

"Autolycus," I said, "I think you are going to be taken back into the service of Prince Florizel and that soon you will again be wearing three-pile velvet; and I certainly hope so. Take my good wishes with you and my grateful thanks for a most interesting afternoon."

"Good bye," said Autolycus, "I shall probably never see you again. But shall I go mourn for that, my dear?" Then, with his long and swinging stride, he tripped gaily down the road, singing:

> "Jog on, jog on the footpath way,
>   And Merrily hent the stile-a;

Shakespearian Fantasias

> A merry heart goes all the day,
> Your sad tires in a mile-a."

The song died away; Autolycus melted into the mellow landscape; and I was again alone with the birds and the flowers.

Under the Greenwood Tree

"NOW am I in Arden!" I exclaimed, remembering the words of Touchstone; and, not agreeing with his impressions, I paraphrased his opinion, adding: "When I was at home I was certainly not in a better place!"

And where indeed *could* you find a more enchanting place than the Forest of Arden?

To eyes accustomed to the wild and primeval woodlands of the New World (which have their own beauties and their own charms) the word *forest* seems a misnomer. It would be more descriptive and more correct to speak of the English greenwood as a *park*.

Beneath the trees, instead of the crisp and russet and fading leaves of yesteryear, the brown and slippery pine-needles, and the underbrush (both growing and withering), you find a soft, smooth carpet of emerald grass, very short, like the pile of velvet, and so uniformly perfect that it is hard to believe this sward is not kept closely clipped and rolled and watered every day like the lawn of a gentleman's estate. And there are great open spaces of this grassy sward, or lawn, in every direction, diversified here and there by hawthorn trees, holly bushes, clumps of pollard willows, groups of ancient oaks, and groves of beeches.

There are no "wild flowers" as we understand the word: no trailing arbutus peeping up through the thick

Shakespearian Fantasias

mat of ancient and decaying leaves on the ground — there are no ancient and decaying leaves on the ground, anywhere — there are no clumps of snowy dogwood, no mountain laurel, no merry little blue eyebrights fluttering in the breeze, no gleaming golden-rod, no crimson and garnet sumach, no perforated queen's lace handkerchief, no golden and speckled jewel-weed, and no white-crowned and yellow-centered daisies. You find, on the other hand, great patches of pink, white, and purple heather, pale primroses, bold oxlips, nodding violets, roses, honeysuckle, wreathing periwinkle, lady-smocks, kingcups and other blossoms that are very close relatives of simple and beloved garden flowers.

Perhaps the most striking feature of the English forest is the beech-tree. You have to come to England to make the acquaintance of the beech. We have nothing like it in America. The peculiar color — a watery green — that is spread over the entire tree, gives it a strange, weird charm. This green is very pronounced on the large trunk — smooth and shiny as satin, where splotches and splashes of darker green and lighter green and black and greenish white appear with fantastic irregularity. The large, luxuriant, and thickly massed leaves are uniform in hue and they tower upward and they spread outward like a canopy. The grass grows thickly and richly underneath the beech all the way up to the dappled trunk and it fills in all the crevices and spaces between the high and rippling roots that flow outward in all directions; and these roots of enormous size extend beyond the radius of the canopy of leaves and grip the ground with the ferocity and tenacity of an ogre's gnarled, wrinkled, and powerful

Under the Greenwood Tree

talons.

One of the indescribable beauties of the beech is the sensitive way the leaves keep moving, thereby permitting the sun to play above, below, and around them, so there is, in consequence, a ceaseless weaving of light and shadow, of the kind that Wagner has depicted musically in his superlatively beautiful *Waldweben* in the second act of *Siegfried*. And throughout all that shimmer of gold there stands out conspicuously — like the fundamental pedal-point in *Das Rheingold* — that great dominant note of watery green — a green that is cool, translucent, and suggestive of phosphorescence — the green of cool grottoes in the ocean's depths; the green of the flowing hair of water-nymphs; the green on the bellies of certain fish; the green on the spring waistcoat of the frog; the green on the torch of the glow-worm; the green of the fire-fly's lamp; and the green in the lantern of the Will-o'-the-wisp.

For a long time I sat here on a high, mossy root with my back against the trunk of a magnificent beech, listening to the birds and watching the sunshine dancing on the leaves while I constantly repeated aloud:

> "Under the greenwood tree,
> Who loves to lie with me,
> And turn his merry note
> Unto the sweet bird's throat.
> Come hither, come hither, come hither;
> Here shall he see
> No enemy,
> But winter and rough weather."[62]

---

[62] *As You Like It* (II.5).

Shakespearian Fantasias

After a time I was surprised to hear these words sung some distance away by a man's voice, clear and very musical. The tune was unfamiliar; but it had the characteristic Elizabethan lilt and it seemed as if birds, leaves, and echoes took up the song. Indeed, "all the woods made answer and the echoes rang" with

> "Under the greenwood tree,
> Who loves to lie with me,
> And turn his merry note
> Unto the sweet bird's throat.
> Come hither, come hither, come hither;
> Here shall he see
> No enemy,
> But winter and rough weather."[63]

What was that?

I thought I saw the figure of a man appear among some very tall ferns about twenty feet away, and then vanish behind a tree.

I leaned forward, tense, with fixed and astonished gaze.

Who could it be?

Perhaps, after all, it was only a deer!

No, I objected promptly, the sound was that of a human footstep! Besides I was sure I had seen a man's form.

I had come so far into the Forest that I fancied I was alone. Yet this idea was in the face of it absurd. Some other lover of the greenwood might have wandered also into its leafy heart. The Forest of Arden was not created exclusively for *me*. I should remember this in all humility.

---

[63] *As You Like It* (II.5).

Under the Greenwood Tree

All was now silent again; and I tried to persuade myself that I was fanciful. Yet the incident had disoriented me, disconcerted me, dumbfounded me. The stillness became oppressive. I began to wish that I might hear that soft, little rustling noise among the green ferns — that little soft swish in the silence, once again, twice again, many times again — anything rather than this solemn quiet. I envied the birds calling to one another and holding excited conversations high above me among the leaves. Perhaps they were talking about me. Like Siegfried I longed to understand the language of the forest birds. At any rate, it was very disconcerting to be so entirely alone in a spot that was vibrating so intensely with life, manifested in so many forms, all of which were communicating with each other; and I alas! too dull to take a part!

Then I began to feel uncomfortable in another way. It seemed as if eyes were fixed upon me — human eyes, bright, piercing, and analytical. I became more and more affected by this scrutiny, which was all the more potent, because the hypnotizer was invisible. I could not move: my throat and lips went dry; I was cold and hot by turns; and I trembled and shivered.

Who could it be who was affecting me thus?

The dropping of an acorn — a soft sound indeed, but seemingly quite loud to my nervously excited hearing — caused me to look in the direction of an ancient oak; and there, behind its enormous trunk, I caught sight first of a very tall, heron-feather; and then of a green cap into which it was jauntily stuck; then of a pair of brightly burning eyes — eyes of a light amber or hazel color —

Shakespearian Fantasias

then the face of a young and extremely handsome man, and, finally, of his entire figure. This young man was dressed in a forester's suit of Lincoln green, fashioned in the style of Robin Hood, which showed to the greatest advantage his slender, *svelte*, debonair, and graceful lines.

Perceiving that he had been discovered, the handsome young man advanced towards me, doffing his cap, and with a courtly bow, requested, in a voice of infinite culture and charm:

"I pr'ythee let me be better acquainted with thee."

I bowed permission.

"They say I am a melancholy fellow," the young gentleman volunteered. "I am so. I do love it better than laughing. I am sometimes called Monsieur Melancholy. 'Tis good to be sad and say nothing."

"I should think it would be better to be merry and speak volumes," I retorted, rather surprised at having found my voice; and, remembering the song I had lately heard from Autolycus, I added: "You know

> A merry heart goes all the day,
> Your sad tires in a mile-a."[64]

The courtly young gentleman flashed a piercing glance upon me, but he did not take up the argument. However, he looked at me very intently as he continued:

> "I have neither the scholar's melancholy, which is emulation; nor the musician's which is fantastical; nor the courtier's, which is proud; nor the soldier's, which is ambitious; nor the lawyer's which is politic; nor the lady's, which is nice; nor the lover's, which is all these: but it is a melancholy of mine own, compounded of many

---

[64] *The Winter's Tale* (IV.3).

Under the Greenwood Tree

> simples, extracted from many objects; and, indeed, the sundry contemplation of my travels, in which my often rumination wraps me in a most humorous sadness."[65]

"How now, my worthy lord?" I ventured.

> "A heavy heart bears not a nimble tongue."[66]

"Pretty and apt!" the young courtier replied, mockingly; but, nevertheless, he took off his cap gallantly and made me a bow of appreciation, accompanied by a most ingratiating smile.

I smiled in response, for I felt rather proud that I had been able to answer him in such fashion that a basis was created for us to meet upon, and on equal terms.

After a short pause, I queried: "You have been a traveler?"

"Yes, I have gained my experience," was the reply.

"And your experience makes you sad?" I asked sympathetically, adding: "I had rather have a fool to make me merry than experience to make me sad."[67]

"You have a nimble wit," he answered. "I think it was made of Atalanta's heels. I will sit down beside you and we two will rail against the world and all our misery."[68]

"I am not in a humor for railing, good sir," I answered. "I would far rather tune a merry note unto the sweet bird's throat."

Taking no notice of this observation, my companion proclaimed sententiously:

---

[65] *As You Like It* (IV.1).
[66] *Love's Labour's Lost* (V.2).
[67] *As You Like It* (IV.1).
[68] Paraphrased from *As You Like It* (III.2).

Shakespearian Fantasias

> "All the world's a stage,
> And all the men and women merely players;
> They have their exits and their entrances;
> And one man in his time plays many parts,
> His acts being seven ages."[69]

And then he told me what these seven ages were;

> "the infant mewling and puking in the nurse's arms; the whining school-boy creeping unwillingly to school; the sighing lover; the bearded, quarrelsome soldier; the severe justice; the lean and slippered age; and, last of all, second childishness, sans teeth, sans eyes, sans taste, sans everything."[70]

"Oh!" I exclaimed. "I know you now! You are the melancholy Jaques!"

"Yes," he admitted with his handsome, sad smile:

> "I am not as I seem to be,
>   For when I smile I am not glad,
> A thrall, although you count me free,
>   I, most in mirth, most pensive sad."[71]

And then, looking at me questioningly, he added:

> "Sweet Mistress, what your name is else I know not,
>   Nor by what wonder you do hit on mine,"[72]

how did you find your way into this Forest of Arden?

"In good sooth, I know not," I answered, "unless I was wafted hither by enchantment; but whether I came here through enchantment or not, out of this wood I have no

---

[69] *As You Like It* (II.7).
[70] Paraphrased from *As You Like It* (II.7).
[71] The first four lines of a poem first published in *Paradise of Dainty Devices* (1576) and attributed to E.O., who is thought to have been Edward Oxenforde, Earl of Oxford.
[72] *The Comedy of Errors* (III.2).

Under the Greenwood Tree

desire to go."

"No one ever wants to leave this Forest of Arden," observed the melancholy Jaques. "You should know that several years ago the reigning Duke was banished by his younger brother. Instead of protesting, the old Duke put himself into voluntary exile. Three or four loving lords came with him; and, as their lands and revenue were taken to enrich the younger Duke, the latter gave them all good leave to wander." Here the melancholy Jaques laughed sarcastically. "The old Duke's daughter, Rosalind," he continued, "remained at the Court with the new Duke's daughter, Celia; and never two ladies loved as they do. The old Duke came here to this Forest of Arden and a many merry men followed him. The watchword of one and all was

> 'Now go we in content
> To liberty and not to banishment.'[73]

"In sooth, many young gentlemen flocked to him every day, and now he has a great number; and they all live here like the old Robin Hood of England, fleeting the time carelessly as they did in the golden world."

"And how long have *you* been here, good Master Jaques?" I asked.

"Oh, I came among the first," he answered, "It was just after I had returned from Italy.[74] The Forest is getting to be full of strange people," he continued; "there is a Fool in

---

[73] *As You Like It* (I.3).
[74] Jaques, a fictional character, of course never went to Italy. But Edward de Vere did, and he lived there for almost a year. Some Shakespeare scholars have pointed out similarities in the character and disposition of Jacques and de Vere.

Shakespearian Fantasias

motley roaming about and uttering strange saws and modern instances, and then there is a swashing young page, who calls himself Ganymede and who wears a gallant curtle-axe upon his thigh and carries a boar-spear in his hand. He has lately come into the Forest and has bought a shepherd's cottage, flock, and pasture, over there under that little tuft of olive trees, where he lives with his sister and the motley Fool, whose name is Touchstone. They all wander about as they please."[75]

"Oh, I *hope* I shall see them," I exclaimed enthusiastically.

"Oh, you probably will," the melancholy Jaques answered, indifferently.

After a short interval, the melancholy Jaques continued his information: "Then there is a man haunts the Forest that abuses our young plants with carving Rosalind on their barks; hangs odes upon hawthorns and elegies on brambles; all, forsooth, deifying the name of Rosalind. Here, for instance, is one just behind you";[76] and, stretching out his long, graceful arm, my new friend pulled from a hawthorn branch, bright with pink blossoms, a paper, on which a verse was written. "Listen to this," he said, mockingly:

> "From the east to Western Ind,
> No jewel is like Rosalind.
> Her worth, being mounted on the wind,
> Through all the world bears Rosalind.
> All the pictures fairest lin'd.
> Are but black to Rosalind.
> Let no face be kept in mind,

---

[75] Partially paraphrased from *As You Like It* (I.3).
[76] Paraphrased from *As You Like It* (III.2).

Under the Greenwood Tree

But the fair of Rosalind."[77]

"I do not like the name," he added.

"Perhaps there was no thought of pleasing you when she was christened," I suggested.

"Well," he smilingly replied, "Love is a madness anyway, and, I tell you, deserves as well a dark house and a whip as madmen do; and the reason they are not so punished and cured is that the lunacy is so ordinary that the whippers are in love, too.[78] Now to prove how true this is, there is a young shepherd in the Forest who is in love with a proud, disdainful shepherdess; and, by my faith, I see no more in her than in the ordinary of nature's sale-works — he is a far more properer man than she a woman — and this piece of scorn and pitiless disdain has fallen in love with the pretty youth, Ganymede, who disdains her in his turn. And the Fool in motley has picked up a silly, country wench named Audrey, who tends goats; and he protests that he is going to marry her. Indeed, he told me this very morning that Sir Oliver Martext, vicar of the next village, has promised to couple them one day soon, here in the Forest, under a bush or a tree. And that will be an odd marriage, I promise you!"

"Well," I laughed, "some men must love my lady and some Joan."[79]

Again the melancholy Jaques looked at me searchingly; "you talk very strangely," he said, "almost like one of *us*!"

"Perhaps you do not know what it is to love?" I

---

[77] *As You Like It* (III.2).
[78] Same.
[79] *Love Labour's Lost* (III.1).

Shakespearian Fantasias

queried, hoping to give the *blasé* courtier a little taste of his own playful mockery.

But the handsome Jaques took my question seriously. He lifted one of his eyebrows and his hazel eyes glowed for a brief moment, as he answered with a great deal of sentiment:

"I have sighed upon a midnight pillow."[80] Then, after a pause, during which memories were evidently running through his mind, he added:

> "I, too, like Orlando — that's the name of the young man who makes all the trees and bushes break into bloom with songs and odes to Rosalind — have written verses to my mistress's eye-brow and to the fairest and softest things in all the world — her eyes! I know the wound invisible that Love's keen arrows make.[81]

"But my verses are very different from Orlando's. Hear this!" And the melancholy Jaques, with a half stifled sigh, drew from an invisible pocket in his belted green doublet, a slip of paper. As he unfolded it I noticed the exquisite handwriting that expressed the characteristics of scholar, gentleman, and artist. The tone in which he read the following stanzas was most musical, most melancholy; and while he was reading them I tried to imagine what his history could have been. Was it one *woman*, or *many women*, who had brought such wide knowledge to his mind, such bitter gall to his lips, and such pinching pain to his heart? I shall never forget the subtle music that seemed to flow from his voice as he read the following:

---

[80] *As You Like It* (II.4).
[81] *As You Like It* (III.5).

Under the Greenwood Tree

"If women could be fair and yet not fond,
    Or that their love were firm, not fickle, still,
I would not marvel that they make men bond,
    By service long to purchase their good will,
But when I see how frail those creatures are,
I muse that men forget themselves so far.

"To mark the choice they make, and how they change,
    How oft from Phoebus do they flee to Pan,
Unsettled still like haggards wild they range,
    These gentle birds that fly from man to man,
Who would not scorn and shake them from the fist
And let them fly, fair fools, which way they list?

"Yet for disport we fawn and flatter both,
    To pass the time when nothing else can please,
And train them to our lure with subtle oath,
    Till, weary of our wiles, ourselves we ease;
And then we say, when we their fancy try,
To play with fools, O what a fool was I."[82]

As the melancholy Jaques finished he folded up the paper very thoughtfully and tucked it again into his doublet. I fancied I saw tears in his eyes, which he quickly winked away. I could not help but wish that I had the ordering of human affairs. I would in this case have bestowed the white hand of heavenly Rosalind, or of saucy Beatrice, or of gracious Portia upon the handsome courtier who was sitting on the greensward beside me. Anyone of these three *perfect* women would have been a fitting companion and play-fellow to Jaques, stimulating his brilliant intellect, delighting his fastidious taste, feeding his sparkling wit, soothing his sensitive nature,

---

[82] Jacques is reciting a poem attributed to the Earle of Oxenforde in the Rawlinson Manuscript. It was published, set to music, by William Byrd in 1587.

Shakespearian Fantasias

sympathizing with his tender heart, and matching, in like kind, his polished manner. It had not taken me long to see that Jaques's melancholy was produced by a super-sensitive soul and that his cynical philosophy was the result of his worldly experience, which had been wide and varied. And, as the brightest sun casts the darkest shadow, Jaques was himself a paradox. Therefore, solemn sadness and merry wit, dark philosophy and delicate poetry, cutting satire and tender sentiment played in and out of his mind just as the sunlight was playing on the leaves of the beech-tree above us. The more the melancholy Jaques talked to me — and he talked long and earnestly — the more privileged I considered myself to share the inner thoughts of this young aristocrat, poet, and philosopher, who sought to hide his delicate nature beneath a masque of cynicism. That Jaques had been a gallant lover I had not the slightest doubt. The verses he had just read to me were not the mere fruit of imagination. I longed to know what the experience of his heart had been and who was the fair cruelty who had made him mistrust all other women. Yet, of course, I dared not intrude any questions upon a man of such high-bred dignity, and so reserved and so sensitive withal.

Our eyes met once again in mutual sympathy and, in my ardent look, I tried to tell him that all he had confided to me would be given an understanding but no tongue and that I would never speak of this that I had heard. With a quick involuntary motion I laid my finger on my lips and just as quickly removed it; but the melancholy Jaques had caught the gesture. Again he flashed upon me his brilliant glance and his enchanting smile, accompanied this time

Under the Greenwood Tree

by a little nod of graceful acknowledgment of my comprehending sympathy; and then, suddenly jumping to his feet, he suggested brightly:

"Shall we to the Duke?"

"With all my heart," I answered.

Another moment later and we were crushing through the tall ferns.

"Is it far?" I asked, as the melancholy Jaques led the way down a gently sloping hill and across a patch of purple heather.

"No," he answered, "just over that second hill we shall find the Duke, for it is now his dinner-time.

It was an extraordinary picture that burst upon my vision as we walked down the grassy incline and passed into a larger and finer grove of beeches than I had yet seen. Beneath one of the most majestic trees stood a long table, or rather a board on trestles, covered with a snowy cloth. At the centre of the table with his back towards the trunk of the tree and his face towards the open, so that he might see the approach of friend or foe at long range, sat the Duke, a man of middle age with the kindest and gentlest of faces. Several of his companions sat at the table with him and on the one side only, while others were lounging about on the grass, or sitting on folding-stools. All the men, including the Duke, were dressed in Lincoln green cloth, the suits made like that of Jaques with tight hose and well-fitting doublets. Each man wore, like Jaques, a jaunty green cap with tall heron's feather. In today's parlance they would be described as a body of well set-up and extremely "smart" looking men. All were talking and laughing merrily as they ate and drank.

Shakespearian Fantasias

A more careful scrutiny of the table informed me that in front of the Duke stood a large venison pasty and, besides there were several manchet loaves, a neat's tongue, and nut-brown ale served in pewter mugs and tankards. My new-found friend stepped quickly ahead of me and whispered a few words to the Duke before he introduced me, whom I surmised he considered the very strangest of all the strange persons now roaming the forest of Arden.

The Duke received me with the utmost cordiality and hospitality. One of his lords arose immediately and offered me his seat on the Duke's right, which I accepted. Another lord brought me a pewter platter on which he had placed a large slice of the venison pasty, and a third lord handed me a pewter mug filled with foaming ale.

Involuntarily I looked for a knife and fork, but I remembered very quickly that forks were not in use in Elizabethan times and that I should have to eat with my fingers. I hoped with all my heart that my hosts had not noticed my *faux-pas*.

I observed, however, that the Duke and all his men were watching me with the most intense curiosity. However, they were a merry lot; and laughter and jests soon began to circulate as they had evidently gone the rounds before my advent. Presently the Duke asked Jaques where he had hidden himself all the morning: everyone had been searching for him, whereupon Jaques burst out with:

> "A fool, a fool! — I met a fool i' the forest,
> A motley fool; — a miserable world! —
> As I do live by food, I met a fool,

Under the Greenwood Tree

> Who laid him down and bask'd him in the sun,
> And rail'd on Lady Fortune in good terms,
> In good set terms — and yet a motley fool.
> *'Good morrow fool,'* quoth I: *'No sir,'* quoth he,
> *'Call me not fool till heaven hath sent me fortune.'*
> *And then he drew a dial from his poke,*
> *And, looking on it with lack-lustre eye,*
> *Says very wisely, 'It is ten o'clock.*
> *Thus may we see,'* quoth he, *'how the world wags,*
> *'Tis but an hour ago since it was nine;*
> *And after one hour more 'twill be eleven;*
> *And so, from hour to hour, we ripe and ripe,*
> *And then, from hour to hour, we rot and rot;*
> *And thereby hangs a tale.'* When I did hear
> The motley fool thus moral on the time,
> My lungs began to crow like chanticleer,
> That fools should be so deep contemplative;
> And I did laugh, sans intermission,
> An hour by his dial! — O noble fool!
> A worthy fool! — Motley's the only wear."[83]

"What fool is this?" asked the Duke.

But Jaques burst out again:

> "O worthy fool! One that hath been a courtier,
> And says, 'if ladies be but young and fair,
> They have the gift to know it!'"[84]

At this all the foresters laughed long and lustily.

"And in his brain," Jaques continued,

> "Which is as dry as the remainder biscuit
> After a voyage, he hath strange places cramm'd
> With observation, the which he vents
> In mangled forms. — O that I were a fool!

---

[83] *As You Like It* (II.7).
[84] Same.

Shakespearian Fantasias

I am ambitious for a motley coat!"[85]

"Thou shalt have one," laughed the Duke.

"I must have liberty withal," the melancholy Jaques stipulated,

> "As large a charter as the wind,
> To blow on whom I please; give me leave
> To speak my mind, and I will through and through
> Cleanse the foul body of the infected world,
> If they will patiently receive my medicine."[86]

Laughter and cheers went round and round in approbation and tankards and mugs were refilled with the foaming ale.

"And how like you this Forest life?" said the Duke turning to me.

"I am enchanted with the Forest of Arden," I replied.

"And so are we," the Duke asserted, "we find this life more sweet than that of painted pomp"; and then, out of the fullness of experience, he added, with deep sincerity:

> "Are not these woods
> More free from peril than the envious court?
> Here feel we but the penalty of Adam —
> The season's difference: as the icy fang
> And churlish chiding of the winter's wind,
> Which when it bites and blows upon my body,
> Even till I shrink with cold, I smile and say
> This is no flattery: these are counsellors
> That feelingly persuade me what I am."[87]

All the men were listening intently, evidently agreeing with what their leader had so feelingly

---

[85] *As You Like It* (II.7).
[86] Same.
[87] *As You Like It* (II.1).

Under the Greenwood Tree

expressed, for all were, like the Duke, experienced men of the world.

Then talking more to himself than to his men or to me, the Duke began again:

> "Sweet are the uses of adversity,
> Which, like the toad, ugly and venomous,
> Wears yet a precious jewel in his head;
> And this our life, exempt from public haunt,
> Finds tongues in trees, books in the running brooks,
> Sermons in stones, and good in everything.
> I would not change it."[88]

"There is contentment in this Forest," I murmured in reply, "and peace and sincerity. I would fain stay here forever."

"We must have some music now," the Duke said abruptly; and, looking at young Amiens, who had given me his seat at the table, said: "Good cousin, sing."

Amiens, picking up a lute, tuned it very quickly and adroitly and, after two or three preliminary chords, his rich, clear voice — the same I had heard an hour or so ago singing *Under the Greenwood Tree*, rang out with:

> "Blow, blow, thou winter wind,
> Thou art not so unkind
>   As man's ingratitude;
> Thy tooth is not so keen,
> Because thou art not seen,
>   Although thy breath be rude.
> Heigh-ho! sing, heigh-ho! unto the green holly:
> Most friendship is feigning, most loving mere folly:
>   Then, heigh-ho, the holly!
>   This life is most jolly.

---

[88] *As You Like It* (II.1).

Shakespearian Fantasias

> "Freeze, freeze, thou bitter sky,
> Thou dost not bite so nigh
>   As benefits forgot:
> Though thou the waters warp,
> Thy sting is not so sharp
>   As friend remembered not.
> Heigh-ho! sing heigh-ho! unto the green holly:
> Most friendship is feigning, most loving mere folly:
>   Then, heigh-ho, the holly!
>   This life is most jolly!"[89]

"The world hasn't changed in these many hundred years," I observed, half-talking to myself; "that song might easily have been written today. It has a very *modern* appeal."

"What do you mean by a 'very modern appeal' and what do you mean by the world hasn't changed in these *many hundred years?*" asked the Duke, with a puzzled expression on his handsome face. "I do not understand you at all."

"My second *faux pas!* Oh why had I not kept my thoughts to myself? How was I to convey to the Duke any comprehension of the *modern* world? Moreover, I did not care to introduce into this peaceful Forest of Arden the perplexities and the vexations of the Twentieth Century. Then, too, I realized that a great deal of what we call modern today, with so much superficial assurance and pretentious arrogance, is not progress nor will it be permanent, being but a fleeting phase that our shell-shocked world is passing through before it can right itself again — if it ever will — whereas everlasting is the culture expressed by this forgiving, and kindly, and

---

[89] *As You Like It* (II.7).

Under the Greenwood Tree

gracious Duke and by the tenderhearted, although cynical and melancholy, Jaques, lover of beasts and birds and hater of intrigues and shams, cruelty and deceit. Here, in the Forest of Arden, I have found the Eternal Verities and all the Humanities; and that is the reason I should like to dwell here. But how can I explain all this to the puzzled and wondering Duke?

I therefore decided to evade the question.

But the Duke intends to be answered.

"What is *modern*?" he repeats.

"Why *you* are, my good Lord Duke, and your melancholy Jaques and your heavenly daughter Rosalind," I answered.

"O Rosalind!" the Duke explained with a tender, proud, and amused smile.

"O Rosalind! Rosalind thinks I do not recognize her in the page Ganymede, roaming the Forest in doublet and hose. I meet her frequently among the trees. Last week I had much question with her. I asked her of what parentage she was, allowing her to think I was interrogating an unknown boy, and she answered. 'As good as you.' So I laughed at her impudence and let her go. Orlando is in love with my Rosalind, whom he thinks is still at Court; and Rosalind is having him woo her in the guise of the page, doubly enjoying the courtship and the jest. Orlando is the son of my much-loved friend, Sir Rowland de Bois, and so I am going to let him marry my daughter. The nuptials will take place tomorrow, here in the Forest. Will you stay for this wedding? If so, Jaques and Amiens will take you now to the little cot beneath the tuft of olives where we will all join you tomorrow morning."

"I do desire it with all my heart," I answered; and then, I set forth to find heavenly Rosalind, escorted by the melancholy Jaques and by Amiens, the latter gaily singing:

> "Under the greenwood tree,
> Who loves to lie with me,
>   And tune his merry note
>   Unto the sweet bird's throat,
> Come higher, come higher, come higher;
>   Here shall he see
>   No enemy,
> But winter and rough weather."[90]

---

[90] *As You Like It* (II.5).

Lady Sylvia

I WAS fortunate in witnessing, or rather in over-hearing and over-seeing, a most charming little love-scene, which took place in a richly-furnished apartment in the Duke of Milan's Palace. An astonishingly handsome and extremely attractive young gentleman was standing there among the carved walnut chairs and settees, the brightly-painted and heavily-gilded *cassoni*, and the rich tapestries and velvets on the walls, talking earnestly to his servant who had just handed him a lady's glove, a kid gauntlet richly embroidered with gay silks and seed pearls, fringed and heavily perfumed, which he had picked up on the floor. The young gentleman recognized the glove as belonging to the Lady Sylvia, daughter of the Duke, at whose Court the young gentleman had lately arrived from Verona. The Clownish Servant, Speed, was twitting his master about Madam Sylvia. He has watched him gazing on her most ardently as she sits at supper. Oh yes, indeed, Sir Valentine has now all the marks of the love-smitten Sir Proteus, whom he mocked at and laughed at only a few weeks ago in Verona! But what a change! Now Sir Valentine relishes a love-song like a robin-redbreast, he walks alone, he sighs, he weeps, he fasts! "You were wont when you laughed," continues Speed, "to crow like a cock; when you walked, to walk like one of the lions; when you fasted, it was

Shakespearian Fantasias

presently after dinner; when you looked sadly, it was for want of money; and now you are metamorphosed with a mistress that, when I look on you, I can hardly think you my master."

Sir Valentine admits that he has loved the Lady Sylvia ever since he first saw her; that her beauty is exquisite and her favor, infinite. "Last night," Sir Valentine tells Speed, "she enjoined me to write some lines to one she loves."

"And have you?" asks Speed, smiling.

"I have," Sir Valentine replies, adding with a deprecatory sigh, "and they are writ as well as I can do them."

Then, seeing a lady approaching from the distance, he softly exclaims: "but peace, here she comes!"

Heralded by a strong wave of perfume, in which sweet roses, spicy carnations and pungent musk predominated, and the rustle and swish of stiff, silken skirts, the Lady Sylvia entered the room.

What a striking costume the dashing lady wore! Her dress was of Genoa velvet, of cream-colored background on which stood forth heavily-raised leaves and flowers of green, crimson, and orange; a tall, standing-ruff of Venetian lace towered above her snowy neck; and white satin slippers peeped from beneath her voluminous skirts. Several ropes of Oriental pearls were wrapped about her throat and fell to her waist, and in her auburn hair, so artfully arranged above her low forehead in tiny crisp curls, twinkled and gleamed several diamond rosettes and diamond stars.

The Duke's daughter had fallen in love with Sir

Lady Sylvia

Valentine — I was told this afterward — as Sir Valentine had fallen in love with her, at first sight, on the very first moment the attractive young gentleman was received by her father, the Duke of Milan, and made welcome to the Court. The Lady Sylvia had given Valentine every encouragement to press his suit during the past few weeks and she had even resorted to several pretty subterfuges to lead him on to declare his love, realizing that all he needed was a little help. Aware that Sir Valentine was very often in this particular apartment of the Palace, the Lady Sylvia had passed through it a short while previously and had purposely dropped her glove for Sir Valentine to find. She hoped he would pick it up and cherish it; and it was, therefore, with great delight that she had seen him take it from Speed and had heard his declaration of love for her and his professed admiration of her beauty. But why was he so slow and so shy about telling her this? She now came forward to get the letter she had asked Sir Valentine to write for her "to someone she loves"; and she had said this with a glance full of meaning, hoping that Sir Valentine might divine who the person was to whom the letter should be addressed.

But alas! her delicate wile did not carry any meaning, for Sir Valentine took the matter very literally. Indeed, he was deeply pained to think that the Lady Sylvia loved someone whose name he did not know and regarding which he was too delicate and too courteous to inquire. It gave him a quick stab in the heart to realize that the Lady Sylvia would ask him to write for her to another man. It proved, of course, that she only entertained a pleasant

Shakespearian Fantasias

friendship for him. Why could she not read the longing in his glance and the love in his heart? Still it was something to be accepted by the Lady Sylvia as her *cavaliere servente*, her devoted servant!

And now took place that delightful little comedy of manners that I was fortunate enough to see; and it seemed to me that the Lady Sylvia enjoyed the little comedy as much as I did, although she was not at all satisfied at its dénouement.

And so the Lady Sylvia floated in with her light and graceful step, and she carried her rich dress so proudly that she suggested a ship with all sails set. With charming dignity and elegance of manner, her face radiant with smiles and her eyes twinkling with the humor of the device she had planned, the Lady Sylvia swept forward.

Speed, hurrying behind the arras, where I was hidden, to watch the little scene, did not show any surprise at my presence — indeed, he seemed to take it as a matter of course — but he held up his forefinger and formed with his rounded lips the word "Hush!" However, I needed no such caution.

Sir Valentine, doffing his hat, nearly brushed the floor with its plumes as he made a low bow and flourish that described a wide half-circle, saying, or rather almost singing, the words as he did so: "Madam and mistress, a *thousand* good morrows."

The Lady Sylvia acknowledged the salutation with a deep curtsey, her rich dress falling around her in many folds, and, in a voice like liquid silver, returned: "Sir Valentine and servant, to you *two* thousand."

Speed, turning to me, whispered: "Here's a million of

Lady Sylvia

manners!"

And so it was — a million of manners! And such lovely manners! Such mingling of playful and rich courtesy; such real and such mock deference; and such tender smiles and such arch glances! Finally Sir Valentine handed Sylvia the letter, saying as he did so: "As you have enjoined me I have writ your letter unto the secret, nameless friend of yours, which I was much unwilling to proceed in but for my duty to your ladyship."[91]

The Lady Sylvia thanked him and admitted, as she examined it carefully, "'Tis very clerkly done."

Sir Valentine then explained that it was difficult to write, inasmuch as he was ignorant of the person to whom it should go. And so these adorable lovers bantered words back and forth for several moments, exchanging meanwhile many furtive and ardent glances. Sir Valentine, however, failed to see that the Lady Sylvia was in love with him; and, consequently, her pretty little device to bring him to terms failed completely.

The Lady Sylvia, however, would carry it on a little longer, in the hope that Sir Valentine might wake up. She, therefore, handed him back the letter, making a more direct appeal:

"It is for *you*; I would have had it writ more *movingly*."

Again her lover failed to understand her pretty, delicate play. He fears she is not satisfied and offers to write her ladyship another one.

"And if you do so," the Lady Sylvia agrees, "and you like it, then take it for your pains; and so, good morrow,

---
[91] *The Two Gentlemen of Verona* (II.1).

servant"; and, with another sweeping curtsey, the Lady Sylvia sailed through the open door and down the long passage-way.

Sir Valentine looked lovingly and longingly after her retreating figure; but his reverie was interrupted by Speed, who leaped from behind the tapestry laughing at his master's stupidity: "Why it is as plain as a nose on a man's face, or a weather-cock on a steeple. It was an excellent jest of the Lady Sylvia, indeed was there ever heard a better! That thy master, being scribe, to *himself* should write the letter?"

But love has made Sir Valentine stupid: he cannot imagine what Speed is reasoning about and he persists that the Lady Sylvia is displeased with his efforts.

Speed cannot persuade his master to believe the truth; and so, reminding him that it is dinner-time, they both disappeared down the long passage-way.

For several days I wandered about Milan hoping that I might again chance to see the Lady Sylvia and Sir Valentine, or, at least, to catch a glimpse of Speed running through the streets; but in vain.

On the last day of my sojourn I decided to visit the Ducal Palace again. Once more I went to the rich apartment where I had seen the Lady Sylvia and Sir Valentine; and, while I mused there in the late afternoon, I was amazed and delighted to see Sir Valentine stepping from behind the tapestry, and even more amazed and delighted when he accosted me cordially:

"Speed told me about you," he said, "and I have been trying to see you for the last few days. I thought you

Lady Sylvia

would like to hear that I have married the Lady Sylvia and we are living here in the Palace; and my friend, Sir Proteus, and Julia, his sweet lady, are also married and are living here, too. So we have, therefore, 'one feast, one house, one mutual happiness.'"[92]

"Heaven give you many, many merry days!" was the only appropriate thing I could think of to say on the spur of the moment. And then I added in a less formal tone: 'Please tell me all about it."

"There is a great deal to tell," Sir Valentine replied, "for much has happened. The past few days were sad and trying; but eventually everything worked out for everyone's happiness, and we are all very, very content. But first let me speak of Sylvia."

"I have seen her," I said, "and she is both a heavenly saint and an earthly paragon."

"Yes," Sir Valentine agreed, "she is. And I as rich in having such a jewel,

> As twenty seas, if all their sand were pearl,
> The water nectar, and the rocks pure gold.[93]

"Sylvia is fair, Sylvia is celestial, Sylvia is perfect," Sir Valentine continued. "All our swains commend her. Let me read to you a poem that was sung under her window a few nights ago." And, taking a paper from his pocket, Sir Valentine unfolded it and read me the following:

> "Who is Sylvia? What is she,
>   That all our swains commend her?
> Holy, fair, and wise is she,

---

[92] *The Two Gentlemen of Verona* (V.4).
[93] *The Two Gentlemen of Verona* (II.4).

Shakespearian Fantasias

> The heavens such grace did lend her,
> That she might admired be.

> "Is she kind as she is fair?
>   For beauty lives with kindness:
> Love doth to her eyes repair,
>   To help him of his blindness;
> And, being help'd, inhabits there.

> "Then to Sylvia let us sing
>   That Sylvia is excelling:
> She excels each mortal thing
>   Upon the dull earth dwelling.
> To her let us garlands bring."[94]

"It is nice to talk to you and to read to you," Sir Valentine went on, "you are so sympathetic. I came here a few weeks ago from Verona, where I left my dear friend, Proteus. You must know we were so devoted that at home they called us the 'Two Gentlemen of Verona.' When I decided to see the wonders of the world abroad, Proteus tried to detain me; but I answered him that 'homekeeping youths have ever homely wits.' I took a fond farewell of him, caviling at love and mocking at Proteus for being Love's slave. And so I came to Milan.

"Arriving with letters to the Duke, I was warmly received and lodged in the Palace. The moment I saw the Duke's daughter I fell in love with her. And, indeed, 'whoever loved that loved not a first sight?' And then everything altered! I did penance for countemning love, and I was punished with high imperious thoughts, with bitter fasts, with penitential groans, with nightly tears, and daily heart-sore sighs. Does this bore you?" he

---

[94] *The Two Gentlemen of Verona* (IV.2.)

Lady Sylvia

suddenly asked.

"No, indeed, on the contrary, I am terribly interested," I assured him. "Do go on."

> "Love hath chased sleep from my enthralled eyes
> And made them watchers of my own heart's sorrow.[95]

"I did not think Sylvia, who is now mine own, loved me; but at last she made me believe so and we were betrothed. As her father intended her to marry a foolish young knight named Sir Thurio, we decided to run away. I procured a rope-ladder and everything was ready. Unfortunately, I told Sir Proteus, who had come to Milan. Proteus, who had fallen in love with Sylvia, being jealous, informed the Duke, who was furious and, consequently, banished me. In the Forest between Milan and Mantua I was captured by outlaws, who, after some parley, saved my life and made me captain of the band. Sylvia followed me, Proteus followed Sylvia, Julia followed Proteus, and the Duke followed us all, bringing Sir Thurio. So here we all were in the Forest! Sir Thurio showed himself cravenhearted and the Duke turned from him and gave Sylvia to me. The page that had followed Sir Proteus proved to be Julia in disguise; and Sir Proteus, looking on her again, was touched by her devotion and felt his old love return. The Duke gave us all his blessing and we returned to Milan, where we were married. We are still having our revels and festivities, still feasting on the wedding cates and meats. You must have some of them and crush a cup of wine with us."

"I'd like to see Julia," I said.

---

[95] *The Two Gentlemen of Verona* (II.4).

Shakespearian Fantasias

"Oh, you won't see Julia," replied Sir Valentine, "Julia is too fascinated with the Lady Sylvia to leave her for a moment; for Sylvia has used her so kindly that Julia hath professed deep, undying love for my lady mistress and my lady wife; and it is arranged that on state occasions Julia is to bear my lady's train. And, in good sooth, Julia is a fair, sweet lady herself, beautiful, true, and devoted."

"Why did Sir Proteus come to Milan?" I inquired.

"Oh, his father sent him because *I* was here," replied Sir Valentine. "He thought it would be great impeachment in his age in having known no travel in his youth. Proteus protested, for he did not want to leave Julia. Nevertheless, he had to go. A few days later Julia followed in a very pretty page's suit, as perhaps you know."

"Oh, yes, I know that," I answered; "but none of you travelled very far. You can hardly call it far from Verona to Milan! Now *can* you?"

"It seems pretty far to me," responded Sir Valentine.

"What on earth would you say to the trip *I* have just taken, all the way across the Atlantic Ocean from New York?"

"New York," questioned Sir Valentine, looking at me queerly, "New York? Where is New York? I have never heard of it!"

"Oh, I forgot!" I apologized; and my brain began to spin around like a top as I realized I was talking to a man who was living long before Henry Hudson sailed into Manhattan Bay!

It was extremely puzzling, because only a few months before I had bought at an auction-sale in that very New York an Italian *cassone* exactly like the one my eyes were

Lady Sylvia

now looking upon, painted, so it was supposed, by Benozzo Gozzoli, and framed in Renaissance gilt scrolls. Moreover I had also purchased a small piece of cream-colored Genoa velvet with large green leaves and red and orange flowers in high relief, just like the dress the Lady Sylvia appeared in when I first saw her. And now Sir Valentine had swept away several hundred years.

Sir Valentine, however, was entirely oblivious of my confusion and went on to tell me that when Julia arrived nobody knew her, not even Proteus. Meanwhile Sir Proteus had fallen in love with Sylvia and was trying to gain her love by every possible means. And Julia, disguised as a page, was witness to it all.

"Poor Julia!" I exclaimed, "what a faithless lover!"

"Yes," said Sir Valentine, "poor Julia was all sighs and tears."

"And what a faithless friend!" I also remarked.

"Yes," replied Sir Valentine, "a faithless friend! I caught him one day talking to himself, here in this very room. And this is what I heard:

> 'To leave my Julia, shall I be forsworn;
> To love fair Sylvia, shall I be forsworn;
> To wrong my friend I shall be *much* forsworn;'[96]

"And then he went on:

> 'At first I did adore a twinkling star,
> But now I worship a celestial sun.'[97]

"And finally he concluded:

> 'I will forget that Julia is alive,

---

[96] *The Two Gentlemen of Verona* (II.6).
[97] Same.

Shakespearian Fantasias

> Remembering that my love to her is dead;
> And Valentine I'll hold an enemy,
> Aiming at Sylvia as a sweeter friend.'[98]

"And then he ran off to tell the Duke of our intended elopement. But Sylvia would not listen to Sir Proteus, nor would she accept his presents. He sent her a little pet dog by his servant, Launce, and made Julia carry to her the very ring that Julia had given him! Sylvia wept when Julia told her how Proteus had abandoned his love; and the next time Sylvia saw Proteus again she told him that he was a subtle, perjured, false, disloyal man; and she swore by the pale queen of night that she would ever despise his wrongful suit; and, moreover, that she was betrothed to me and would evermore be faithful. Indeed, indeed Sylvia

> Excels each moral thing upon this dull earth
> dwelling."[99]

"Indeed, indeed, she does!" I agreed, "I think her perfect."

"Proteus is, after all, my dear friend," continued Sir Valentine. "He is a poet and a philosopher. I often think of his remark:

> 'Cease to lament for that thou can'st not help,
> And study help for that which thou lament'st.'[100]

"Julia was so happy when Sir Proteus again looked upon her with love; and then he, full of remorse, said to me, 'Valentine, were man but constant he were perfect: that one error fills him with faults,' We again became

---

[98] *The Two Gentlemen of Verona* (II.6).
[99] *The Two Gentlemen of Verona* (IV.2).
[100] *The Two Gentlemen of Verona* (III.1).

Lady Sylvia

good friends."

"Oh, you men are deceivers ever," I sang out:

> "One foot on sea and one on shore,
> To one thing constant never!"[101]

"Well," Sir Valentine continued, "Proteus sacrificed his tears, his sighs, and his heart upon the alter of Sylvia's beauty; but all for nothing. Sylvia is mine; and oh to me:

> What light is light if Sylvia be not seen?
> What joy is joy if Sylvia be not by?
> Except I be by Sylvia in the night
> There is no music in the nightingale;
> Unless I look on Sylvia in the day
> There is no day for me to look upon:
> She is my essence.[102]

"I wish I might have the privilege of seeing her again," I said, "she is so unutterably lovely!"

"Well, you can," replied Sir Valentine, "for her she comes!"

I looked down the long passage-way and, sure enough, there floated toward us, swishing and rustling in her stiff robes and heralded by waves of delicious perfume, the Lady Sylvia, more beautiful than ever, now that her lover had yielded to her persuasion. She was miraculously handsome in a lustrous, daffodil-colored satin ablaze with diamonds and she advanced to me with a radiant smile and her hand gracefully extended.

"Speed told me that you were here," she said, "and I have come to bid you welcome to our home. You are *very* welcome."

---

[101] *Much Ado About Nothing* (II.3).
[102] *The Two Gentlemen of Verona* (III.1).

Shakespearian Fantasias

"May I be so bold as to congratulate your ladyship," I asked.

"You may," she sweetly replied. "You certainly may, for of all my lovers, Sir Valentine is the best"; and turning to Sir Valentine with an arch glance remarked half teasingly:

> "I have no other but a woman's reason;
> I think him so because I think him so."[103]

"I, on the other hand," replied Sir Valentine with a charming smile, "have no other but a man's reason to love you; and I love you with reason and without reason, and beyond reason and below reason, and in reason and out of reason; and I will reason you with reasons as long as you will listen to reason. Hear this. So Valentine then read to us both:

> "Let not my love be call'd idolatry,
> Nor my beloved as an idol show,
> Since all alike my songs and praises be,
> To one, of one, still such, and ever so.
> Kind is my love today, tomorrow kind,
> Still constant in a wondrous excellence;
> Therefore, my verse, to constancy confin'd
> One thing expressing, leaves out difference.
> Fair, kind, and true, is all my argument,
> Fair, kind, and true, varying to other words;
> And in this change is my invention spent,
> Three themes in one, which wondrous scope affords.
>   Fair, kind, and true, have often liv'd alone,
>   Which three, till now, never kept seat in one."[104]

"Yes," I echoed,

---

[103] *The Two Gentlemen of Verona* (I.2).
[104] Sonnet No. 105.

Lady Sylvia

> "She is kind as she is fair
> For beauty lives with kindness."[105]

The Lady Sylvia smiled graciously. "Now," she said to Sir Valentine, "*I* want to talk to this stranger. You come from some outlandish country, do you not?" she queried, looking at me searchingly.

"I come from New York, if that is outlandish; and, indeed, I sometimes think it is," I added laughingly.

"New York?" she asked wonderingly. "Where is New York? What is New York? I never heard of it."

"New York!" I hesitated. How was I to give her any idea of New York. "New York is in the United States of America," I began, "it is one of the great cities of the world. We have, I think, about six millions of people. Now we are larger than London, I believe."

The Lady Sylvia shook her head. "You must be mistaken," she said quietly, "London has only fifty thousand people. What do you mean by the United States of America? What a peculiar combination of words. I don't understand you at all. You say '*New* York,' but you mean *York*, don't you? There is no such place as *New* York. Did you buy that peculiar dress you have on in New York?" she asked, laughing gaily; and then she added: "Pardon me if I am a little bold of speech; but your costume is so amusing and so outlandish! We are going to have a masked dance tonight and I hope you will come. Will you go with us? I will lend you one of my gowns. I am sure my clothes would fit you and my tiring-maid will crisp your hair and arrange it properly. I will lend you

---

[105] *The Two Gentlemen of Verona* (IV.2). "Who is Sylvia?"

Shakespearian Fantasias

some of my jewels, too. Will you come?"

"With the greatest pleasure," I responded.

"Very well then," the Lady Sylvia answered with one of her flashing smiles. "Come with us now, for it will take quite a little time to dress you properly. You see *I* am already dressed."

As we walked down the long passageway, Sir Valentine and the Lady Sylvia chatting merrily, I paused to look at a gorgeous piece of tapestry representing Venus and Adonis in a leafy landscape; and when I turned to join my companions, they had vanished! It was strange — very strange — but they were irrevocably gone!

By Spangled Starlight Sheen

DO YOU believe in fairies?

You certainly would never doubt their existence had you spent Midsummer Night with me in Epping Forest last June.

My idea in going into the forest on Midsummer Night was to be among the ferns at fairy-time; for, if old traditions are to be credited, the fern blossoms exactly at twelve o'clock on St. John's Eve.

What happens is this. First of all the fern suddenly puts forth a bud, which expands rapidly into a full-blown flower of a brilliant ruby color, and which, like a precious ruby, gleams, and glows, and sparkles with weird radiance, illuminating everything in its immediate vicinity. I had long known that if you wish to procure this magic fern-flower, you must steal quietly into the forest a little before the midnight hour, choose a fern and draw a circle around it; and you must stand within this circle, keeping your eyes fixed on the fern. You must be ready at the precise moment the flower is fully open — not a minute too soon and not a minute too late — so that you may pick the flower quickly; and you must be sure to gather the seed as well as the blossom. With these magical possessions you will be able to find hidden treasure; to become invisible whenever you please; and to enjoy many other privileges, not the least of which is

Shakespearian Fantasias

the ability to obtain all your fondest desires.

Another thing you have to bear in mind, or you may not succeed in gathering either the fern-flower or the seed, is that Oberon, the Fairy King, is always on the lookout to guard his fairy plant from the profane hand of mortals.

I reasoned in this wise.

If I should not be able to gather the magic fern-flower, I might see Oberon! Then, if I succeeded neither in gathering the fern-flower nor in seeing Oberon, it would be, at any rate, a thrilling experience to stand among the tall, dark-green, and dewy ferns at the witching hour in a romantic English Forest beneath whose centenary oaks and beeches Oberon and Titania and their train of fairies had disported themselves for hundreds of years. And so I decided to visit Epping Forest on Midsummer Night.

It was all true: the fern did flower according to tradition and schedule; and, although I was not quick enough to pluck the magic blossom, I was able to gather the seed. I immediately sprinkled some of the precious seed into my shoes and the rest into my left hand glove, saying to myself as I did this: "Now, perhaps, this fern-seed will make me invisible to any mortals who may be roaming about in the Forest tonight; and, better still, perhaps it will make visible to me the Little People who are certain to be flying around on this hallowed night. I shall have several hours to watch for them, for fairy-time always lasts from midnight until dawn."

There was a brief moment when everything became perfectly still and silent; and in this silence a curious, tense feeling seemed to develop. Every leaf on every tree,

By Spangled Starlight Sheen

and bush, and tiny plant seemed to stand at attention — as if the entire Wood were expectant.

"Perhaps the Fairies are coming!" I said to myself.

Suddenly the moon slipped from a great bank of snowy clouds and the dreaming Wood became a silver world.

"Be careful and please don't step on me," I heard a bell-like voice say; and here at my feet was a fragile little Fairy standing beside a gold-coated and ruby-freckled Cowslip, very intently occupied in hanging in his ear a lustrous dew-drop pearl.

"I hope I am not intruding," I apologized, half afraid to speak lest the little Fairy might vanish.

"Oh, no, not in the least," the little Fairy replied, "in fact, if you wish, you may stay and watch me at work. I have a great deal to do tonight. I have got to go through the entire Wood and hang a pearl in *every* Cowslip's ear. The Cowslips are the Queen's Pensioners, you know, the Queen's bodyguard, and they have to be very gorgeous tonight; for the Queen, with all her elves, comes here anon. The only trouble is that the Cowslips are so very tall it is hard for me to reach their ears.

"Won't they lean down a little?" I suggested.

"Oh, they would if they could, but they can't," the little Fairy explained, "their gold coats are so stiff with embroidery that they can hardly move. So I have to stand on tip-toe and stretch out my arms, and it is very hard, for these big pear-shaped pearls are dreadfully heavy."

Where do you find the pearls?" I asked.

"Oh, on the bladed grass," the little Fairy answered. "Phoebe decks with liquid pears the bladed grass, you

Shakespearian Fantasias

know. I have a basket full of them. See! Then I have also to make sure that the fairy-rings of grass, where we dance, are all properly decorated and sparkling with dewdrops."

At this moment a shrewd and knavish little sprite landed on a leaf beside the little Fairy with:

"How now, spirit, whither wander you?"

Of course, I had no difficulty in recognizing that merry wanderer of the night, even if the little Fairy had not addressed him both as Puck and as Robin Goodfellow. I was most interested to listen to their conversation.

Puck announced that the King was going to keep his revels in the Wood tonight and had selected this very spot. So he warned the little Fairy to take heed that the Queen not come within his sight. Then, looking straight at me, Puck explained that Oberon and Titania were at odds about a little changeling that Titania had stolen from an Indian king. "Oberon wants the pretty boy for his train," he said, "but Titania will not relinquish him"; and then Puck added very solemnly:

> "And now they never meet in grove or green,
> By fountain clear or spangled starlight sheen,
> But they do square; that all their elves, for fear,
> Creep into acorn-cups and hide them there."[106]

I asked Puck:

"What do you mean by square? 'But they do square,' you say?"

"Quarrel," Puck explained; and then, in alarm, he cried out:

---

[106] *A Midsummer Night's Dream* (II.1).

By Spangled Starlight Sheen

"But room, Fairy, here comes Oberon!"

"And here my mistress," gasped the little Fairy, "would that he were gone!"

At this moment, a delicate fanfare was heard from elfin horns and Oberon and Titania entered from opposite sides of the Wood, each accompanied by a large and brilliant train of attendants. It was a scene of marvelous beauty, although the figures were so very tiny that each one could at need hide in an acorn-cup and find plenty of room there, besides. With magnificent *hauteur* Oberon took a proud pose and accosted his Queen:

> "Ill met by moonlight, proud Titania."[107]

And the tiny Queen, equally proud and even more disdainful, retorted:

> "What! jealous Oberon! Fairies, skip hence;
> I have forsworn his bed and company."[108]

Some of the fairies scattered; but most of them remained, and I remained also. I heard a very heated argument that nearly developed into a quarrel; and I also learned that Oberon and Titania had both come into the Wood to bring joy and prosperity to Theseus and Hippolyta, who were to be married in a day or two. At the end of the discussion Titania invited Oberon to dance in her round and to take part in her moonlight revels; but Oberon made the surrender of the Indian changeling a condition, whereupon Titania swept away indignantly with her Fairies.

---

[107] *A Midsummer Night's Dream* (II.1).
[108] Same.

Shakespearian Fantasias

"Well, go thy way," exclaimed Oberon, looking after Titania, as she spread her gossamer wings and darted off in the midst of a brilliant flutter and flight of wings and a dazzling sparkle of jewels from the tips of wands and starry coronals:

> "Thou shalt not from this grove
> Till I torment thee for this injury."[109]

I had the fancy to try to follow the flight of the Queen and her elves and so I ran across the dewy glades, winding in and out of groves and copses and clumps of bushes; but as the speed of the little company was "swifter than the moon's sphere," I soon lost sight of the Fairies. This, indeed, was a night devoted to mysterious, immortal, and starry things.

I gazed fascinated by the unearthly beauty of the Wood so brilliantly illuminated with *sentient* moonlight, moonlight so intense that I am reminded of the old English nursery rhyme that so charmed me in my childhood:

> "Girls and boys come out to play
> The moon doth shine as bright as day."[110]

The entire scene is flooded with fantastic radiance from our mysterious sister-world. This "moonlight sleeps upon every bank," "tips with silver all the fruit-tree tops" and pours liquid silver upon, around, and under the ancient trees, coating with metallic sheen their great trunks and their huge and sprawling roots. Some of the willows drip in cascades of tiny, feathery, silver leaves

---

[109] *A Midsummer Night's Dream* (II.1).
[110] An old English nursery rhyme.

By Spangled Starlight Sheen

while other willows trail long, dewy, silvery fronds of fringe; luxuriant clumps of fern and broom lift tall plumes of silver that throw the blackest of shadows upon the gleaming ground. Patches of heather tinkle their tiny bells of pink, white and purple, in this ethereal moonlight. Hawthorn and lilac bushes are so still and quiet you would think they were carved and painted were it not for the delicate and delicious incense they are offering to the moon-goddess. On banks sheeted with moonlight wild thyme, bold oxlips, and drowsy violets nodding in their dreams send forth delicious perfumes that rise and mingle with the fragrant honey dripping from thick canopies of lush woodbine, sweet musk roses, and pink eglantine.

Under dark leaves I catch glimpses of dull, phosphorescent glowworms and every now and then I hear the clamorous owl hooting from some hidden and leafy cell. I see "spotted snakes with double tongues," thorny hedgehogs," "weaving spiders," and black beetles scuttling away from these fairy "bowers of dances and delight," whence come fairy voices chanting to the accompaniment of nightingales a charm-song to banish all ugly, crawling, creeping things on this Midsummer Night. My eyes open to more and more beauty. I see Titania's elves and fairies flitting here and there and everywhere, busy upon their nightly offices: "some are killing cankers in the musk-rose buds"; some are making war upon the dusky bats to get their leathern wings for coats; some are gathering apricots; some are picking dewberries; some are robbing the squirrel's larder for nuts; some are stealing the honey-bags from heavily-

Shakespearian Fantasias

laded bees; some are plucking the wings from "painted butterflies" to use for fairy fans; some are swinging in the bells of flowers; some are hiding in acorn-cups. I also see Master Cobweb with weapons in hand aiming at a "red-hipped bumble bee on top of a thistle" and I recognize Peaseblossom, Moth, and Mustardseed flying about on various errands for Titania.

"Well, and how do you like our Midsummer Night in the Wood?" a merry voice beside me asked.

"O Puck!" I exclaimed, "where did *you* come from?"

"Where did *I* come from?" he repeated a little petulantly, "where did *I* come from? Why I came from everywhere — the entire empyrean! I have been all around the world since I first saw you an hour or so ago in another part of the Wood. Oberon sent me to find a special flower, which, squeezed on the sleeping eyelids of man or woman, will make that man or woman madly dote on the first creature seen on awakening. Oberon intends to squeeze the flower on Titania's eyes — in fact, he is probably doing it now at this very moment — so that she will be full of hateful fantasies when she wakes. Perhaps you heard Oberon say that Titania should not leave this Wood until he tormented her for the injury."

"O yes, I remember perfectly," I answered, "and I wondered what he was going to do."

"Well," answered Puck, "now you know! See here — this is the flower! It is called Love-in-Idleness. I flew all around the earth to find it. It took me forty minutes. I put a girdle round about the earth in forty minutes!"

"I call it a Pansy," I replied, taking the flower in my

By Spangled Starlight Sheen

hand for a moment and then handing it back to Puck, "more precisely, indeed, I would call it a Johnny Jump-Up! What are you going to do with it? I hope you are not waiting for *me* to go to sleep!"

"Oh, no indeed, I am not," laughed Puck; "Oberon gave it to me for a special purpose. A sweet Athenian lady is here in the Wood and in love with a disdainful youth. I am on my way now to anoint his eyes; and Oberon has enjoined me to

> 'Effect it with some care that he may prove
> More fond on *her* than *she* upon *her* love.'"[111]

"Can't I come along and see you do it?" I requested.

"Certainly, you can if you want to," Puck acquiesced, "and if you are not afraid to trust yourself with me? You know that I am very mischievous and I warn you that I am just as likely to play a trick on you as on anybody else." And then he sang merrily:

> "Up and down, up and down;
> I will lead them up and down:
> I am fear'd in field and town;
> Goblin, lead them up and down."[112]

"I'll take a chance," I said; "who would refuse to wander about in an English forest with Puck on Midsummer Night? Not I, for one!"

The tiny, short, moss-like grass was so thickly spangled with dewdrops that I hesitated to walk upon it: I felt as if I were crushing diamonds and pearls with every footstep. The long stretches of open sward glimmered in

---

[111] *A Midsummer Night's Dream* (II.1).
[112] *A Midsummer Night's Dream* (III.2).

Shakespearian Fantasias

the intense moonlight and looked almost as if covered with cold hoarfrost. Every time I brushed by a bush, or walked under the low-hanging bough of a beech, or passed through the long, dangling fringe of a willow-tree, a shower of diamonds and pearls fell upon me. All the cups of the roses and all the cornucopias of the honeysuckles that carpeted the banks or that climbed upon each other to make bowers and canopies were full of crystalline drops redolent of perfume and richly lacquered in silver moonlight. All the flowers, too, had taken on ethereal colors transformed by the cold fire of the moon's rays; and every moment the perfumes grew more and more intense. In addition to the scents of many flowers that I knew so well, I noticed new and unfamiliar aromas from hundreds of modest little plants that were sending forth into the heart of the night subtle essences from leaf and stalk and tiny blossom.

Enchanting night! Mysterious moonlight! Spangled starlight sheen!

And now in addition to the soft, delicate, and radiant colors, the liquid silver pouring down in sheets from the moon, the black shadows lying everywhere, and the intoxicating perfumes from flowers and leaves, another delight was added — nightingales! Nightingales began to trill in every leafy copse.

A night made for Fairies, and for moonfolk, and for *me!*

We went on and on, Puck and I, looking for the delinquent lover, Puck and I, through the night and silence — silence except for the trilling of the

By Spangled Starlight Sheen

nightingales.

At last Puck stopped suddenly:

"Who is here?" he exclaimed. "This surely is he, for weeds of Athens he doth wear; and besides here's the maiden sleeping sound on this dank and dirty ground." And Puck squeezed the flower-juice on the eyelids of the sleeper, chanting as he did this:

> "Churl, upon thy eyes I throw
> All the power this charm doth owe."[113]

There was a little pause and then Puck said: "Now I must to Oberon"; and we resumed our wanderings.

Before very long we came to a cleared place where the turf was particularly soft, and thick, and green. There were many hawthorn brakes and bushes and mossy banks and other banks covered with herbs and flowers. Here we found six rude mechanics very excitedly talking about a play called *Pyramus and Thisbe* that they had come here to rehearse, hoping that they might be allowed to play it before Duke Theseus on his wedding-day at night. Peter Quince, the carpenter, had just called the actors by the scroll. These were Nick Bottom, the weaver; Francis Flute, the bellows-mender; Robin Starveling, the tailor; Thomas Snout, the tinker; and Snug, the joiner.

"What hempen homespuns have we swaggering here, so near the cradle of the Fairy Queen!" exclaimed Puck. "Come here!"

Sure enough, just to the right of this group and unseen by the Clowns, Titania was sleeping in the loveliest spot my eyes had ever beheld.

---

[113] *A Midsummer Night's Dream* (II.2).

Shakespearian Fantasias

This was a gently sloping bank thickly covered with wild thyme, which has a delicious aromatic scent — and one placed high in the scale of perfumes by the Elizabethans — and sprinkled lavishly with oxlips and violets. Above this bed of thyme there was a luxuriant canopy of lush woodbine, sweet musk roses, and eglantine, and beneath it the dainty and exquisite little Fairy Queen was sleeping, herself as lovely as the roses, sleeping peacefully and happily and as if visited by the gentlest and purest of dreams. Everything in the nature of evil — spotted snakes with double tongue, thorny hedgehogs, newts and blindworms, weaving spiders, beetles black, and worms and snails — had been charmed away by the song of Fairies aided by Philomel. One tiny Fairy Sentinel stood to guard Queen Titania, while all her attendants were busy at their various nocturnal offices. However, the Fairy Sentinel had been powerless to protect the queen from the baleful visit of Oberon; and I knew that those white and deeply fringed eyelids had just been anointed by the angry Fairy King with the juice of the wonder-working flower.

When we returned to the rustic clowns we found them busy discussing the question of bringing in a lion. Bottom was talking.

"To bring in a lion," he said, "among ladies is a most dreadful thing: for there is not a more fearful wild-fowl than your lion living; and we ought to look to it."[114]

Snout suggested that a prologue ought to be written, telling that it was not a real lion.

---

[114] This conversation is a paraphrase of the conversation in *A Midsummer Night's Dream* (III.1).

By Spangled Starlight Sheen

"Nay," objected Bottom, "you must name his name and half his face must be seen through the lion's neck; and he himself must speak through, saying this, or to the same defect — 'Ladies,' or 'Fair Ladies! I would wish you,' or 'I would request you,' or 'I would entreat you, not to fear, not to tremble; my life for yours. If you think I come hither as a lion, it were pity of my life. No, I am no such thing; I am a man as other men are' — and there, indeed, let him name his name and tell them plainly he is Snug the joiner."

The next thing that troubled them was how to bring moonlight into the chamber; for "you know," Peter Quince explained, "Pyramus and Thisby meet by moonlight."

Then they had to consider the question of a wall, "for Pyramus and Thisby," Peter Quince explained again, "did talk through the chink of a wall."

"Oh, you can never bring in a wall," Snug objected. But Bottom was, however, as usual, ready with a solution.

"Some man or other must present Wall," he suggested, "and let him have some plaster, or some loam, or some rough-cast about him, to signify Wall; or let him hold his fingers thus (and Bottom held up his own fingers) and through that cranny shall Pyramus and Thisby whisper."

Everything now being settled, Peter Quince called out: "Come, sit down, every mother's son, and rehearse your parts. Pyramus, you begin: when you have spoken your speech, enter into that brake; and so everyone according to his cue.

Puck, looking at me mischievously, whispered, "I will

Shakespearian Fantasias

be an actor, too, in this play"; and when Pyramus, after having spoken his speech, entered into the bushes, Puck followed him, unseen by Bottom. And suddenly by magic Puck fixed an ass's head on the shoulders of Bottom!

Francis Flute now began Thisby's lines: and at the words:

"As true as truest horse, that yet would never tire,"
Pyramus entered, saying:

"If I were fair, Thisby, I were only thine."

Imagine the terror of the rest when they saw Bottom with a huge ass's head instead of his familiar face!

"O monstrous!" cried Peter Quince, "O strange! We are haunted. Pray, masters! Fly, masters! Help!"

The actors all ran away, frightened out of their wits, and fell over each other in their haste, their clothing catching on the bushes and briars, which retarded their progress. Snout, consumed by curiosity, returned for a moment to look at Bottom.

"O Bottom, thou art changed! What do I see on thee?" he gasped; and then he ran away again.

Peter Quince, likewise, had to take another look at his companion.

"Bless thee, Bottom! bless thee! thou art translated!" he panted in his terror; and Peter Quince also fled.

Puck and I watched this new turn to the dramatic action with the greatest amusement. Puck looked at me mischievously and, pointing to Titania's bower, said insinuatingly: "The best is yet to come!"

Whether Bottom was frightened or not, I had no means of finding out. Bottom liked anything that would give him importance; but, even so, he must have been

By Spangled Starlight Sheen

scared to feel suddenly an ass's great nowl with hairy face and long ears upon his shoulders. He said, quite calmly — and I rather admired Bottom for his composure — "I will walk up and down here, and I will sing, and they shall hear I am not afraid"; and then, in a voice very far from musical, he brayed:

> "The ousel-cock, so black of hue,
>   With orange-tawny bill,
> The throstle with his note so true,
>   The wren with little quill."[115]

There was a slight rustle among the roses and honeysuckle and the lovely little Queen of the Fairies leaned forward, peeping through the leaves and perfumed petals to inquire in the most seductive of voices, gazing at Bottom:

> "What angel wakes me from my flowery bed?"

Puck looked at me, laid his hands on his mouth, and nearly doubled up with silent laughter.

And the sweet little voice continued:

> "I pray thee, gentle mortal, sing again:
> Mine ear is much enamour'd of thy note.
> So is mine eye enthralled to thy shape;
> And thy fair virtue's force perforce doth move me,
> On the first view, to say, to swear, I love thee."[116]

"How Oberon will enjoy this!" Puck whispered, "when I tell him"; and then we listened to Titania, who begged Bottom not to desire to leave the Wood. Then Titania informed Bottom that she would keep him by force, if

---

[115] *A Midsummer Night's Dream* (III.1).
[116] Same.

Shakespearian Fantasias

necessary; that she was a spirit of no common rate; and that she would give him fairies to attend on him — to fetch him jewels from the deep and to bring him everything he might want and wish. And then Titania called Peasblossom, Cobweb, Moth, and Musterdseed and gave them orders to serve Bottom; to feed him with apricocks and dewberries, with purple grapes, green figs and mulberries, and to pluck the wings from painted butterflies to fan the moonbeams from his sleeping eyes. Then she bade them lead Bottom to her bower; and, preceded by Queen Titania and ceremoniously conducted by Peasblossom, Cobweb, Moth, and Mustardseed, Bottom marched along and I saw his long hairy ears disappear behind the curtains of tawny honeysuckles and pink eglantines.

"I am going now to tell Oberon all about this," said Puck; "suppose you stay here and see what happens next."

I found a comfortable seat on the high and moss-covered root of a beech-tree and for a long time I revelled in the beauty of the night. What strange visions I had had! To think that *I* should have had Puck for a companion! To think that *I* should have seen Oberon and Titania! To think that the Fairy World had been revealed to *me!*

Then, by contrast, I thought of the amusing rustic Clowns I had seen and how comical was their interpretation of the old myth of Pyramus and Thisbe. How ridiculous they were, too, in the seriousness of their crude dramatic arrangements and also in their terror when Bottom suddenly appeared wearing the unexplainable ass's head! And yet there was something

By Spangled Starlight Sheen

romantic about these rude workmen meeting on Midsummer Night in the Forest to rehearse their play in glades drenched and sheeted with silver moonlight — using a hawthorn-brake for a tiring-house — with Fairies of the greatest beauty and delicacy flitting around them! And then I thought of how much beauty circles around us that we are incapable of seeing. Like these simple rustic clowns, we are too gross to appreciate what lies beyond the limited gamut of our mortal and human senses. I have had a slight insight tonight into the Fairy World beyond our ken. Could I see and hear a little more I would understand what those nightingales are singing about in that bush over there; and I would understand what these roses and honeysuckles beside me are saying in waves of perfume that come and go, as Lord Bacon remarked, like "the warblings of music."

How glad I am that all this silver beauty has been opened to me! Never after such visions as I have beheld on this Midsummer Night will I cease to believe in Nature Spirits and in the Little People who have the care of the most beautiful and spiritual creations on our planet — *Flowers!*

I do not know how long I was musing here, but I was finally drawn from my reverie by the approach of a tall and handsome young woman with an abundance of light hair, simply arranged in a loose knot at the nape of her neck, and a beautiful face, which was, however, full of distress.

"I am Helena," she said. "Will you let me talk to you? Lysander, Demetrius, and Hermia — they have *all* joined to mock me! Lysander and Demetrius are both in love

Shakespearian Fantasias

with Hermia and they have both been hurling the most cruel epithets upon me.

> O, that a lady of one man refus'd
> Should of another therefore be abus'd![117]

"And Hermia," she continued, "has conspired to bait me with this foul derision! And to think this should happen after all the hours that we have spent together! O, all is forgot. All school-days' friendship and childhood innocence! We grew together like to a double cherry, two lovely berries moulded on one stem, and now Hermia joins with men in scorning her poor friend."

"Poor Helena," I said, "I am *so* sorry for you; but what can I do? What made you come into the Wood and have you seen the Fairies?"

"What Fairies?" questioned Helena. "No, I have seen no Fairies."

"I wish you had," I answered, "for after seeing the Fairies in this ethereal moonlight all human troubles seem to be but dreams and this world of dreams the reality."

"I don't understand what you are talking about; but if you really want to know how I came into the Wood I will tell you," said Helena, dismissing all thought of the Fairy World; and I saw very clearly that this Enchanted Wood meant nothing to Helena but the commonplace background for her own troubles.

"I came here," she continued, "because Hermia and Lysander had decided to steal away from Athens tonight and to pass through this Wood, so I told Demetrius, who

---

[117] *A Midsummer Night's Dream* (II.2).

By Spangled Starlight Sheen

was, not long ago, my devoted lover, but who now dotes on Hermia, knowing that Demetrius would pursue Hermia; and then I followed Demetrius, hoping, at least, to see him and to get his thanks. So now we are all in the Wood and *wood* within the Wood — crazy I mean," she explained, noticing my bewildered look at this use of the word *wood*. "But alas! when Demetrius saw me, he spoke so cruelly to me. Then, as I came along through the Wood I saw Lysander lying on the ground and I did not know if he were dead or alive. So I woke him; and, oh, dear, he jumped up and said that he would run through fire for my sweet sake and that he would address all his powers to me and be my knight forever!"

"Puck's flower!" I said to myself, "and squeezed on the *wrong* eyelids."

"Presently I came across Demetrius, also sleeping," continued Helena, and he woke up and called me his goddess, nymph, and princess."

"Puck's flower!" I again said to myself, "and squeezed on the *right* eyelids!"

"But Demetrius is now in love with Hermia," Helena went on, "and, of course, he only said this to mock me. O spite, O hell, they are all mocking me!" And Helena burst into tears.

"Helena," I said, "be patient. All these cross-purposes are owing to Oberon's magic flower, I am sure Puck will set everything right before this night is over. Oh, how I wish this gorgeous, exquisite Midsummer Night would never end! What a perfect Dream it has been!"

"I don't know what you mean by Oberon's magic flower and by Puck setting everything right, nor what you

Shakespearian Fantasias

mean by saying that it has been a gorgeous and an exquisite night. Oh, what a long and tedious night it has been to *me!*" moaned Helena, who was impervious to the ethereal beauty surrounding us. "One thing I do know," Helena added, "I know that sleep sometimes shuts sorrow's eye"; and poor love-sick and heart-broken Helena tumbled down on the moss and instantly fell asleep.

And now here came Puck with the magic flower and told me that Oberon was about to take the charm off Titania's eyes with a famous fairy herb called Dian's Bud.

"Oh yes," Puck replied in answer to my question, "I am going to squeeze this Love-in-Idleness on Lysander's eyelids, so that when he wakes he will take delight in his former lady." And then he merrily sang:

> "Jack shall have Jill;
> Nought shall go ill;
> The man shall have his mare again, and all shall be well."[118]

Once more darting upon me his mischievous elfin glance Puck mockingly laughed out: "I'd rather leave matters at cross-purposes, for

> "Those things do best please me
> That befall preposterously,
> Lord, what fools these mortals be!"[119]

And then Puck vanished.

---

[118] *A Midsummer Night's Dream* (III.2).
[119] Same.

The Merry Mad-Cap Lord

IT SEEMED to me as if I had stepped into a painting by Watteau, although the scene belonged to the Valois period, a hundred and more years before the time of Watteau. Yet this Park had all the feeling of the out-of-door drawing-room that Watteau provides for his *Fêtes Champêtres* and his *Pastorales galantes*. Yes, I stepped through a Watteau-like transparency into an aërial and dewy veil of golden mist and into irised air that was circulating freely beneath luxuriant trees. Velvet lawns, like soft green carpets, spread out in wide spaces — great open spaces, treeless and flowerless, over which there arched a translucent dome of blue sky which, as it curved towards the horizon, made a delicate background for the stately trees that framed in the Park. Broad carriage drives and narrow bridle-paths of yellow sand, fine, hard, and compact, twisted this way and that as they led into a sequestered grove, a thick forest, or towards the handsome, ornate *Château* in the distance, surrounded by a moat and entered by a drawbridge.

And what a delight to the eye this building of Flamboyant Gothic, its white mass gleaming in the sunlight and standing out so prominently from the green shrubbery around it! What a fine contrast the heavy, round towers capped with inverted funnel roofs made with the lighter features of the architecture — the dormer and the lancet windows, the peaked roof, the open-work galleries, the stone balustrades, the tiny pinnacles, turrets, and finials darting up, here, there and everywhere, the decorative and twirling weather-vanes occasionally flashing in the sun and the wealth of stone-carving on the façade and on every other broad space and odd corner, which showed lace almost like that of Alençon, leaves, fruit, flowers, fantastic animals, and grotesque men and women.

A charming fairy-like effect this building — *château*, palace, manor-house, and villa, all in one!

On the far side of the *Chateâu* there extended a garden of later date than the building — a very modern and up-to-date garden in the style of the High Renaissance — "a curious knotted garden," where the flowerbeds were laid out in intricate geometrical patterns and filled with blooming flowers of every hue. From this "curious knotted garden" an avenue of plantains and mulberry-trees led to a large stone terrace with heavy balustrades, on which stood enormous jars and pots containing bright, blooming plants. Wide steps led down into a sunken garden, where again were beds of flowers and tossing fountains; and beyond this sunken garden extended another great open space of emerald lawn, upon which were placed a number of tents, their rich and gaily colored hangings of brocade and tapestries fluttering in the summer breeze.

What a setting for youth, poetry, gallantry, and love!

But where were the people to whom this lyric scene belonged?

I hoped I should see them.

The Merry Mad-Cap Lord

I soon had my wish.

Beyond a screen of hawthorn bushes — perhaps in a French scene they ought to be called *aubépines* — enchanting chords from a lute now reached me, evidently played by the firm fingers of a man, as the notes were so strong and so rhythmical. A few moments more and a rich and beautifully trained soprano added her melody to the accompaniment and, in the most faultless diction, the words of Ronsard's song:

> "Mignonne, allons voir si la rose
> Qui ce matin avait déclose
> Sa robe de pourpre au soleil
> A point perdu cette vesprée,
> Les plis de sa robe pourprée,
> Et son teint au vôtre pareil.
>
> "Las! voyez comme en peu d'espace,
> Mignonne, elle a dessus la place,
> Las! las! ses beautés laissé choir!
> O vraiment marâtre Nature,
> Puisqu'une telle fleur ne dure
> Que du matin jusques au soir!
>
> "Donc, si vous me croyez, mignonne,
> Tandis que votre âge fleuronne
> En sa plus verte nouveauté,
> Cueillez, cueillez votre jeunesse:
> Comme à cette fleur, la vieillesse
> Fera ternir votre beauté."[120]

While this song was being sung I slipped quietly over the grass towards the hawthorn hedge and peeped through an opening, taking care to keep myself hidden from the sight of the gallant company.

---

[120] "Migonne allons voir si la rose," by Renaissance French poet Pierre de Ronsard (1524-1585).

Shakespearian Fantasias

The lady who was singing I at once recognized as the Princess of France and the gallant who was accompanying her she addressed on the conclusion of the song as Lord Boyet. Around the Princess were grouped three handsome young ladies, their brilliant silks and velvets harmonizing and contrasting with the verdure. Beside and beyond these ladies, lords and attendants were moving about and I gathered that they had just been enjoying an *al fresco* meal.

The Princess waved aside the compliments Lord Boyet expressed to her in flowery speech and proceeded at once to the business of her mission from her ill father to the King of Navarre, concerning certain rights to lands in Aquitaine. The company paid great attention to her announcement that only now, when the little embassy is in sight of the King of Navarre's *Château*, has she learned that the King lately made a vow to engage in ardent study for three years with three companions, during which term no woman may approach his silent court!

"Therefore, before we enter his forbidden gates," the Princess adds, "it seems to us a needful course to know the King's pleasure; and we single you, my good Lord Boyet, as our best moving fair solicitor."

Proud of his errand, Boyet departed.

Turning to her companions, the Princess asked if they knew who the King's vow-fellows are? One Lord mentions Longavill, whereupon Lady Maria announces that she met him at the marriage feast of Lord Perigot and the heiress of Falconbridge in Normandy and describes him as being well fitted in the arts, glorious in arms, and endowed with a sharp wit as well.

The Merry Mad-Cap Lord

"Who are the others?" queries the Princess.

Lady Katherine mentions young Dumaine, whom she met at the Duke Alençon's. Dumaine is too delightful, "indeed he has enough wit to make an ill shape good and shape to win grace though he had no wit."

Lady Rosaline then spoke up, admitting that she had met at the same time the third of these students, Berowne. "I never talked with a merrier man," she says, adding:

> "His eye begets occasion for his wit;
> For every object that the one doth catch,
> The other turns to a mirth-moving jest."[121]

Everybody is enchanted with Berowne, Lady Rosaline continues, "aged ears and younger hearings are quite ravished, so sweet and voluble is his discourse."

"God bless my ladies! are they all in love? "the Princess laughs and looks searchingly at each in turn. Maria, Katherine, and Rosaline blush and smile, but they offer not the slightest denial. Boyet soon returned with the news that he met the King of Navarre and his three companions on their way to pay their respects to the Princess. On hearing this, the princess and her ladies mask, so that the King and his suite may not be forsworn.

As the King, Longavill, Dumaine, and Berowne and their attendants come down the steps of the Terrace from the *Château* into the garden, I have the pleasure and privilege of seeing the courtly etiquette of the Sixteenth Century; and it pleases me extremely. All four lords are dressed in perfect taste and wear their silken doublets,

---

[121] *Love's Labour's Lost* (II.1).

Shakespearian Fantasias

velvet mantles, plumed hats, and jewelled swords with elegance. All have charming manners; but my attention is rivetted on Berowne. After his salutation to the Princess, Berowne, with captivating grace, approaches Rosaline to renew the acquaintance of which that lady spoke to the Princess.

The King soon became deeply engaged with the Princess in a discussion of the Aquitaine matter and apologized for not being able to entertain the embassy in his *Château* on account of the vow. Then he bade the Princess a most elaborate farewell and promised to visit her again on the morrow, regretting that he could not entertain her.

The Princess, with a sweeping curtsey, murmured:

"Sweet health and fair desires consort your grace."[122]

And the King, bowing low and kissing her hand, returned with:

"Thy own wish wish I thee in every place."[123]

The king and his Lords then ascended the Terrace and walked towards the *Château.*

At their departure a gentle melancholy fell upon the group. Boyet noticed that the King has lost his heart and I have noticed that three other hearts have been left behind. It looks to me as if all these four students of philosophy and rhetoric may soon be forsworn!

Silence and solemnity having fallen upon the lovesick ladies, I left the spot to wander through the lovely Park. I

---

[122] *Love Labour's Lost* (II.1).
[123] Same.

The Merry Mad-Cap Lord

soon came upon a strange couple seated under the trees — a courtier and his little page. The man, an odd, fantastical person, I learned later, was Don Adriano de Armado, a native of tawny Spain, "a man in all the world's new fashion planted who had a mint of phrases in his brain and whom the King of Navarre had brought to his court for the purpose of entertaining him and his companions in the interim of their studies."[124]

Don Armado, dressed in the most extravagant costume, was amusing himself in conversation with his witty little Moth, and they were bantering words to such a degree that they did not see me, although I passed right by them.

I lingered quite a long time in the "curious-knotted garden," where I saw many of the same flowers that I had become acquainted with in the Lady Olivia's garden in Illyria and some that I had not seen there. As I passed through the pleachèd arbor, I came abruptly to a small pavilion completely smothered with blooming roses. One of the King's companions was standing at the entrance in a dejected and nonchalant attitude, his arms crossed upon his breast and his eyes upon the ground. It was hard to believe that this melancholy young man was the gay and dashing Berowne whom I had seen addressing Rosaline. Yet, Berowne it was, and none other. I recognized him, although he wore a different costume.

Berowne did not hear my footsteps and began to talk to himself, uttering with deep emotion this confession and complaint:

---

[124] From, loosely, *Love's Labour's Lost* (I.1).

Shakespearian Fantasias

> "O! — and I, forsooth, in love! I, that have been Love's whip;
> A very beadle to a humorous sigh;
> A critic; nay, a night-watch constable;
> A domineering pedant o'er the boy.
> Than whom no mortal so magnificent!
> This wimpled, whining, purblind, wayward boy;
> This senior-junior, giant-dwarf, Dan Cupid:
> Regent of love-rhymes, lord of folded arms,
> The anointed sovereign of sighs and groans."[125]

A pause and then he began again, even more dramatically:

> "O my little heart! —
> And I to be a corporal of his field,
> And wear his colors like a tumbler's hoop!
> What I! I love! I sue! I seek a wife!
> A woman that is like a German clock,
> Still a repairing; ever out of frame;
> And never going aright!"[126]

Another pause. And then with still more vehemence and passion:

> "And I to sigh for her! to watch for her!
> To pray for her! Go to; it is a plague
> That Cupid will impose for my neglect
> Of his almighty dreadful little might.[127]

"If you are sighing for the Lady Rosaline, my good Lord Berowne," I said advancing, "she is in as bad a plight as you. You must forgive me for eavesdropping. I came upon you unawares: I could not help hearing what you said."

---

[125] *Love's Labour's Lost* (III.1).
[126] Same.
[127] Same.

The Merry Mad-Cap Lord

Berowne, recovering his poise instantly, made me a graceful bow and asked me by what miracle I knew his name. Although I hated to tell him that I had heard him so addressed while I was peeping through the hawthorn hedge a little while ago, lest he should consider me a chronic eavesdropper, I thought it best to be honest; and so I confessed how I had been an unseen spectator of the King of Navarre's visit of welcome to the Princess of France.

Lord Berowne smilingly said: "But that visit took place two weeks ago!"

"Why, how could that be?" I exclaimed in surprise. "I have been in this Park only a few hours!"

Lord Berowne looked at me pityingly, as if he thought I must be mad.

Then he asked me with the greatest politeness how I had found entrance into the Royal precincts. Again I concluded that honesty was the best policy; and so, I told the truth.

"I do not know," I said.

Again Lord Berowne looked at me curiously. Then he answered in a charming spirit of friendliness: "I need somebody to talk to. I need some sympathy and you affect me very strangely. Come into the arbor and sit down."

I acquiesced.

For some time we studied each other. I had no means of discovering what Berowne thought of me and of my dress; but I can say what my opinion was of him — that he was one of the most fascinating and elegant men I have ever been privileged to have met.

I will speak of his clothes first, for his costume was

Shakespearian Fantasias

most striking and he wore it with an air that added greatly to its style, distinguished as that style was.

The doublet was a pale violet silk, pinked and ornamented with narrow gold braid in horizontal lines and still further brightened by gold buttons down the front. The collar of the doublet was high and around it a ruff of Venetian lace, quilled up in stiff S-like scrolls and starched, added an elegant touch. Gracefully fastened at his left shoulder, a black velvet mantle lined with silk brocade of the same shade of violet as the doublet fell in long folds. His hat — a kind of toque or bonnet — was black velvet with a small brown and white feather stuck at an odd angle in the back while the brim was adorned with gold buttons in pairs. The doublet was heavily padded and tapered from the shoulders to the waist. Doublet and cloak, bonnet and ruff,[128] all exhaled the subtle and delicious scent which Edward de Vere had lately brought from Italy and which was known in Court circles as "Lord Oxford's Perfume."[129] The costume set off

---

[128] Parts of this description appear to match the Ashbourne Portrait of Edward de Vere, which is now located in the Folger Shakespeare Library in Washington, D.C.

[129] In *The Pictorial Edition of the Works of Shakspere*, Charles Knight reports on page 384 that, "Autolycus has offered for sale 'Gloves as sweet as damask roses.' Howes, who continues Stow's Chronicle, thus describes the introduction of perfumed gloves in the early part of the reign of Elizabeth: 'Milliners or haberdashers had not then any gloves embroidered, or trimmed with gold or silk, neither gold nor embroidered girdles and hangers; neither could they make any costly wash or perfume until, about the fourteenth or fifteenth year of the queen, the right honourable Edward de Vere, Earl of Oxford, came from Italy, and brought with him gloves, sweet bags, a perfumed leather jerkin, and other pleasant things; and that year the queen had a pair of perfumed gloves trimmed only with four tufts or roses of couloured silk. The queen took

The Merry Mad-Cap Lord

the attractions of the wearer, who was rather undersized, but who carried himself with such dignity and had been so exercised in knightly accomplishments that one soon forgot Berowne was "a little fellow."[130] His bonnet, pushed back quite far on his head, worn at the fashionable angle, showed to advantage an extraordinarily high forehead, white and dome-shaped, with slight eye-brows trained in a semi-circle or made up like a half moon with a pen. Beneath these glowed very large, elongated, and handsome eyes, full, hazel, brilliant, and heavily lidded; and Berowne had, moreover an attractive way of occasionally dropping his lids, or veiling his eyes, as if in thought, and then suddenly opening his eyes very wide and looking at you searchingly. His long, commanding nose gave evidence of a strong will. Perhaps his mouth was his most attractive feature — it was so tender, sensitive, refined, honest, witty, and charming, the upper lip lightly shaded by a thin and much cultivated moustache. His smile was most enchanting and his manner most ingratiating.[131] Altogether this young aristocrat was "a peerless fellow."[132]

---

such pleasure in those gloves, that she was pictured with those gloves upon her hands, and for many years after it was called the Earl of Oxford's perfume."

[130] Thomas Nashe, in *Strange News* (1593) described Edward de Vere as "a little fellow:" "Mark him [de Vere] well. He is but a little fellow, but he hath one of the best wits in England. . . . I myself . . . enjoy but a mite of wit in comparison of his talent."

[131] This description matches that of Edward de Vere as portrayed in the Ashbourne Portrait, now in the Shakespeare Folger Library in Washington, D.C.

[132] This phrase was used twice to describe Edward de Vere: 1) as "a fellow peerless in England" by Angel Day, in *The English Secretary*

Shakespearian Fantasias

Everything about Lord Berowne expressed the most intensive cultivation of body and mind — he was *point device* in every respect.

And he was just as delicate in speech: every word was carefully selected; every word was fastidiously pronounced; and the intonations, modulations, and inflections of his voice were like music. Lord Berowne was "the most goodly fashioned man I ever saw; from head to foot in form, rare and most absolute."[133] He fascinated me.

"Perhaps you do not know," Lord Berowne began, "and if you do not I will tell you, that a few months ago the King of Navarre decided to make his Court the wonder of

---

(1586). Day was Oxford's secretary, and *The English Secretary* was dedicated to him. And 2) vividly caricatured by Gabriel Harvey in *Speculum Tuscanismi* (*Mirror of Tuscanism*) (1580) as:

> Delicate in speech, quaint in array, conceited at all points,
> In courtly guiles a passing singular odd man,
> For Gallants a brave Mirror, a Primrose of Honour,
> A Diamond for nonce, a fellow peerless in England.

[133] Yet another phrase used in real life to describe Edward de Vere. From George Chapman's *The Revenge of Bussy d'Ambois* (III, iv, ll. 84-115) (1610):

> I overtook, coming from Italy
> In Germany, a great and famous earl
> Of England, the most goodly fashion'd man
> I ever saw; from head to foot in from
> Rare and most absolute; he had a face
> Like one of the most ancient honor'd Romans,
> From whence his noblest family was deirv'd;
> He was beside of spirit passing great,
> Valiant and learn'd, and liberal as the sun,
> Spoke and writ sweetly, or of learned subjects,
> Or of the discipline of public weals;
> And 'twas the earl of Oxford;

The Merry Mad-Cap Lord

the world, by establishing a little Academy for a three years' study of philosophy, art, and poetry. He selected three fellow-students who pledged themselves to see no woman, to fast, and to sleep but little. Although I protested at this war against our affections, I subscribed with Dumaine and Longavill to the vow. Now, almost as we had signed, the French King's daughter came in embassy. Exultingly I told Navarre that study was now overshot and that necessity would make us all forsworn three thousand times within this three years' space!

"When we paid our devoirs to the Princess, Dumaine, Longavill and I discovered that we had previously met the ladies-in-waiting. In good sooth, Longavill was already in love with Maria, Dumaine with Katharine — "

"And you, my lord," I interjected, "had you not been stabbed by the black eyes of Rosaline when you danced with her in Brabant?" Berowne merely smiled an acknowledgment and went on to say that all eyes saw how the King's eyes were enchanted with the Princess.

"Well, you are all certainly in a mess," I exclaimed. "What are you going to do about it?"

"We tried to hide our feelings from each other," Berowne continued, "but mark what happened. We had all been studying to compose sonnets in the manners of Ronsard, Joachim du Bellay, Estienne Jodelle and other members of the Pléiade; but we little thought, while working on the art of poetry, that we would soon find use for it to sing the praises of our mistresses! I think I was the first," laughed Berowne, "to sing in a sonnet like a nightingale. At any rate, I did write one."

"Won't you tell it to me?" I pleaded.

Shakespearian Fantasias

"Certainly I will," Berowne responded most obligingly, "but I do not think mine as good as the King's or Longavill's. But this is what I wrote:

> "If love make me forsworn, how shall I swear to love?
> > Ah! never faith could hold if not to beauty vow'd!
> Though to myself forsworn, to thee I'll faithful prove;
> > Those thoughts to me were oaks, to thee like osiers bow'd.
> Study his bias leaves, and makes his book thine eyes;
> > Where all those pleasures live that art would comprehend:
> If knowledge be the mark, to know thee shall suffice;
> > Well learned is that tongue that well can thee commend:
> All ignorant that soul that sees thee without wonder, —
> > Which is to me some praise that I thy parts admire, —
> Thy eye Jove's lightning bears, thy voice his dreadful thunder
> > Which, not to anger bent, is music and sweet fire.
> Celestial as thou art, O pardon, love, this wrong,
> > That sings heaven's praise with such an earthly tongue.[134]

"I like it very much," I said. "I only wish you had written it to *me! I* would not flout you as the Lady Rosaline does. Could you not find me a gallant just like yourself?"

Berowne's indifference to my remark told me plainly that he was quite surfeited by compliments from the fair sex and he continued, much amused at his own recital, as follows:

"I addressed this sonnet to the snow-white hand of the most beauteous Lady Rosaline and I gave it to Costard, the Clown, to deliver, making sure of his interest with a guerdon. Then I walked slowly through the Park,

---

[134] *Love's Labour's Lost* (IV.2). The first line is also in *The Passionate Pilgrim*.

The Merry Mad-Cap Lord

meditating upon another sonnet. Presently the King came along with a paper in his hand, sighing 'Ah me!' So I climbed a tree."

"Eavesdropping!" I said, "like your present audience!"

"Delighted indeed was I to know that Navarre had been shot by Cupid's bird-bolt. The King, believing he was alone, read his sonnet — really a loving thing — beginning:

> 'So Sweet a kiss the golden sun gives not
> To those fresh morning drops upon the rose.'"[135]

"That is beautiful," I exclaimed. "It makes one smell the roses when they are sweet with the morning dew; and is there anything more delicious in the way of perfume than 'morning roses newly washed with dew'?"

"Just as the king finished his sonnet Longavill appeared, crying 'Ah me, I am forsworn.' The King concealed himself and Longavill read his sonnet. Wonder of Wonders! Dumaine came sauntering by, sighing 'O most divine Kate!' Here were four woodcocks in a dish! Again I saw how love can vary wit, for Dumaine read an ode! Then he exclaimed 'O would the King, Berowne and Longavill were lovers, too!'

"Longavill then came out of hiding and began to chide Dumaine, upon which the King stepped forth and reproved Longavill for scolding Dumaine when he was just as great an offender, saying:

"'I have been closely shrouded in this bush and marked you both for you both did blush. I heard your

---

[135] *Love's Labour's Lost* (IV.3).

Shakespearian Fantasias

guilty rhymes.' Then he added: 'What will Berowne say?

> 'How will he scorn! how will be spend his wit!
> How will he triumph, leap, and laugh at it!
> For all the wealth that ever I did see
> I would not have him know so much by me.'[136]

"'Now step I forth to whip hypocrisy,' I said to myself and descended from the tree. How I railed at them all! How I mocked them! How satirically I laughed and triumphed! I asked Navarre how dared he reprove those worms in loving when he was most in love. I jested at their sonnetting, their sighs, their groans, and told them I was betrayed by keeping company with moon-like men of strange inconstancy. I started to leave the three guilty loves when Jaquenetta and Costard ran into me with a letter for the King! I took it, and, by cock and pye, it was my sonnet to Rosaline! They had another letter to deliver from Don Armado — have you seen him yet? — to the King; and they made a mistake, giving Don Armado's letter to Rosaline and were about to hand my sonnet for Rosaline to the King! I tore up the paper; but Dumaine picked up the pieces and there was nothing to do but confess. So I cried out:

> 'Sweet lords, sweet lovers, O let us embrace!
>   As true we are as flesh and blood can be;
> The Sea will ebb and flow, heaven show his face;
>   Young blood will not obey an old decree:
> We cannot cross the cause why we were born;
>   Therefore of all hands must we be forsworn.'[137]

"Then we all began to praise our mistresses; and,

---

[136] *Love Labour's Lost* (IV.3).
[137] Same.

The Merry Mad-Cap Lord

finally, the King appealed to me to find some way to cheat the devil and make the loving lawful!"

"How did you get out of the difficulty?" I asked.

"I made a fine case," replied Berowne, "and I concluded with this:

> 'Let us once lose our oaths to find ourselves,
> Or else we lose ourselves to keep our oaths:
> It is religion to be thus forsworn;
> For charity itself fulfils the law,
> And who can sever love from charity?'[138]

"My fellow companions were all delighted.

"'Saint Cupid, then! and, soldiers, to the field!' cried the king.

"So we resolved to woo these girls of France. We have planned some entertainments for them in their tents. We have already sent them presents of diamonds and chains of pearls and perfumed gloves; and this afternoon we are to appear before them like Muscovites, or Russians, with music, so that we may have a dance and press our love-suits. And, moreover, we are preparing to have a pageant of the Nine Worthies performed to amuse the Princess and her ladies, which we have given to Don Armado to arrange, as he is good at what he calls 'such eruptions and sudden breakings out of mirth.'"

"And what if these flouting ladies should meet your loves as but a pleasant jest of merry mocking lords?" I inquired.

"Then," answered Berowne, "we will do our best in honest plain words to make them believe our love is

---

[138] *Love's Labour's Lost* (V.1).

Shakespearian Fantasias

sound."

"Tell me about this Don Armado?" I requested. "Who is he? And is he named for the Spanish Armada?"

"Don Armado," replied Berowne, "is a fantastical Spaniard, a Monarcho, whom the King keeps here to make sport for us. Don Armado has adopted Euphuism in the highest degree."

"And what is Euphuism?" I asked.

"Oh, Euphuism," Berowne replied, "is a new literary movement — I am surprised you do not know this when all Europe is affected by it — to enrich language by graceful rhetoric and choice words of new fashion. The name came from a book called *Euphues, the Anatomie of Wit*, written by my fellow-worker, John Lyly, and printed a few years ago."[139]

"Do you remember the date?" I asked.

"Oh, yes," Berowne replied, "*Euphues* appeared in 1579. I am supposed to be Philautus. In the next year, Lyly published *Euphues and his England*, which he dedicated to *me*; and he wrote here: 'whoso compareth the honor of your Lordship's noble house with the fidelity of your ancestors may well say which no other can truly gainsay, *Vero nihil verius.*'[140] But to go on. Euphuism has spread into every country. La Pléiade here is one expression: the King, Dumaine, Longavill and myself are all Euphuists; and we enjoy seeing ourselves mocked in Don Armado,

---

[139] Here Berowne is speaking in the voice of Edward de Vere. John Lyly was de Vere's private secretary for ten to twelve years in the 1570s and 1580s. Although *Euphues, the Anatomie of Wit* is often attributed to Lyly, the first edition states only that it was compiled by him.

[140] See previous note. *Vero nihil verius* was de Vere's motto.

The Merry Mad-Cap Lord

who, in the words of Master Holofernes 'draws out the thread of his verbosity finer than the shape of his argument.' Don Armado is a soldier and a man of travel that hath seen the world; but we call him, however, a plume of feathers, a vane, and a weather-cock. The letter that he writ to Jaquenetta — and Jaquenetta is only a country wench — and which was delivered to Rosaline by mistake, Rosaline gave to me. There is a phrase in it which I think Don Armado intended as a hidden allusion to me and I should like to know if you agree with me. I hope you will."

Unfolding the letter, which he took from his pocket, Berowne read:

"By heaven, that thou art fair is most infallible; true that thou art beauteous; truth itself that thou art lovely. More fairer than fair, beautiful than beauteous, *truer than truth itself.*[141]

"Is not truer than truth itself my motto, *Vero nihil verius?*"[142]

"I cannot see how any one can doubt it," I exclaimed most emphatically.

"I am glad you believe this," said Berowne, with much feeling. "I knew I had your understanding sympathy from the first moment I saw you. Perhaps you will understand, as well, the allusions in this poem on *Labor and Its Rewards!* I will repeat two verses of it:

> "The idle drone that labors not at all,
>   Sucks up the sweet of honey from the bee;

---

[141] *Love's Labour's Lost* (IV.1). "Truer than truth itself" is one possible translation of *Vero nihil verius*.

[142] See previous note. Berowne is clearly channeling Edward de Vere.

Shakespearian Fantasias

> Who worketh most to their share least doth fall,
> > With due desert reward will never be.
>
> So he that takes the pain to pen the book
> > Reaps not the gifts of golden goodly muse;
> But those gain that, who on the work shall look,
> > And from the sour the sweet by skill shall choose;
> For he that beats the bush the bird not gets,
> > But who sits still and holdeth fast the nets.[143]

"Now, I must go," he said, making me a graceful bow, "and put on the Muscovite dress, for my companions stay for me. Farewell!"

---

[143] From "Labour and Its Reward" by Edward de Vere, Earl of Oxenforde. First published in 1573 in his preface to Thomas Bedingfield's translation of *Cardanus Comforte*, which was published by the Earl's command. It was republished in 1576.

In Such a Night

I WAS the interested spectator a few evenings ago of a most extraordinary and delightful homecoming.

During one of my fantastic adventures I found myself in the grounds of a romantic Italian estate. It was quite a little while before I could identify it as *Belmont*, the famous home of the more famous Portia.

The *Villa Belmont*, a long rectangular house of white stucco with red tiles, stood on a prominence looking down proudly over the valley from its wide-bricked terrace with heavy balustrade entwined with thick masses of eglantine and ornamented with noble statues and pots of blooming flowers. Around the house innumerable cypress-trees lifted their tall, dark, pointed spires, like green velvet in softness and depth, exactly as we see them in the pictures by Benozzo Gozzoli of the Fifteenth Century.

From the terrace a series of gardens gradually fell away into emerald lawns and ultimately broke into wild and distant walks, which apparently continued until they were lost in the low violet hills that framed in the horizon.

Those various gardens were embellished with pergolas that supported cascades of pale purple wistaria, pink, yellow, and red roses, and starry white jessamine and that sheltered beneath their trellises azaleas, lilies, and other flowers that love the shade.

Shakespearian Fantasias

In the more exposed gardens hollyhocks, tall Madonna lilies, marigolds, larkspur, Canterbury-bells, and yellow snapdragons made such rainbows of color that you wondered if Iris had not dropped her scarf there by mistake.

At intervals, along the stone parapets, on the balustrades, along the sides of the broad steps leading from the garden, and outlining the paths, great jars containing orange-trees, lemon-trees, pomegranates, and oleanders added decorative beauty.

There is magic in moonlight. Sometimes the rays of the moon have power over the mind, as well as over the body, and can capture the imagination and carry one into the realms of fantasy.

There are places where the moon shines in peculiar splendor and with peculiar power: in our southern States, for instance, in Egypt, in Carthage, in Venice, and elsewhere in Italy.

It was on one of these eerie moonlight nights that I found *Belmont*; and the reason I knew that I had found *Belmont* was because I saw a young man and a young woman walk out of the house and down the broad steps of the terrace into the first garden on the slope. The young man, putting his arm around the young woman's waist, spoke as follows:

> "The moon shines bright! — In such a night as this,
> When the sweet wind did gently kiss the trees,
> And they did make no noise; in such a night,
> Troilus, methinks, mounted the Trojan walls,
> And sigh'd his soul toward the Grecian tents,

In Such a Night

Where Cressid lay that night."[144]

And then the young woman took up the duet:

> "In such a night
> Did Thisbe fearfully o'ertrip the dew,
> And saw the lion's shadow ere himself,
> And ran dismay'd away."[145]

Then the young man began again:

> "In such a night
> Stood Dido with a willow in her hand
> Upon the wild sea-banks, and wav'd her love
> To come again to Carthage."[146]

The young woman again spoke:

> "In such a night
> Media gather'd the enchanted herbs
> That did renew old Aeson."[147]

The young man now made a modulation from poetry to realism:

> "In such a night
> Did Jessica steal from the wealthy Jew
> And, with an unthrift love, did run from Venice
> As far as Belmont."[148]

There was no difficulty in my knowing where I was after that!

I crept softly up among the dewy eglantines, wishing to enjoy the full beauty of the scene and fearful lest my slightest footfall might disturb the lovers — and they

---

[144] *The Merchant of Venice* (V.1).
[145] Same.
[146] Same.
[147] Same.
[148] Same.

Shakespearian Fantasias

seemed so very happy!

I must be honest, however, and confess that my studied silence was not entirely unselfish. I wanted of all things to saturate myself with the beauty of the scene and to meet the people who dwelt in this enchanting Italian villa, if such a thing were possible.

The threads that bound me to the spot and its owners were far too delicate to permit of any sudden connection. My contacts must be made with the most extreme caution; otherwise, I feared the whole scene might melt away in this fantastic moonlight.

I listened to the banter of Lorenzo and Jessica until at last Jessica playfully accused her newly-made husband of "stealing her soul with many vows of love and ne'er a true one." Lorenzo met this remark with

> "In such a night
> Did pretty Jessica, like a little shrew,
> Slander her love, and"

with a pause

> "he forgave it her."[149]

Then, catching Jessica to his heart, Lorenzo gave her a rapturous kiss.

Jessica laughingly remarked that she would outnight him "did nobody come"; but that she heard the footsteps of a man.

At this I listened attentively, but I could hear nothing. Lorenzo, however, had started to his feet in a defensive attitude, and his hand instinctively felt for the delicate

---

[149] *The Merchant of Venice* (V.1).

In Such a Night

little dagger worn at the side of his plum-colored velvet doublet.

"Who comes so fast in silence of the night?" Lorenzo called loudly.

"A friend," was the answer that rang out over the cascades of moon-drenched flowers in the tangled gardens.

"A friend! What friend?" Lorenzo called in reply. "Your name, I pray you, friend."

It proved to be Stephano, one of the *Belmont* servants. Stephano came with good news. His mistress, the Lady Portia, would be back at *Belmont* before the break of day. She was travelling slowly because she stopped at all the holy crosses on the wayside to pray for happy wedlock hours.

"Oh, I shall perhaps see Portia!" welled up in my heart with great joy.

"Oh, I shall perhaps see Portia!" And I kept repeating this over and over to myself while I noticed the delight the news gave to Lorenzo and Jessica.

While Lorenzo was consulting Jessica with regard to the kind of welcome they ought to prepare for the mistress of the house, another call was heard through the silent beauty of the silver night.

This time it was Launcelot Gobbo — I recognized him instantly — coming to announce the approach of his master.

"How delightful!" I said to myself. "How delightful! I shall, perhaps, see Bassanio, too! This is, indeed, wonderful!"

Lorenzo then sent Stephano into the house for music

Shakespearian Fantasias

to greet Portia. "Bring the music here," he commanded. The night was far too perfect to go within!

"How sweet the moonlight sleeps upon this bank![150]

Here we will sit," Lorenzo said to his pretty young wife, "and enjoy the sweet sounds of harmony in the soft stillness of the night."

Then Lorenzo directed Jessica's eyes to the sparkling firmament:

> "Look how the floor of heaven
> Is thick inlaid with patines of bright gold;
> There's not the smallest orb which thou beholds't
> But in his motion like an angel sings,
> Still quiring to the young ey'd cherubims."[151]

I now watched several musicians come out of the house carrying their lutes and viols of various sizes and, with a thrill, I realized that these beautiful instruments had come from the workshops of Amati and Stradivari and that I was going to hear some Italian music of the Sixteenth Century while it was still "modern music."

Seeing these men, Lorenzo called out:

> "Come, ho, and wake Diana with a hymn;
> With sweetest touches pierce your mistress' ear,
> And draw her home with music."[152]

Lights now appeared in every window of the house and there was a general feeling of expectancy.

The mistress of *Belmont* was returning!

The members of the little orchestra grouped

---

[150] *The Merchant of Venice* (V.1).
[151] Same.
[152] Same.

In Such a Night

themselves gracefully upon the steps of the terrace and, after tuning their instruments, began to play some deliciously soft and sweet madrigals and *canzoni* with exquisite taste.

It seemed to me advisable to introduce myself to Lorenzo and Jessica at this moment, as there were so many personalities on the scene, so many threads in motion that I hoped if I could not hold firmly on to one, I might to another. Yet is was with some agitation that I approached the moonlit bank on which Lorenzo and Jessica were seated, looking at the stars and listening to the music.

I hated to interrupt the music, but it could not be helped.

"Pardon me for intruding," I began; but Lorenzo and Jessica had both seen me the instant I emerged from the eglantine. They stared at me with much surprise and curiosity; and indeed it must have been somewhat disconcerting for them to look upon a stranger from the Twentieth Century and from a city not on the maps of their day.

But what does a small affair like that matter to people who are sympathetic?

"Lorenzo and Jessica," I began, "I hardly know which one of you to address first and so I choose you both. I may be unknown to you, but *you* are not unknown to *me*. Many a time and oft have I listened to your exquisite verbal duet with the most intense pleasure; but never until tonight have I heard it in its *perfect* setting. Many a time and oft have I tried to imagine *Belmont*, but never until tonight have I visualized this enchanting villa and its gardens.

Shakespearian Fantasias

Surely the cultured and gracious mistress of this place has put something of herself here! *Belmont* is not merely a typical Renaissance villa, but it represents, I feel very sure, Portia's elegant taste."

"You are perfectly right," Lorenzo replied, "it does."

"I have a great favor to beg of you," I continued. "May I stay and see Portia? There is no time for explanations, because I see her coming through the gardens and, consequently, I make the request at once."

"Why, of course, you may," exclaimed Lorenzo and Jessica together.

"Portia will be delighted, I know," added Jessica, "so long as you are not one of those tiresome suitors that always agitate and distress her so much."

"Well, they matter nothing now," Lorenzo returned. "Since Bassanio chose the right casket, Portia is safely married and released from all that anxiety."

The travelers came up the slopes, Portia and Nerissa leading and followed at a respectful distance by several men-servants, who went quietly into the house, leaving Portia and Nerissa.

Portia was even more exquisite than my fancy had painted her.

The first words I heard her say — and in the most melodious and golden of voices that carried far and wide — were: "Music! hark!"

The unusual beauty of the night impressed Portia as it had impressed Lorenzo and Jessica and as it had impressed me; and, placing her hand gently on Nerissa's arm, she murmured softly like a strain of melody:

"Peace, ho! the moon sleeps with Endymion,

In Such a Night

<blockquote>And would not be awaked."[153]</blockquote>

Then for quite a while these two — Portia, and Nerissa — stood, like the statues in the garden, listening to the music.

I suddenly realized that the musicians grouped so gracefully upon the terrace were the same who had been commanded by Portia to play while Bassanio had made his choice of the caskets, so that her lover might make a swan-like end, fading in music were he to fail; or, if he should win, then the music should be as the flourish to a new-crowned monarch — and this music, therefore, possessed an added charm for me.

In a short interval, inspired by a pretty sentiment for welcoming the mistress of Belmont to her home and reminding her of that most important moment of her life, the little group sang, *à capella*, to a lovely melody:

> "Tell me, where is fancy bred,
> Or in the heart or in the head?
> How begot, how nourished?
> > Reply, reply.
>
> It is engender'd in the eyes,
> With gazing fed; and fancy dies
> In the cradle where it lies:
> > Let us all right fancy's knell;
> I'll begin it — Ding dong, bell.
> > Ding, dong, bell."[154]

While all this music was being played and sung I had ample opportunity to observe the gracious Lady of *Belmont*. And in sooth she was a gracious lady; and a

---

[153] *The Merchant of Venice* (V.1).
[154] *The Merchant of Venice* (III.2).

Shakespearian Fantasias

beautiful one besides. As I looked upon her, I thought of Bassanio's words when he first spoke to Antonio about Portia:

> "In Belmont is a lady richly left,
> And she is fair, and fairer than that word,
> Of wondrous virtues; sometimes from her eyes
> I did receive fair speechless messages:
> Her name is Portia; nothing undervalued
> To Cato's daughter, Brutus's Portia.
> Nor is the wide world ignorant of her worth;
> For the four winds blow in from every coast
> Renowned suitors; and her sunny locks
> Hang on her temples like a golden fleece;
> Which makes her seat of Belmont Colchos' strand,
> And many Jasons come in quest of her."[155]

At a pause in the music Lorenzo went forward with Jessica to give the mistress of *Belmont* the proper welcome. On being informed that her husband was returning, Portia bade Nerissa to go in and give order to all the servants that they should take no notice of her absence. "Nor you, Lorenzo; Jessica, nor you," she added cautiously.

At this moment a shrill tucket resounded through the hillside, proclaiming the arrival of Bassanio, Antonio, Gratiano and their suite. Could anything exceed Portia's rippling, joyous reception of Bassanio and her courteous, cordial, and graceful welcome of Antonio, when Bassanio presented this beloved friend?

While these three were engaged in conversation, much of which I could not hear, Gratiano and Nerissa were having high words near the tall post at the end of

---

[155] *The Merchant of Venice* (I.1).

In Such a Night

the terrace steps. Gratiano became vehement:

"By yonder moon, I swear you do me wrong. In faith I gave it to the judge's clerk," he protests.

The noise of the argument reaching Portia's ears, she glides toward Gratiano and Nerissa with

"A quarrel, ho! already! what's the matter?"

Well enough does the merry Portia, who is acting her part so cleverly, know what the matter is, for have not she and Nerissa taken the rings away from their husbands for the very purpose of having fun with them at their homecoming and of hearing them swear that they had given their rings away to men? Portia and Nerissa play their little game most charmingly here in the silver moonlight and they keep the straightest faces, pretending to be horribly outraged.

Gratiano protests that he gave his ring to a little scrubbed boy about the size of Nerissa. But Nerissa is sure that Gratiano gave it to some woman — and Nerissa is right!

Portia reproves Gratiano gently, but severely. It was very, very wrong for him to part so lightly with his wife's first gift. "I gave my love a ring," she murmurs sweetly, "and I dare be sworn he would not pluck it from his finger for the wealth that the world masters!" Glad, indeed, is Portia that such a thing could not happen to her!

Bassanio hears this with dismay. What can he do? "I were best to cut my left hand off and swear I lost the ring defending it," he thinks.

But Gratiano, wanting company in his misery, blurts out: "My lord Bassanio gave his ring away unto the judge that begged it, and indeed deserved it, too; and then the

Shakespearian Fantasias

boy, his clerk, that took some pains in writing, he begged mine; and neither man nor master would take aught but the two rings."

Portia hopes that this was not the ring she gave to Bassanio and pretends to be deeply aggrieved and hurt when she finds out the truth. And how merry Portia — so serious at need — enjoys this play and how she leads Bassanio on until the climax is reached for clearing up the matter! Presently Antonio comes forward to say how distressed he is to be the unhappy cause of all these troubles.

Portia entreats Antonio not to be grieved and assures him that he is very welcome, notwithstanding. Then Portia hands Antonio a ring and asks him to be surety that Bassanio will keep it better than the other, bidding him hand it to Bassanio.

"By heaven, this is the ring I gave the doctor!" Bassanio exclaims.

Following Portia's lead, Nerissa hands Gratiano her ring.

How I do enjoy from my unseen, shadowy spot the amazement of Bassanio, Antonio, and Gratiano when they learn that Portia was the doctor of laws, Nerissa the doctor's clerk, and that they have so newly returned from Venice that they have not even yet entered the house!

And for Antonio Portia has some good news — three of his argosies have suddenly come to harbor. Then Portia adds: "It is almost morning. Let us go in and we will talk over all these events in full and answer all your questions."

These happy people pass up the terrace-steps and

In Such a Night

sweep into the house, from the windows of which a few minutes later another lovely Italian melody, full of sentiment and charm, steals forth from viol and lute.

It seemed to me that I stood here a very long time alone and enjoying the beauty and the perfume of the flowers and watching the large silver moon growing whiter and whiter as it dropped slowly towards the hills on the horizon, where the first wan light of day began to tint the sky. As I looked towards the house I wondered just where was situated the *salon* in which the famous three caskets of gold, silver, and lead stood, to which so many suitors had gone: some with confident strides and high hopes leading them through the tapestried corridors; and some with trembling steps and hearts full of dire forebodings — both types of minds and characters doomed to disappointment. There, too, had Portia trembled.

Since I had beheld Portia I realized how poignant, how bitter, how cruel the disappointment must have been. For the second condition of the contest — that any suitor choosing the wrong casket must never speak to lady afterwards in way of marriage — would mean little or nothing to one of Portia's wooers. For who, indeed, could think of any other woman after having fallen in love with Portia!

My musings were interrupted by Antonio, who came out of the house and stood for a few moments upon the terrace, apparently looking for someone. To my surprise his eyes lighted on me, whereupon he descended the steps and joined me.

Shakespearian Fantasias

"Lorenzo has been telling me about you," said Antonio, "and I came out here to try to find you. It is so nearly morning that it does not seem to me worth while to go to bed. Sleep is also far from visiting my eyelids. Besides, I wanted to see you and I feared that you might vanish into thin air if I did not take advantage of your presence among us."

"I shouldn't think you *would* be able to sleep after all *you* have been through," I remarked.

"Oh, you know about the great trial we have just had in Venice? And Shylock?" Antonio exclaimed.

"Oh, yes indeed I do," I replied, "and my dear Antonio, if you will allow me to call you that, how deeply I have admired you. Oh, what a friend you are! And you did go through an awful experience — didn't you?"

"Well, it's over now," Antonio replied, smiling gently. "Everything came out better than I expected. I prepared for the worst. I was perfectly willing to go to my death for my dear Bassanio."

"I never heard of such a sublime friendship," I said, "I am sure, Antonio, my dear Antonio — I really must call you that, I cannot help it — that your name will stand forever as the symbol of the most exalted, most sublime, most self-sacrificing, most unselfish friendship any man ever had."

"Oh, you praise me far too highly," Antonio protested.

"No, I do *not*," I answered emphatically. "No I do not. You know what Bassanio told Portia about you — well, perhaps you don't know, you were not there to hear it (or here rather, for it was said in this beautiful villa) when the news came to *Belmont* that all you ventures had failed,

In Such a Night

that not one of your vessels — from Tripoli, from Mexico, from England, from Lisbon, from Barbary, and from India — had come to port; and that, in consequence, you were in forfeiture to the fearful and ferocious bond of Shylock."

"Well, what did my dear Bassanio say of me?" asked Antonio, his eyes brightening and his smile a trifle less melancholy.

Bassanio said to Portia, when she asked him who it was that was in such trouble:

> "The dearest friend to me, the kindest man,
> The best condition'd and unwearied spirit
> In doing courtesies; and one in whom
> The ancient Roman honor more appears
> Than any that draws breath in Italy."[156]

"Did Bassanio say *that*?" Antonio murmured. "How glad I am that I risked my life for him! I have done nothing to merit such praise and such affection."

"Oh Antonio!" I said, and I shook my head reproachfully, "you do not know yourself." And then, after a pause, I added: "Do you know how beautifully Portia met the situation, how generously she came to the rescue?"

"No, I do not," said Antonio, "there has not yet been time to hear. Tell me."

"Well, Portia entreated Bassanio," I explained, "to despatch all business and be gone to your aid. Then she said she would give Bassanio six times the amount and then added: 'No, you shall have gold twenty times over to pay the petty debt, and when it is paid bring your true

---

[156] *The Merchant of Venice* (III.2).

Shakespearian Fantasias

friend along.' And then, like the excessively feminine and altogether charming woman that she is, Portia insisted that Bassanio first go to church with her and call her wife. Portia wanted to be sure of her man!"

"Can anybody be sure of a man?" laughed Antonio.

"Well, Antonio, my dear Antonio, I have my theories," I replied. "The world doesn't seem to have changed much. I cannot see that the Shakespearian men and women are any different to those of my Twentieth Century."

Anthony gave a start and, looking at me strangely, asked: "What do you mean by your Twentieth Century?"

It was a dangerous moment. I thought I saw the villa of *Belmont* totter in the wan light as if rocked by a slight earthquake. What could I do to save the moment?

"I don't know what I am saying, Antonio," I hastened to reply, "something foolish and stupid. This moonlight has got into my head. Tell me quickly that I am standing here in *Belmont*, talking to Antonio, the Merchant of Venice."

"Why, of course, you are," Antonio replied, "where else should you be?"

"Oh," and I breathed a deep sigh of relief. "How glad I am that this is not a dream!"

"Why should it be a dream?" Antonio observed placidly.

Hardly hearing him, I murmured:

> "What relish is in this? how runs the stream?
> Or am I mad? or else this is a dream:
> Let fancy still my sense in Lethe steep;

In Such a Night

If it be thus to dream, still let me sleep!"[157]

At the citation of these exquisite lines the trembling, quivering veil which resembled the watery-like haze of a hot summer day that had enveloped the *Villa Belmont* now vanished and everything became stationary and solid once again. It had been a nervous moment and I nearly lost my contacts; but, happily everything was natural again and Antonio and I resumed our conversation.

"Isn't Portia *marvelous?*" I asked him.

"Marvelous!" exclaimed Antonio, "Portia is the most wonderful woman I have ever known — and I have known many!" Then, after a pause, he said, "Who would have thought that Portia was the doctor! I wish you could have been in Venice to have seen Portia dressed like a doctor of laws standing in the Court of Justice, defending me and watching Bassanio all the time as well. Such wisdom, such knowledge of the law, such logical argument, and such self-control have seldom been displayed anywhere. And to think all the time the learned doctor was Portia and we knew her not!"

"There is something else that you have not mentioned, Antonio," I said.

"What is that?" he asked.

"Woman's wit," I answered. "Don't you remember what Rosalind says? 'Make the doors upon a woman's wit, and it will out at the casement; shut that, and it will out at the keyhole; stop that, 'twill fly with the smoke out at the chimney.'"

---

[157] *Twelfth Night* (IV.1).

Shakespearian Fantasias

"Well," rejoined Antonio, "there is no limit to Portia's wit."

"Nor to her beauty, nor to her grace, nor to her charm, nor to her culture, nor to anything that is Portia's," I exclaimed enthusiastically.

"Portia is the most perfect woman that I have ever seen," said Antonio. "I have only been with her a short time, but she is more captivating than I had even imagined."

"Portia certainly possesses every charm," I answered, "and I hardly know which to admire the most — her enchanting playfulness, or her cultivated mind."

"Yes," replied Antonio, "and you should see how that mind is expressed in her home — just as it is in her gardens. Portia's love of beauty is controlled by a fastidious taste. You should see the rare tapestries and the superb paintings that adorn the walls of this villa," said Antonio, waving his hand towards the house. "There are also many antique statues from Rome and the Isles of Greece. The furniture is more than rich: Andrea del Sarto painted many of the gilt mounted *cassoni* and the chairs and sofas are covered with the most gorgeous brocades and velvets from Genoa. On the *bancs*, or settees, of carved walnut are soft Turkey cushions boss'd with pearl and from the windows hang valences of Venice-gold in needlework. The cabinets contain the rarest gems and carvings of ivory, exquisite Murano glass, and filigree work of gold and silver. Handsome majolica from Diruta and Urbino is plentiful. The book-cases show hundreds of rare editions of classical works printed by Aldus and the latest poems and romances of our living writers; and

In Such a Night

there are many viols and lutes of exquisite shape and exquisite ornamentation. Poets and painters flock to visit Portia and they say: 'At the sound of her name all the Muses rise and do reverence.' Indeed, Portia is *la prima donna del mondo*."

"And such is the beautiful house that Portia gave with her beautiful self to Bassanio," I exclaimed. "Did Bassanio tell you what she said?

> 'Myself, and what is mine, to you and yours
> Is now converted: but now I was the lord
> Of this fair mansion, master of my servants,
> Queen o'er myself; and even now, but now
> This house, these servants, and this same myself
> Are yours, my lord. I give them with this ring,
> Which when you part from, lose, or give away,
> Let it presage the ruin of your love,
> And be my vantage to exclaim on you.'"[158]

Suddenly I noticed Antonio's face. There was an unmistakable expression upon it.

"And you did all this for Bassanio when you wanted Portia for yourself?" I murmured.

"You have surprised my secret," said Antonio, "stolen it from me unawares. But now that you have guessed the cause of my melancholy, you might as well know all the rest.

"I was about to embark as another Jason for the Golden Fleece of Colchos' strand, to hazard my all for heavenly Portia, when Bassanio came to ask my help in furnishing him with money to make a pilgrimage to *Belmont*. Of course, I could not stand in the way of my

---

[158] *The Merchant of Venice* (III.2).

friend. I assured him that my purse, my person, and my extremest means were all unlocked for his occasions. Unfortunately, all my fortunes were at sea; and I had no money, nor commodity, to raise the sum. All my argosies were tossing on the ocean.

"And it was a rather large sum, too," I interrupted.

"To raise the sum," Antonio continued, "it was, therefore, necessary to see what my credit could do in Venice. You know the rest."

"No, I don't know all," I replied, "I don't know about *you*! Please tell me, if I may be permitted to make such a request."

"Yes," said Antonio, "of course, you see, I had to withdraw."

"No, I don't quite see that," I answered, "I'm not so unselfish as you are, Antonio."

"Well, I *did* withdraw; and Bassanio never knew and never will; and I had to stifle all thoughts of Portia. I, too, had seen fair Portia's counterfeit. My friend, Veronese, painted her portrait a few months ago and brought it to his studio in Venice. I do not know if he, too, were a suitor for her hand, but he would never talk of her. I wanted to buy the portrait — I would have given all my ships in exchange for it. Veronese would not sell it. But many a time and oft did I visit the studio to look upon that flower-like face, those gently parted lips — parted with such sugar breath — those soft, yet brilliant, eyes, and that splendid hair — a golden mesh to entrap the hearts of men. Bassanio, when describing the mistress of Belmont to me, little dreamed how well I knew the face of that thrice fair lady.

In Such a Night

"When I first fell in love with Portia through Veronese's portrait of her, I did not really know that I was in love. Solanio and Salarino, friends of mind and Bassanio's, questioned me one day about my melancholy. All that I could say was:

> 'In sooth, I know not why I am so sad:
> It wearies me; you say it wearies you;
> But how I caught it, found it, came by it,
> What stuff 'tis made of, whereof it is born,
> I am to learn.
> And such a want-wit sadness makes of me
> That I have much ado to know myself.'[159]

"Solanio and Salarino both thought that I was sad because of my great ventures on the sea; but I assured them this was not the case. Then Solanio insisted that I must be in love. But I said 'Fie! Fie!' to that. One moment more and I began to realize that this was so; and I determined there and then that I would go to *Belmont* and knock at Portia's door to try my fate with the caskets of gold, of silver, and of lead. But I also had a strange presage that there was no happiness for me! Soon after that the merry-hearted Grantiano, with his skipping spirit, found me marvelously changed; and my secret nearly broke from me when I said to Gratiano:

> 'I hold the world but as the world, Gratiano –
> A stage, where every man must play a part,
> And mine a sad one.'[160]

"When Bassanio told me of his desire to woo Portia there was nothing left for me in life."

---

[159] *The Merchant of Venice* (I.1).
[160] Same.

Shakespearian Fantasias

"Oh, Antonio, my dear Antonio, and all are so happy now except you! Bassanio and Portia, Gratiano and Nerissa, Lorenzo and Jessica, but *you*! Oh, my dear Antonio! Oh, if it could only have been Portia and *you*!"

"Hush! Hush!" said Antonio, very softly, his eyes full of tears and the sweetest of melancholy smiles upon his handsome lips.

"Oh, Antonio, my dear Antonio!" I sighed; and I buried my face deep in the dewy eglantines of Portia's garden and wept bitterly.

They

"THRICE to thine, and thrice to mine,
And thrice again, to make up nine —
Peace! — the charm's wound up."[161]

I heard these words chanted in a strangely penetrating and monotonous voice and repeated several times, at first very faintly and then increasingly, little by little, from a faint tone to a stronger one, until the words became both audible and distinct.

In like manner, an apparition gradually arose before me — dim and vague at first and then, by degrees, growing clearer and brighter until it finally became tangible and corporeal.

This vision was far from beautiful. I will not attempt to describe it.

I had no difficulty, however, in identifying the creature — a secret, black and midnight hag, withered and wild in her attire, with skinny lips, choppy finger, a coarse, sparse beard, straggly hair, and evil eye — as one of Macbeth's witches.

"I came," the creature said, "because you have been pondering over our Macbeth and Lady Macbeth, two of the most wonderful persons we have ever enticed into our Realm of Darkness and Evil.

---

[161] *Macbeth* (I.3).

Shakespearian Fantasias

"You have been trying to discover if the Evil Powers dwelt in their own hearts, or if Macbeth and Lady Macbeth were controlled by the Powers of Darkness. I can explain everything to you. First, you must know that we, Weird Sisters, belong to the Powers of Darkness and that we are always on the lookout for agents to do our work. To our great delight, we found a situation ready for our hands and the characters as well.

"Hovering around the Castle of Inverness one dark midnight, we overheard Macbeth and Lady Macbeth discussing how they might obtain the Scottish crown. There was but one way that we, Weird Sisters, could see; and that was the nearest and the blackest way. We whispered something in their ears; but they dared not speak to each other of it. We, Weird Sisters, laughed in glee and danced a round to the wind that was whistling among the battlements; for we knew that we had gathered two rare and marvelous prizes into our Realm of Darkness.

"Instantly we placed a croaking raven over the entrance to the Castle of Inverness; and, amid a wild outburst of thunder, lightning, and rain, we hastened to our favorite heath, where we set our Cauldron to boil and laid all our plans.

"Tell me everything you can," I said, a little fearful of addressing my uncanny visitor.

"List, list oh list," replied the Weird Sister. "Once — not long ago — a handsome lady dwelt here in Scotland, small and fair, with blue eyes, very graceful in figure, movement and gesture, and very charming in manner. This was Lady Gruach, the granddaughter of Kenneth the

They

Fourth, King of Scotland, and one of the heirs to the throne. Now, Kenneth, King of Scotland, had a brother, Malcolm, who deposed him: and, in order to keep the throne, this Malcolm murdered the father of Lady Gruach, her brother, her husband, and fifty of the latter's friends, by setting fire to the Castle where they were all feasting. Not long after this happened, Lady Gruach married her first cousin, Macbeth, who was also a grandchild of Kenneth the Fourth. Consequently, the Macbeths were *both* heirs to the Crown of Scotland. In course of time, Malcolm's grandson, Duncan, became King; and Duncan was, as you see, the second cousin of both Macbeth and of Lady Macbeth.

"Now it will be easy for you to comprehend how it was that Macbeth and Lady Macbeth looked upon the Crown as *rightfully* belonging to them and how they regarded King Duncan as a usurper. Macbeth and his wife frequently talked of getting the throne back and we, Weird Sisters, visited the Castle of Inverness nightly, to plant seeds in their hearts and to give them thoughts in their dreams. Moreover, we kept before Lady Macbeth's eyes the picture of Malcolm's murder of her father, her first husband, and her brother and their company. It was a bloody family," continued the Witch; "and 'blood will have blood,' as we, Weird Sisters, taught Macbeth to say."

"Khama," I interposed, "which came to Duncan!"

"Yes, answered the Witch, "Khama; but how did *you* know? What do *you* know about Khama? We, Weird Sisters, work out the laws of Khama — evil Khama — of course. Well, to go on," she continued, "it was just the kind of family that we, Weird Sisters, like to play with. Such

Shakespearian Fantasias

people are ready-made puppets for us to work with. We can so easily make them the agents for our Dark Purposes and our Evil Schemes. So you can easily understand that it was not difficult for us to bend Macbeth and Lady Macbeth to our will, although they knew nothing about this.

"Neither was it difficult for us to materialize before Macbeth, because Macbeth had a most magnificent imagination; and while he was a villain in his heat, he was a poet with his brain. We hovered around him all the time until he began to *feel* our presence; and then one day we burst upon his astonished vision. We, Weird Sisters, thought it best to remain for a brief moment only; and then we vanished as suddenly as we had appeared. Within a few days we appeared again to Macbeth (although we had stayed by him, unseen, all the time to keep our influence strong) and we answered a few of his questions, very vaguely, of course, and with a veiled allusion to his ambition of obtaining the Crown. Then we stopped coming to him for some time, to make him desire us the more. Artful? Why, of course we, Weird Sisters, are artful."

"Did you ever appear to Lady Macbeth?" I asked. "Did she ever see you?"

"Oh no," replied the Weird Sister, "we never appeared to her. Lady Macbeth was too practical. She was unable to see visions and hard no patience with Macbeth when he told her about them. She always contemptuously said: 'O proper stuff!' Lady Macbeth always preferred to act directly and promptly. She was the person for *action*, not *dreams*. She never let

They

'I dare not wait upon I would,
Like the poor cat I' the adage.'[162]

"No, we, Weird Sisters, never appeared to Lady Macbeth; but she knew all about us from her husband. However, we managed to get her under our influence and *she believed in us although she never could see us.* Moreover, it was not necessary for us to appear to her: we could work through Macbeth. Macbeth was an easier tool for us; and Macbeth was the one we chose for our Evil Purposes. We kept Macbeth wondering about us and longing so to see us that he frequently solicited our supernatural aid; but the time had not come for his absolute surrender to our will until he won a great battle for King Duncan. We knew that Duncan would reward him with the title of Thane of Cawdor, as the Thane of Cawdor had forfeited it, a new event of which Macbeth did not know. Through the death of his father, Sinel, Macbeth was already Thane of Glamis. So, after the battle on the heath near Forres, we, Weird Sisters, appeared to Macbeth and Banquo, another of Duncan's generals and a great friend of Macbeth's.

> "'All hail, Macbeth! hail to thee, Thane of Glamis!' I cried.
> "All hail, Macbeth! hail to thee, Thane of Cawdor!' the Second Witch cried.
> "'All hail, Macbeth! that shalt be King hereafter!' the Third Witch cried.[163]

"Macbeth was startled at our greeting and our great prediction of noble having and of royal hope. Banquo then asked us to look into the seeds of time and speak to

---

[162] *Macbeth* (I.7).
[163] *Macbeth* (I.3).

Shakespearian Fantasias

him; and we, Weird Sisters, promised Banquo that he should get kings but be none. When Macbeth arrived at the Palace of Forres, Duncan gave him the title of Thane of Cawdor; and Macbeth remembered our prediction of a few moments before, and began to believe in the third and greatest promise. At the same moment, Duncan made his son, Malcolm, Prince of Cumberland, which, perhaps you know, is the title for the heir to the Crown of Scotland. When Macbeth heard this we whispered something in his ear, which caused him to exclaim:

> 'Stars, hide your fires!
> Let not light see my black and deep desires:
> The eye wink at the hand! yet let that be,
> Which the eye fears when it is done to see.'[164]

"The King then decided to visit Macbeth's Castle of Inverness, and Macbeth, with our black thoughts in his heart and our golden dreams in his mind, rode ahead to inform Lady Macbeth of the approaching visit of Duncan. The rest you know."

The Weird Sister paused for a moment and then continued:

"But there was one trouble. Duncan had proved himself a fine King and a saintly man and he was greatly beloved. He called Macbeth 'a peerless kinsman' and he brought a beautiful diamond to Lady Macbeth. Macbeth, therefore, hesitated about killing Duncan, whom he said had borne his faculties so meek and had been so clear in his great office that his virtues would plead like angels against the murder. We found it very hard to keep

---

[164] *Macbeth* (I.4).

They

Macbeth firm in purpose; and when he said to his wife that, as both Duncan's host and kinsman, he should shut the door against the murderer not bear the knife himself, we thought we had lost him.

"Now, before going to Forres, Macbeth had written a letter to his wife and had despatched it to the castle of Inverness by a quick messenger. Let me recall it to you:

> 'They met me in the day of success (They, of course means us, the Weird Sisters); and I have learned by the perfectest report, they have more in them than mortal knowledge. When I burned in desire to question them further, they made themselves air, into which they vanished. Whiles I stood rapt in the wonder of it, came missives from the King, who all-hailed me Thane of Cawdor; by which title before, these Weird Sisters saluted me, and referred me to the coming on of time, with *Hail King that shalt be!* This have I thought good to deliver thee, my dearest partner of greatness; that thou mightst not lose the dues of rejoicing, by being ignorant of what greatness is promised thee. Lay it to thy heart, and farewell!'

"And to our great delight, for we, Weird Sisters, had travelled with the letter, Lady Macbeth put herself under our guidance. We heard Lady Macbeth read the letter aloud and watched her face as she did so, emotion flickering all over it like our lightning flashes. What a majestic figure she was standing in her tapestried chamber, her rich robe flowing around her in graceful folds and her jewels sparkling in the light of the big fire of logs burning in the great stone fireplace! We placed a golden crown upon her head which she seemed to feel was there in reality and we filled her heart with the one thought of gaining this golden crown at all costs.

Shakespearian Fantasias

Remember that Lady Macbeth was not actuated by sordid ambition, but that she was a *queen in her own right* and she was a queen in her every movement and gesture. Yet, she was so afraid of her woman's heart and so afraid of future remorse that she felt the need to rely on supernatural powers. We wanted to appear to her at this moment; but Hecate forbade us to do so. However, we were ready when Lady Macbeth cried:

> 'Come, you spirits
> That tend on mortal thoughts, unsex me here;
> And fill me from the crown to the toe, top-full
> Of direst cruelty! Make thick my blood,
> Stop up the access and passage to remorse,
> That no compunctious visitings of nature
> Shake my fell purpose.'[165]

"We, Weird Sisters, remained in the Castle until Macbeth arrived and we kept close by, planning all the arrangement for the murder while Lady Macbeth voiced it and thought it was her idea. Yet all this was the work of the Weird Sisters. Then my two sisters went to the heath to brew a wicked charm in our Cauldron and I stayed in the Castle to manage Macbeth and Lady Macbeth and to show our dagger in the air to Macbeth, and move it on by magic to Duncan's chamber. *That dagger was created in our boiling Cauldron of hell-broth on the heath and sent to me through the air.*

"The mysterious voice that Macbeth heard just after he had murdered the sleeping Duncan, banishing sleep from Macbeth's eyelids forever, was *mine*," said the Witch triumphantly with a horrid laugh that sent an icy chill

---

[165] *Macbeth* (I.5).

They

through me. "It was *I* who cried 'Sleep no more'; and, although it was Macbeth alone who heard me (he did not see me, for I purposely made myself invisible to be the more mysterious and the more awful), I cried it to all the house! I chanted on one great deep note:

> 'Sleep no more!
> Macbeth does murder sleep, the innocent sleep;
> Sleep, that knits up the ravell'd sleave of care,
> The death of each day's life, sore labor's bath,
> Balm of hurt minds, great nature's second course,
> Chief nourisher in life's feast.'[166]

"I paused for a moment in the silent, cold house, now full of such delightful horror and then I continued:

> 'Sleep no more!
> Glamis hath murder'd sleep: and, therefore, Cawdor
> Shall sleep no more. Macbeth shall sleep no more.'[167]

"My voice," said the Witch, "like a great dark wave from the Ocean of Sound carried this baleful charm as it went reverberating down the stone halls, down the narrow passages, down the long corridors, down the winding stairways, into the courtyards, into the sleeping-rooms, into the banquet-hall, with its minstrel-gallery, into the kitchen-offices, into the pantries, into the vaults and dungeons, out of the great keep and across the moat and back again, up, up, up, to the very top of the battlemented towers and then down again and through the loop-holes and the arched windows and the wide doorways and back again to the door before Duncan's chamber, where Macbeth stood petrified with the horror

---

[166] *Macbeth* (II.2).
[167] Same.

Shakespearian Fantasias

of his deed.

"It was *my* voice that made Macbeth first realize what he had done; and I cried the charm three times! Never again would sleep visit the tired eyelids of black Macbeth! It was a wild, unruly night," the Witch continued, gloating over the memory of it. "We arranged that it should be so. Chimneys were blown down; lamentings heard i' the air; and strange screams of death. Owls hooted and shrieked and screamed; crickets cried and chirped; and cocks crew and clamored the live-long night. On the heath my sisters were boiling their Cauldron and

> 'Prophesying, with accents terrible,
> Of dire combustion and confus'd events,
> New hatch'd to the woeful time.
> Some say the earth was feverous and did shake.'[168]

"'Twas a rough night, even for the Weird sisters. So the Cauldron boiled and bubbled and the dagger was made and also the charm to banish sleep."

"Do you know?" the Witch added, looking at me with a wild glare, "do you know that one of the worst curses that we Evil Powers can place upon mortals is the loss of sleep? Do you know what the loss of sleep means? Do you comprehend what the function of sleep really is?"

"What do *you* say it is?" I responded.

"Every creature and everything on this whirling Earth needs repose and refreshment to repair the body after its work of the day and needs, even more than that, the release of the astral body for those mysterious voyages into the ether, where it gets experience and training. No

---

[168] *Macbeth* (II.3).

They

creature can do without sleep. Once there was a sailor's wife who was munching chestnuts. I asked her for some and the rump-fed ronyon cried 'Aroint thee, Witch,' Do you know how I punished her? I knew that her husband was master of the Tiger and on his way to Aleppo. So I sailed to Aleppo in a sieve! — yes, a sieve, ha! ha! ha! and I decreed that

> 'Sleep should neither night nor day
> Hang upon his pent-house lid;'[169]

also that he should dwindle, peak, and pine, as anyone must do who suffers loss of sleep. You see I had had experience in pronouncing the charm against sleep and that is why Hecate sent me to Inverness on that memorable night of nights."

Again the Witch paused. "Yes," she muttered, "we had a difficult time with Macbeth and Lady Macbeth. We had to poison their souls and to inflame their minds in order to make them first *want* to do the deed and then go into action. Macbeth was so vacillating. He nearly gave up the murder of Duncan and we had to work very hard through Lady Macbeth to force him to do it; and as soon as it was accomplished Macbeth repented. Yet once he was steeped in blood, we found it easy to make Macbeth commit crime after crime until at last he had no feeling left. The deterioration of Macbeth's character was complete and he grew indifferent to suffering, and even the death of Lady Macbeth made no impression upon him. The only thing that affected him was the report that Birnam Wood was moving towards Dunsinane, which we

---

[169] *Macbeth* (II.3).

Shakespearian Fantasias

had prophesied; and Macbeth knew then that the end had come for him. Macbeth was such a cold, selfish, and heartless creature, both satisfactory and unsatisfactory to us.

"Our great trouble with Macbeth was that he would stop everything to muse, to dream, and to moralize; but this had its advantages, too, because as he had the gift of seeing with his mind's eye, we could show him visions and appear to him ourselves."

"Yes," I replied, "think of a man planning a frightful murder and then saying to his wife:

> 'Ere the bat hath flown
> His cloister'd flight; ere, to black Hecate's summons,
> The shard-borne beetle, with his drowsy hums,
> Hath rung night's yawning peal, there shall be done
> A deed of dreadful note.'[170]

"And again breaking out with

> 'Light thickens; and the crow
> Make wing to the rooky wood:
> Good things of day begin to droop and drowse;
> While night's black agents to their prey do rouse.'[171]

"And then again, think of a murderer looking on his bloody hands and pronouncing these matchless lines:

> 'Will all great Neptune's ocean wash this blood
> Clean from my hand? No; this my hand will rather
> The multitudinous seas incarnadine,
> Making the green one, red.'"[172]

"With Lady Macbeth the question was very different,"

---

[170] *Macbeth* (III.2).
[171] Same.
[172] *Macbeth* (II.2).

They

remarked the Witch, ignoring my references to Macbeth's poetic flights. "Lady Macbeth was much the harder of the two to manage. She was a proud and dignified queen — first an *uncrowned* and then a *crowned* queen. She could act well: she understood how to 'look like the innocent flower, yet be the serpent under it.' She was deeply affectionate. She loved her husband and she tried to stimulate his weak points; and she, who was infinitely more honest with herself than Macbeth was with himself, could not possibly understand how he was afraid to be the same in act and valor as he was in desire. Her affection mastered her when we, Weird Sisters, on that glorious night of blackness, seeing how vacillating Macbeth was, sent her first to kill Duncan. Duncan looked so like his uncle, Lady Macbeth's father, as he lay asleep, that she was overcome; and, consequently, she failed us. Then she was terribly frightened when she returned down the stairs after taking the daggers back to the room and heard the owls and the crickets shriek and cry; and, more frightened still, when the knocking at the gate began.

"Yes," I interpolated," I know that Lady Macbeth lived over the horrors of that night when she walked in her sleep at Dunsinane Castle. Isn't that true?"

"Yes, that is true," the Witch answered. "You see it was *I* who made it impossible for her to sleep naturally. The curse 'Macbeth shall sleep no more' fell upon her, too! Haunted by fear of the dark and the Evil Powers that dwell in it, afraid of the Weird Sisters whom she had never known, except by Macbeth's descriptions of us, she had light by her continually; and every night, when she walked in her sleep through the chilly rooms and

Shakespearian Fantasias

corridors of Dunsinane Castle, she always carried a lighted candle."

After a short pause the Witch continued:

"Lady Macbeth nearly betrayed herself the morning after Duncan's murder when she came into the hullabaloo and calmly asked what was the matter; and when she was told of the murder she appeared far too astonished by saying 'What, in our house?' that was a great blunder. We had to try to repair it. So we threw the attention on Macbeth. We made him speak at great length; and Lady Macbeth was so astonished to hear her husband *describe* what a short time ago he was *afraid to look on*, that she fainted. We had a great deal of trouble to keep matters going our way and in the confusion Malcolm and Donalbain, Duncan's two sons, escaped — the one to England, the other to Ireland.

"For a long time we had used Lady Macbeth as a support for her weak husband, but after Duncan's murder we needed her no longer. When Macbeth told his wife:

> 'I am in blood
> Stepp'd in so far, that, should I wade no more,
> Returning were as tedious as go o'er,'[173]

we knew he was wholly ours. Oh, yes, it was we, Weird Sisters, who filled Macbeth's mind with scorpions!"

"I have always thought that the Weird Sisters controlled both Macbeth and Lady Macbeth and I am glad to have my impressions confirmed," I said.

"Would you like to see my sisters and the boiling of our Cauldron?" the Witch asked me with a grin of

---

[173] *Macbeth* (III.4).

They

excruciating ugliness, again ignoring my remarks. "Our heath is a delightful place."

"I don't know," I answered hesitatingly, "it is most kind of you to ask me, and I appreciate it; but I am rather afraid of sinister things."

"Oh, I'll take care that nothing shall happen to you," said the Witch comfortingly. "Everything and everybody is afraid of the Weird Sisters — you, too, it seems" — and then she added: "Well, whether you want to come or not does not matter in the least, you *are* coming with me and I am going to reproduce for you one of our most splendid nights. Now listen to me attentively: you will have to obey me. You must stand still while you watch our performances and you must not utter a single word."

Immediately heavy thunder began to roll and rumble and crack and lightning darted about in vivid forks, burst into balls of fire, and occasionally threw great sheets of pink upon the blue black sky, making an uncanny glow. By these brilliant flashes I soon found that I was standing alone on a very solitary and arid Scotch heath — terribly frightened by the place and the storm – and in full view of a dark Cave. In the centre of the Cave, a large Cauldron was boiling over a lurid fire — a gigantic gipsy pot — and three Witches entered the Cave. They were all alike; but I recognized the voice of the one that spoke first as the Weird Sister that had brought me here.

"Thrice the brinded cat hath mewed," she intoned in that dark and terrible voice that had echoed through the halls of Inverness to banish sleep from the House of Macbeth. Then this Witch walked around the Cauldron, throwing the most horrible ingredients into it. When she

Shakespearian Fantasias

had finished, all three Witches took hands and danced around the Cauldron chanting:

> "Double, double toil and trouble;
> Fire, burn; and, cauldron, bubble."[174]

The second Witch threw in fillet of a fenny snake, eye of newt, toe of frog, wool of bat, tongue of dog, adder's fork, blind-worm's sting, lizard's leg, and owlet's wing, "for a charm of powerful trouble," And again the three Witches took hands and danced around the Cauldron, chanting:

> "Double, double toil and trouble;
> Fire, burn; and, cauldron, bubble."[175]

The third Witch had even worse things to add to the brew that was making a great bubbling noise and sending forth clouds of brownish-gray steam and horrible odors. Again, the Witches circled around their charmèd pot, chanting their

> "Double, double toil and trouble;
> Fire, burn; and, cauldron, bubble."[176]

The dance suddenly stopped and the second Witch shrieked:

> "Cool it with a baboon's blood,
> Then the charm is firm and good!"[177]

At this moment Hecate flitted in, accompanied by her bats and owls, and approved of all that had been done. Hecate also commanded that the dance be repeated; and,

---

[174] *Macbeth* (IV.1).
[175] Same.
[176] Same.
[177] Same.

They

after singing her song:

> "Black spirits and white,
> Red spirits and gray;
> Mingle, mingle, mingle,
> You that mingle may,"[178]

the Queen of Darkness vanished.

The second Witch suddenly cried:

> "By the pricking of my thumbs,
> Something wicked this way comes."[179]

It was Macbeth.

The Weird Sisters were all ready for him: their Cauldron was full of potential visions to show Macbeth his destiny.

There was no wavering in Macbeth's determination this time and no fear in his voice as he demanded to know his fate. And the poet within him spoke too:

> "I conjure you, by that which you profess,
> (Howe'er you come to know it) answer me:
> Though you untie the winds, and let them fight
> Against the churches: though the yesty waves
> Confound and swallow navigation up;
> Though bladed corn be lodg'd, and trees blown
>   down;
> Though castles topple on their warder's heads;
> Though palaces and pyramids do slope
> Their heads to the foundations; though the treasure
> Of nature's germins tumble all together
> Even till destruction sicken, answer me
> To what I ask you."[180]

---

[178] *Macbeth* (IV.1).
[179] Same.
[180] Same.

Shakespearian Fantasias

The Witches agreed; and, to a terrific crash of thunder, an Armed Head rose from the Cauldron. In solemn tones it warned Macbeth to beware of Macduff.

Another terrific clap of thunder; and this time, a Bloody Child arose from the hell-broth, saying that "none of woman born shall harm Macbeth." The third apparition to issue from the Cauldron, also to fearful thunder, was a Child, crowned, with a tree in his hand, who promised that Macbeth would never vanquished be until great Birnam Wood should come to high Dunsinane hill.

At this Macbeth broke out into an ecstasy of delight, feeling so sure of his safety; but I remembered that Hecate had said: *"Security is mortal's chiefest enemy."*

"Yet my heart throbs to know one thing," Macbeth cried to the Weird Sisters, "tell me (if your art can tell so much), shall Banquo's issue ever reign in this Kingdom?"

"Seek to know no more," the Witches yelled."

But Macbeth persisted.

Suddenly the Cauldron sunk and a weird melody was heard from some unseen hautboys.

To this melody the Weird Sisters intoned:

> "Show his eyes and grieve his heart;
> Come like shadows, so depart."[181]

Eight kings now appeared, one by one, and passed across the heath, each one wearing a crown, some of them carried two-fold balls and treble sceptres. The eighth king had a glass in his hand, which showed many more kings to follow. Last of all, Banquo appeared, who smiled at Macbeth and pointed to the long line of Stuart Kings as his progeny.

---

[181] *Macbeth* (IV.1).

They

Macbeth gazed at the royal procession amazedly. The Weird Sisters gave then a short, triumphant dance, and vanished.

> "Infected be the air whereon they ride
> And damn'd all those that trust them,"[182]

Macbeth exclaimed wildly; and, in another moment Macbeth, also, was gone.

A blinding flash of lightning, accompanied by a ferocious roll of thunder, made me close my eyes. When I opened them, the blasted heath had disappeared; but I thought I heard, out of a far distance, the voices of "They" — the Weird Sisters — chanting darkly:

> 'Show his eyes and grieve his heart;
> Come like shadows, so depart.'[183]

---

[182] *Macbeth* (IV.1).
[183] Same.

Saucy Beatrice

I WAS standing on the Terrace of an Elizabethan manor house a few days ago and as I was admiring the elegance of its lines, the justness of its proportions, the soft hues of its bricks, the piquancy of its pointed gables, the richness of its ivy-covered, mullioned windows, the quaintness of its chimney-pots, and the beauty of its Terrace with tall jars of blooming flowers and wide steps that led down to the river softly purling among the rushes and water-lilies, one of the most fascinating women that I have ever seen appeared at the door and stepped out upon the red-bricked pavement.

Suddenly the lady saw me and for several minutes she looked at me with undisguised curiosity. Then, evidently deciding that it was perfectly safe to make my acquaintance, she accosted me with charming grace.

While she had been staring at *me*, I had been staring at *her*.

I think her beauty lay more in expression than in her actual features, although these would have satisfied any painter's ideals. Her figure was tall, slender, and *svelte*; and she moved with the lightness of a snowflake. Vivacity was expressed in her every motion — a vivacity that was never violent, nor jerky, but graceful, rippling like a wave, or, better still, like the play of a sparkling jewel.

And I think Beatrice — for that was her name —

Saucy Beatrice

should be compared to a jewel, for she was so brilliant, so flashing, so full of color, and there were so many facets in her precious mind. Beatrice was as proud in bearing as she was proud in feature and expression — and I admired her no less for this, for I like *hauteur* — and although she was friendly and merry in her manner and conversation, I saw that she could be disdainful, scornful, and mocking when she pleased. Beatrice told me later that she was born under a dancing star and I think that describes her scintillating wit and her enchanting vivacity better than any words of mine could do. Her dress, too, was very artistic and most becoming — "cloth of gold and cuts and laced with silver set with pearls, down sleeves, side sleeves and skirts, underborne with a bluish tinsel."[184] Diamonds twinkled in her hair and a necklace of very large pearls lay around her throat.

After we had had quite a long conversation, during which I satisfied Beatrice that she was not unknown to me (although I was unknown to her), and that she could depend upon my friendship were she to honor me with it, she took my hand in hers and placing her left hand over it said as she did so that she would fain trust me and that she would bestow upon me not friendship alone, but confidence as well.

"Come with me," she added, "I will take you to a place that is very dear to me — our pleachèd bower, where honeysuckles ripened by the sun forbid the sun to enter, and there I will tell you the story of my heart."

Then Beatrice and I walked down the steps of the

---

[184] *Much Ado About Nothing* (III.4).

Shakespearian Fantasias

Terrace, turned to the right and passed under the long pleachèd arbor that led into Leonato's orchard. This pleachèd arbor might best be described as an arcade, or a leafy tunnel, where roses, honeysuckles, clematis, grapevines, and rosemary were climbing over one another in carefully trained, yet riotous, beauty. Finally, we came to a bower at the very end of the arcade entirely covered with honeysuckles, so thick and luxuriant that the masses of dark green leaves and the buff and creamy blossoms did indeed forbid the sun to enter; and yet the sun, which was shining with its full golden heat on the outside flowers, had ripened them to such enormous size and perfection that the perfume excelled the perfume of any honeysuckles that I had ever seen before.

"It was here in this bower," Beatrice said very tenderly, and with the very sweetest of smiles, "that I learned that Benedick loved me. You will not wonder, therefore, that the honeysuckle is my favorite flower, will you? The French have a pretty name for it; they call it *cher feu*, and indeed the 'dear flame' was kindled for us both here, in this very bower, for my dear Benedick, too. Let us sit down while I tell you all about it."

"I cannot express to you how much I appreciate your telling me this," I said; but Beatrice was too intent upon her story to notice my acknowledgment of her favor.

"One day," Beatrice began, "one day just after dinner, when I was sitting in the parlor talking to Don Pedro and Claudio, who was betrothed to my cousin, Hero (the daughter of my uncle, Leonato), Margaret, who is one of Hero's attendant gentlewomen, came running in and whispered in my ear that Hero and Ursula (Hero's other

Saucy Beatrice

gentlewoman) were walking in the orchard and that all their discourse was of *me*; and she advised me to steal into the honeysuckle-bower so that I might overhear their talk. Of course, I ran as fast as I could and couched myself in the woodbine coverture.

"Hero and Ursula, who were walking up and down the pleachèd alley, came closer to the bower and I heard Hero say to Ursula that Claudio and the Prince had told her that Benedick loved me entirely and that they had entreated her to acquaint me of it. Hero then said she had persuaded them, if they love Benedick, to wish him wrestle with his affection and *never* let me know of it. Ursula asked her why she did so and if she did not think Benedick was deserving of me? 'O god of Love!' Hero exclaimed, 'Benedick doth deserve as much as may be yielded to a man; but nature never framed a woman's heart of prouder stuff than that of Beatrice. Disdain and scorn ride sparkling in her eyes'; and then she went on to say that I turned every man the wrong side out and that I carped and mocked at every gentleman no matter how wise, how noble, how young, or how rarely featured he might be. 'Benedick,' she continued, 'will have to waste inwardly and consume himself in sighs like covered fire.'

"Ursula suggested that Hero tell *me*.

"'Oh, no,' Hero answered, 'I would rather go to Benedick and counsel him to fight against his passion. Moreover, I will devise some slanders to stain my cousin with.'

"'Oh, do not do your cousin such a wrong,' Ursula begged; and then she said that I had so swift and excellent a wit I surely could not refuse so rare a gentleman as

Shakespearian Fantasias

Signor Benedick. Then, after praising Benedick's figure, his bearing, his intellect, his valor, and his splendid reputation, they began to talk about Hero's approaching wedding; and then they walked away.

"Can you imagine how I felt? What fire was in mine ears? How distressed I was to be so condemned for pride and scorn? And to think I was beloved by the one man with whom I have always engaged in a kind of merry war and whose wit I have always so admired! I knew better than all reports what my Signor Montano deserved and so I said to the honeysuckles:

> 'And, Benedick, love on; I will requite thee;
> Taming my wild heart to thy loving hand.'[185]

"Now you must know," Beatrice continued after a pause, "that until this moment I always had mocked all my wooers out of suit. I could not endure to hear talk of a husband. For one thing," Beatrice explained sententiously, "I had observed that wooing, wedding, and repenting is as a Scotch jig, a measure, and a cinque-pace: the first is hot and hasty like a Scotch jig, and full as fantastical; the wedding, mannerly modest as a measure, full of state and ancientry; and then comes repentance, and, with his bad legs, falls into the cinque-pace faster and faster till he sinks into the grave. And yet," she added a little pensively, "I had Signor Benedick's heart once — he lent it to me awhile — and then I lost it. Ever after that he called me my dear Lady Disdain and I called him Signor Montanto, and we never met but we had a skirmish of wit between us."

---

[185] *Much Ado About Nothing* (III.1).

Saucy Beatrice

"Why did you object so strongly to marriage?" I inquired.

"I don't know," answered Beatrice, "I suppose for the same reasons that Benedick railed so long against marriage, whatever those reasons were! At any rate, I used to say that it would grieve me to be overmastered with a piece of valiant dust and to make an account of my life to a clod of wayward marl! And I used to tell my uncle whenever he said he hoped he would see me one day fitted with a husband: 'No, uncle, I'll none. Adam's sons are my brethren; and truly I hold it a sin to match in my kindred'; and when people mocked me and told me that I would have to lead apes in hell I laughed at them and answered, 'I will deliver up my apes and away to Saint Peter for the heavens; he shows me where the bachelors sit, and there live we as merry as the day is long.'"

"Well, Lady Beatrice," I broke in, "you evidently knew where you would find Signor Benedick; and may I ask if that was not the reason you looked forward with such confidence to sitting with the bachelors and being as merry as the day was long?"

"Perhaps that is true," Beatrice laughed back, a conscious blush stealing over her face.

"Now tell me about Benedick. How did he change his mind?"

"It all happened in this very honeysuckle-bower," she answered, "and on the very same day, but just before dinner. Benedick was sitting here reading — he reads and writes nearly all the time — when Don Pedro, my uncle Leonato, and Claudio came by; and Don Pedro said in a loud voice to my uncle, so that Benedick would be sure to

Shakespearian Fantasias

hear, 'What was it you told me of today — that your niece, Beatrice, was in love with Signor Benedick?' And my uncle told him that I simply doted on Benedick, although in my outward behaviours I seemed ever to abhor him; and then Claudio added, 'Hero thinks she surely will die, for she says she will die if he love her not and she will die ere she makes her love known'; and so they went on talking of me. Then Don Pedro said, 'I am sorry for your niece. Shall we go see Benedick and tell him of her love?'

"'Never tell him, my lord,' Claudio advised, 'let her wear it out with good counsel.'

"'Well,' said Don Pedro, 'we'll hear further of it by your daughter: let it cool the while. I love Benedick well; and I could wish he would modestly examine himself to see how much he is unworthy to have so good a lady.'

"'Then Leonato said: "My lord will you walk? Dinner is ready.'

"When they left Benedick exclaimed: 'They seem to pity the lady. Love me! Why it must be requited. I hear how I am censured: they say I will bear myself proudly if I perceive the love come from her; they say, too, that she will rather die than give any sign of affection. I did never think to marry. They say the lady is fair; 'tis a truth, I can bear them witness: and virtuous — 'tis so, I cannot reprove it; and wise, but for loving me. I may chance have some odd quirks and remnants of wit broken on me because I have railed so long against marriage; but doth not the appetite alter? A man loves the meat in his youth that he cannot endure in his age. When I said I would die a bachelor, I did not think I should live till I were married. — Here comes Beatrice. By this day, she's a fair lady: I do

Saucy Beatrice

spy some marks of love in her.'"

"How did you know all this?" I asked.

"Oh, Benedick told it all to me. But to continue," she said. "Now my uncle sent me to call Signor Benedick to dinner and so I came to the arbor, and said very saucily: 'Signor Benedick, against my will I am sent to bid you come in to dinner.'

"'Fair Beatrice, I thank you for your pains,' he answered; and he gave me such a strange new look and there was such a light in his eyes and such a tone of love in his voice that I thought it best to reprove him, so I replied very mockingly. 'I took no more pains for those thanks than you take pains to thank me; if it had been painful I would not have come.' Benedick looked at me with even more fire in his glance as he quickly retorted: 'You take pleasure, then, in the message?'

"So I bade him farewell, with a very mocking and disdainful curtsey, and ran back to the house. Of course, I could not make anything out of Benedick's change in manner; and all during dinner he gazed at me most fondly. After dinner he walked away in a melancholy mood."

"And were you as merry as usual yourself?" I questioned.

"No, I do not believe I was," Beatrice replied, "and while Don Pedro and Claudio were talking to me in the parlor after dinner, I did not hear much of the drift. Then it was that Margaret came for me — and I ran here. I have told you all the rest. Yes, there is something more to tell you," Beatrice laughingly admitted. "The fact is Benedick and I were both victims of a trick. Don Pedro, my uncle, and Claudio decided to make a match between us and took Hero into their confidence; and they planned that they would contrive to practice on Benedick and that Hero and her gentlewomen must spread the same net for me; and they chose this honeysuckle-bower for the place."

"Were you and Signor Benedick angry when you found out how you had both been caught in the snare?" I asked.

Beatrice darted a very merry glance at me as she laughingly replied: "Not a bit. We had already been writing sonnets to one another; and our floutings and wit-crackings were only a part of our love-making; for, as Benedick said: 'We were too wise to woo peaceably.'"

"You must have been subject to many jeers!" I remarked.

"Oh, yes," answered Beatrice, "but Benedick got a worse drubbing than I did. The very next morning, Don Pedro, my uncle, and Claudio laughingly said that Benedick's heart was as sound as a bell and that Cupid did not dare shoot at him. But Benedick replied: 'Gallants, I am not as I have been.'

"'Yes, you do seem sadder,' my uncle admitted.

"'I hope he's in love,' Claudio said.

"'If he's sad, he wants money,' Don Pedro laughed back; and so they teased Benedick, one after the other. Claudio persisted that he was in love; he knew the signs: Benedick brushes his hat; he paints his face; he perfumes himself with civet! Finally, Benedick took my uncle by the arm and walked away with him, saying he had eight or nine words to speak with him.

Saucy Beatrice

"'About Beatrice,' Don Pedro guessed — and he guessed right."

"And you?" I asked, "what did the ladies do to you?"

"Oh, they teased me, of course; and when I said I was feeling ill, Hero advised me to get some distilled "Carduus Benedictus" to lay on my heart; and Margaret said that Benedick was just such another.

"We dressed for Hero's wedding; but things were not destined to go smoothly. When we were all assembled in the church and were standing before the altar, Claudio refused to marry Hero and made a dreadful accusation against her. Hero protested her innocence and swooned away. We all thought she was dead; and Claudio and Don Pedro left in sorrow. If it had not been for Benedick I think I should have swooned away, too. Our dear Friar, who had come to marry Hero and Claudio, advised my uncle to give out that Hero was really dead; for he said so wisely that she would be lamented and pitied and that Claudio would begin to mourn for her and to wish that he had not accused her thus.

"'For it so falls out,' he said,

> 'That what we have we prize not to the worth
> Whiles we enjoy it; but being lack'd and lost,
> Why, then we rack the value; then we find
> The virtue that possession would not show us
> Whiles it was ours.'[186]

"Then the dear kind Friar assured Hero that her wedding-day was only postponed, or prolonged, and exhorted her to have patience.

---

[186] *Much Ado About Nothing* (IV.1).

Shakespearian Fantasias

"Then Benedick told me over and over again that he loved nothing in the world so well as me and I told him that I loved him with all my heart; and then he promised me that he would challenge Claudio and avenge my sweet, slandered cousin, Hero.

"It was not very long before the truth was discovered by the Night Watch, so we planned to have Hero come to life again. Claudio told my uncle he could choose his revenge and my uncle said then he must marry a niece, the very counterpart of Hero; and his revenge would die there. It was a beautiful morning for the next wedding, very early. The gentle day before the wheels of Phoebus had just dappled the drowsy east with spots of gray when the same wedding-party assembled in my uncle's house. Hero was masked; and my uncle made Claudio take her hand and swear before the holy Friar that he would marry her. When Claudio had done this, Hero unmasked and Claudio found that he had the *real* Hero. Then we all went into the Chapel of our house and Benedick and I were married at the same time."

"You seem to be very happy," I observed; and Beatrice answered, smiling sweetly:

"I were little happy if I could say how much."

"And is Benedick as happy as you are?" I asked.

"He can speak for himself," said Beatrice, "for here he comes."

"I came to seek you, Beatrice," the handsome Elizabethan gallant began; but, catching sight of me, he doffed his plumed velvet hat and made me an elegant bow.

"This is a stranger from an outlandish country,"

Saucy Beatrice

Beatrice explained. "I don't quite understand how it is, but she seems almost like one of us. She is much interested to hear how we both railed against marriage and how we have been converted."

"Peace: I will stop your mouth," said Benedick, kissing her. "I have come to read you a sonnet that I have just written to you. Will the stranger permit me?"

"I shall be much honored to hear it," I said.

"Whereupon Benedick, unfolding a little paper which he had been holding in his hand, read:

> "The forward violet thus did I chide;
> Sweet thief, whence didst though steal thy sweet
>   that smells,
> If not from my love's breath? The purple pride
> Which on thy soft cheek for complexion dwells,
> In my love's veins thou hast too grossly dy'd.
> The lily I condemned for thy hand,
> And buds of marjoram had stolen thy hair;
> The roses fearfully on thorns did stand,
> One blushing shame, another white despair;
> A third, nor red nor white, had stolen of both,
> And to his robbery had annex'd thy breath;
> But for his theft, in pride of all his growth,
> A vengeful canker eat him up to death.
> More flowers I noted, yet I none could see,
> But sweet or color it had stolen from thee."[187]

"And to think," said saucy Beatrice, laying her hand on Benedick's shoulder, "and to think that only a few weeks ago you asked Don Pedro to send you on the slightest errand to the antipodes: to get a toothpicker from the farthest inch of Asia; to bring the length of Prester John's foot; to fetch a hair off the great Cham's beard; do any

---

[187] Shakespeare's Sonnet No. 99.

Shakespearian Fantasias

embassage to the Pigmies rather than hold three words conference with *this* harpy!"

"Well, you know now, saucy Beatrice, that I live in thy heart and am buried in thy eyes," Benedick answered.

"Did you not say, Signor Benedick," I ventured to remark, "that till all the graces be in one woman one woman should not come in your grace? And, if you will permit me to pay this compliment, I think your lady is possessed of all the graces. Your lovely sonnet describes her perfectly."

"I think I like Benedick's poem on Love even better than the sonnet to me," said Beatrice and she drew from a hidden pocket in her gown, which, as its folds were moved, set forth a delicious whiff of the famous Lord Oxford perfume,[188] which all the Court ladies and gallants were using, a paper from which she read:

> "'Is he god in peace or war?
> What be his arms? What is his might?
> His war is peace, his peace is war:
> Each grief of his is but delight;
> His bitter ball is sugared bliss;
> What be his gifts? How doth he pay?
> Sweet dreams in sleep, new thoughts by day.'"[189]

"Don't you like that?" said Beatrice. "It certainly jumps with my humor."

"I do, indeed," I answered. "It reminds me of something I know," I said. "Where have I heard that unique melancholy rhythm? That musical lilt? That

---

[188] See notes 128 (p. 138) and 131 (p. 139).

[189] From the second and third stanzas of Edward de Vere's poem, "What is Desire?" Benedick, then, has apparently written poems by both William Shakespeare and Edward de Vere.

Saucy Beatrice

choice and delicate touch? Oh, I know now," I added, "hear this:"

> 'Tell me, where is fancy bred,
> Or in the heart, or in the head?
> How begot, how nourished?
>   Reply, reply.
> It is engender'd in the eyes,
> With gazing fed; and fancy dies
> In the cradle where it lies.
>   Let us all ring fancy's knell;
> I'll begin it — ding dong, bell.'"[190]

"Why, of course," laughed Beatrice, "Benedick wrote that song, too."

While we had been talking I had been admiring this remarkably handsome couple; for Benedick was every bit as charming and as dashing as Beatrice. It was easy to see that they were made for one another. I was rather surprised to find that Benedick was short, but his great presence and his unusual elegance made you forget that he was rather undersized. His forehead was large, intellectual, and curiously domed; his eyes were hazel and burned with fire, sparkled with wit, paled with melancholy, or melted with sentiment; his mouth, ornamented with a light and carefully clipped moustache, was sensitive and sweet of expression; and his smile was captivating. He was noble in appearance and every motion suggested valor and honesty. Much of his grace was owing to his accomplishments as a fencer, in which

---

[190] *The Merchant of Venice* (III.2). So our narrator is saying that de Vere's poem has the same "unique melancholy rhythm," the same "musical lilt" as de Shakespeare's poem. And Beatrice says that the same person wrote them both.

Shakespearian Fantasias

art his skill was so great that Beatrice had nicknamed him Signor Montanto. In addition to his personal charms, Benedick was a delightful conversationalist and his farcical banter added much to this social grace.[191]

"I have not told this stranger how Don John's slander of Hero was discovered," Beatrice said to Benedick. "Suppose you take her to see Dogberry and make him relate the story. I think it might amuse her to see Dogberry."

"Oh, I'd love to see Dogberry," I exclaimed.

"Come on, then," said Benedick, "I will take you to Dogberry, but I cannot stay, for," looking at Beatrice, "we have a supper-party and a masked dance tonight. I will join you, Beatrice, in about half an hour."

How delighted I was to hear this elegant man of such cultured speech pronounce the word hour in two syllables, rhyming with flower!

The honeysuckle-bower was built near a high and thick wall of dull red bricks in which there was a large wooden door painted green and which Benedick unlocked. To my surprise, this door led into the principal street of the little English town discreetly veiled under the name of Messina.

We had not gone very far before Benedick exclaimed: "There's Dogberry now! and Verges, his officer, with him. You will soon hear some odd slandering of the King's English, I warrant you!"

Calling Dogberry to his side, Benedick ordered him to tell me all about Don John's villainy; and then, with a

---

[191] The description of Benedick in this paragraph could easily have been applied to Edward de Vere. See footnote 129 on page 124.

Saucy Beatrice

profound bow and the word "Farewell!" pronounced with his enchanting smile, Benedick re-entered the gate and was gone!

Dogberry began at once. "I was out with the Watch," he said, "and I had chosen the most desertless man to be constable, George Seacoal. God hath blessed him with a good name and he could read and write. To be a well-favored man is the gift of fortune; but to read and write comes by nature."

It does to *some* people," I interrupted, "to Signor Benedick, for instance; and, if it were not for the sake of modesty, I could mention somebody else."

"George Seacoal," continued Dogberry, not noticing my remark, "was the most senseless and fit man for the constable of the Watch and he, therefore, bore the lantern and I gave him charge to comprehend all vagrom men and to bid any man stand in the Prince's name. I also told my honest neighbors to watch about Signor Leonato's door; for the wedding, being there tomorrow, there was a great coil tonight. Two men came and stood under the penthouse, for it was drizzling rain. One told the other how he had that night wooed Margaret, Lady Hero's gentlewoman, by the name of Hero, out of her mistress's chamber-window. 'I should first tell thee,' he said, 'how the Prince Claudio and my master, planted and placed and possessed by my master Don John, saw afar off in the orchard this amiable encounter. Away went Claudio enraged and swore he would meet her in the temple and there before the whole congregation shame her with what he saw overnight and send her home again without a husband.'

Shakespearian Fantasias

"'We charge you in the Prince's name stand,' said my first Watch.

"'We have recovered the most dangerous piece of lechery that was ever known in the commonwealth' said my second Watch.

"I went with Verges, here," continued Dogberry, pointing to his companion, "to Prince Leonato's house and I said to Prince Leonato, 'I would have some confidence with you that decerns you nearly.'

"'Marry, sir,' clapped in Verges, 'our Watch tonight, excepting your worship's presence, have ta'en a couple of as arrant knaves as any in Messina.'

"'Our Watch, sir,' I said, 'have indeed comprehended two auspicious persons, and we would have them this morning examined before your worship.'

"The Prince would not stay, for he was going to the wedding and he told us to take the examination ourself.

"When the offenders came before me I said to one: 'What is your name, friend?' 'Borachio,' he said. 'Pray write down Borachio,' I said. I asked the other: 'Yours sirrah?' 'I am a gentleman, sir, and my name is Conrade,' he said. I said 'Write down Master gentleman Conrade.' I said 'Masters, do you serve God?' 'Yes, sir, we hope,' they said. I said: 'Write down that they hope they serve God and write God first, for God defend but God should go before such villains.'[192]

"The Watch said that Borachio said he had received a thousand ducats off Don John for accusing the Lady Hero wrongfully. 'Flat burglary as ever was committed,' I said.

---

[192] From *Much Ado About Nothing* (IV.2).

Saucy Beatrice

'And that Count Claudio did mean, upon his words to disgrace Hero before the whole assembly and not marry her.' 'O villain!' I cried 'thou wilt be condemned into everlasting redemption for this.'

"'You are an ass, you are an ass,' Conrade said to me. He did not suspect my place; he did not suspect my years; and Seacoal was gone that did write. Oh, that he had been here to write me down as ass! Oh, that I had been written down an ass!"

"Well," I asked, "and did you tell Signor Leonato?"

"Yes," answered Dogberry, "as we walked along, with Borachio and Conrade bound, we met Don Pedro; and Borachio confessed his villainy, and by that time our sexton had reformed Signor Leonato of the matter."

"Thank you, Dogberry," I said, "it is a wonderful story. I think you understand how to train your Watch."

"I told them," said Dogberry, evidently pleased with my compliment, "if you meet a thief, you may suspect him, by virtue of your office, to be no true man; and for, such kind of men, the less you meddle with them, why, the more is for your honesty."

"Tis very true," observed Verges solemnly.

"Good-night," said Dogberry to me, very abruptly, "but though it is not written down, yet forget now that I am an ass. Come, neighbor."

I watched the quaint figures of Dogberry and Verges, in their curious Elizabethan gown of office, as they retreated slowly down the street, and then I decided I would return to Leonato's mansion, hoping to find again Beatrice and Benedick; but when I turned, lo! the brick wall and the green door that opened into Leonato's

Shakespearian Fantasias

orchard had melted away. In another moment one of those beautiful and fantastic amethystine mists of England spread softly over the scene and completely blotted out the little town of Messina.

Cock-A-Doodle-Doo

> "Hark, hark! I hear
> The strain of strutting chanticlere
> Cry, Cock-a-doodle-doo!
> *The Tempest, Act I, Scene ii*

STARTLED from a reverie by a clarion call that had the quality of magic in its last long-drawn-out note, I opened my eyes to see standing in front of me a game Cock of unusual beauty.

I have never been particularly interested in barnyard fowls, but the gorgeousness and the majestic mien of this bird magnetized my attention. Everything about him was perfect. In the first place he was built for speed: thin and trim and sharply pointed fore and aft, taut and clean of line. Instinctively I thought of a racing yacht and then of a thoroughbred horse. The little Cock's movements were as agile and graceful as those of a cat and he turned his head as if it were worked by a screw as he looked upon me first with his right eye and then with his left eye — little round, sparkling beads of black and ruby encircled by a thread of gold. His feathers were so lustrous that they seemed to be coated with enamel, having a *niello* brittle brilliance and their colors were a confused mass of gold, maroon, canary, garnet, cinnamon, and ginger with high lights of scarlet and orange here and there and burnished greens that changed to bronze as they caught the light and back

Shakespearian Fantasias

again to green and purplish blue. His tail was a splendid cascade of flowing and quivering greens, all a-shimmer with golden iridescence. His serrated and perpetually nodding comb was like a piece of lobster coral and he shook it haughtily before he hunched up his neck-ruffles and dropped his sharp beak, shaped like the prow of a Roman galley, into these plumes. Then, surveying me again, he trumpeted forth another clarion call, long and shrill.

As he drew himself up in position for his impressive vocal effort, I noticed that his little legs were so slim that I wondered how they could support his body — light and lithe as that was — and indeed they could not have done so if he had not possessed the secret of perfect balance. Moreover, these delicate little putty-colored legs were equipped with a pair of long and very sharp spurs. The little Cock seemed to be excessively proud of them, as he swung about, so delicately poised on his tiny toes, furnished with long almond-shaped nails that tapered to a fine point, reminding me of the nails that a Chinese mandarin cultivates with such care and protects by metal sheaths. This brilliant Cock was not unlike those fantastic and brightly-hued cocks we see on precious Chinese and Japanese porcelains.

The dashing bird seemed to be as much interested in me as I was in him. Every now and then, as he whirled around on his graceful little toes that seemed almost like the hands of a beautiful woman, ruffled his neck feathers, shook his comb and his coral *jabot*, or took a quick peck at the grass, he would fasten first one bright little eye upon me and then the other, as if he were trying his best

Cock-A-Doodle-Doo

to establish a relationship between us.

For a long time I could get no farther than this, for I was trying to puzzle out the question as to which one of us was real and which one of us was the dream. I had not as yet understood what the cock had undoubtedly understood from the first — that we had met in the Fourth Dimension.

Strange things happen in dreams; and the stranger they are, the more natural they are — in *dreams*. Consequently, all of a sudden, we began to talk; and I am going to record as much of the experience as I can remember.

Communication was brought about in a curious way. The branch of a tree a little above my head suddenly waved to-and-fro in the breeze — I had not noticed before that I was sitting under an apple-tree in full flower — and the delicious perfume from "the blossom that hangs on the bough" seemed to clear my senses — it was so sweet — and at the same instant I heard a silvery, flute-like, boyish voice singing:

"And sweet sprites the burden bear;"[193]

And then, "dispersedly," all around, and above, and even below me, myriads of soft, yet crystal-clear voices broke out in a merry catch, the words and musical phrases all mingled in a sort of organized confusion:

"Hark, hark!
Bowgh, wowgh,
The watch-dogs bark:
Bowgh, wowgh,

---

[193] *The Tempest* (I.2).

Shakespearian Fantasias

> Hark, hark! I hear
> The strain of strutting chanticlere
> Cry, Cock-a-doodle-doo![194]

I looked at the Cock and smiled, And the Cock looked at me and laughed:

"Aha!" he chuckled, "You know me at last, do you? Well, it took you a long time, didn't it? *Of course*, I am Ariel's cock. Ding, Dong, Bell."

I was so entranced that I could say nothing, for the air was full of voices still singing the merry catch and from the distance there came faint barkings and crowings and ringing of bells.

"And I am more than that," the Cock explained. "I am," and he twirled around madly on his dainty toes before he stretched himself proudly to his full height, "I am Shakespeare's Cock. Yes," he added, "Shakespeare's Cock. I have called up every beautiful Shakespearian morning that you love so well. More than this, I can bring them all before you. Perhaps you would like to enjoy some of those golden hours with me?

"But," the Cock continued, looking at me inquisitively. "You are a great puzzle to me. I cannot, for the life of me, place you. I do not seem to remember you in any of the Plays; yet you have the Shakespearian atmosphere around you. Tell me, did Shakespeare create you?"

"No, I'm afraid not," I answered, "I wish he had."

"Undoubtedly it would have been better," remarked the Cock, "very *much* better. You would have been so much more interesting; and, besides, you would have

---

[194] *The Tempest* (I.2).

Cock-A-Doodle-Doo

been *real*. As it is, you are very transitory. You wander from the stupid materialistic world of yours into our world of imagination; but the trouble is you don't stay here long enough. Why do you go back and forth? It is rather unusual though that you can get here at all."

"Well, you see," I tried to explain, "I live a great deal in the Shakespeare World, so much so that it has become a very real world to me."

"Ah! that partly accounts for it," replied the Cock. "I am glad to hear you say that. You will then be able to see what I should like to show you. But still I cannot understand how you crossed the border-line. I wonder if you ever knew Shakespeare?"

"I sometimes fancy so," I answered.

"Good!" exclaimed the Cock. "Now, look!"

Astonishing!

It has turned very cold. The air was nipping and eager. The icy blast had blown away my spring-tide apple-tree and in its place was standing a massive gray stone tower, very awe-inspiring in the pale light of the waning moon that slipped in and out of the ragged rifts and banks of clouds, a round, cold, and silvery moon. All was grim and silent in this alternate play of bright light and dark shadow except for the plash and boom of the waves as they broke on the beach far below. I was standing on a high turretted platform of the Castle of Elsinore and a deep-toned bell was ringing out the hour of twelve. A guardsman was shivering at his post — Bernardo, of course, and it was Francisco who came to relieve him. I also recognized Horatio and Marcellus, now arriving. I was deeply interested in their courteous Elizabethan greetings and still more so in the conversation that ensued.

Marcellus remarked:

> "Horatio says 'tis but our fantasy,
> And will not let belief take hold of him
> Touching this dreaded sight, twice seen of us:
> Therefore I have entreated him along
> With us to watch the minutes of this night;
> That, if again this apparition come,
> He may approve our eyes and speak to it."[195]

"Tush, tush, 'twill not appear," Horatio interrupted.

And then Bernardo begged them to sit down and hear the strange story.

"Last night of all," Bernardo began, pointing with his lance to a bright star,

> "When yon same star that's westward from the pole
> Had made his course to illume that part of heaven
> Where not it burns, Marcellus and myself,
> The bell then beating one — "[196]

Marcellus interrupted with

> "Peace, break thee off: look where it comes again!"[197]

Did it walk? Did it stalk? Did it float, Did it sail? Did it glide? — that buried "majesty of Denmark" — that ghost of Hamlet's father, across the platform of Elsinore? Armed from top to toe, from head to foot, in a suit of silver mail that gleamed weirdly blue in the cold moonlight, his vizor up, showing a beard like sable silvered, his face pale, his countenance more in sorrow than in anger, and his

---

[195] *Hamlet* (I.1).
[196] Same.
[197] Same.

Cock-A-Doodle-Doo

staring eyes fixed upon space, appeared King Hamlet.

"Thou art a scholar, speak to it, Horatio," entreated Marcellus; but the Ghost stalked away. Suddenly Horatio exclaimed:

> "But soft, behold! Lo, where it comes again!
> I'll cross it, though it blast me. — Stay, illusion!"[198]

And then he broke out in a sort of chant having a weird, musical cadence:

> "If there be any good thing to be done,
> That may to thee do ease, and grace to me,
> Speak to me:
> If thou art privy to thy country's fate,
> Which, happily, foreknowing may avoid,
> O, speak!
> Or if thou hast unhoarded in thy life
> Extorted treasure in the womb of earth,
> For which, they say, you spirits oft walk in
>   death — "[199]

(and now the Cock, who had been standing beside me all the while gave his shrill clarion call.)

"Speak of it: — stay, and speak! — Stop it, Marcellus."

"Shall I strike at it with my partisan?" asked Marcellus.

"Do, if it will not stand," replied Horatio.

"'Tis here!" exclaimed Bernardo.

"'Tis here!" exclaimed Horatio.

"'Tis gone!" whispered Marcellus and then added:

> "We do it wrong, being so majestical,
> To offer it the show of violence;

---

[198] *Hamlet* (I.1).
[199] Same.

Shakespearian Fantasias

> For it is, as the air, invulnerable,
> And our vain blows malicious mockery."[200]

"It was about to speak when the cock crew," Bernardo observed; and Horatio added:

> "And then it started like a guilty thing
> Upon a fearful summons. I have heard,
> The cock, that is the trumpet to the morn,
> Doth with his lofty and shrill-sounding throat
> Awake the god of day; and at his warning,
> Whether in sea or fire, in earth or air,
> The extravagant and erring spirit hies
> To his confine: and of the truth herein
> This present object made probation."[201]

And Marcellus continued:

> "It faded on the crowing of the cock.
> Some say that ever 'gainst that season comes
> Wherein our Saviour's birth is celebrated,
> The bird of dawning singeth all night long:
> And then, they say, no spirit can walk abroad;
> The nights are wholesome; then no planets strike,
> No fairy takes, nor witch hath power to charm;
> So hallow'd and so gracious is the time."[202]

"Did you know that?" asked the Cock, turning to me. "Did you know that we birds of dawning have a part in the solemnities of Christmas eve? And did you notice that Shakespeare calls me the 'trumpet of the morn' and declares that I awake the god of day? Ah, yes indeed," added the Cock sententiously, "where would your days be if it were not for me and my kind?" his little beady eyes burning like jewel-fire, "and where indeed would you be

---

[200] *Hamlet* (I.1).
[201] Same.
[202] Same.

Cock-A-Doodle-Doo

if there were no mornings?"

The moon had now disappeared and had taken with her all the silver and blue and violet lights. The world was pale and wan for a few brief moments; and then athwart the thick gray turrets of Elsinore and over the tumbling waters of the Sound breaking below on the beach, there travelled softly a rosy light, faint and delicate as the petals of the eglantine. As it deepened into a richer pink, Horatio called to his companions, Marcellus and Bernardo:

> "But, look, the morn, in russet mantle clad,
> Walks o'er the dew of yon high eastern hill:
> Break we our watch up."[203]

"That is not a mere figure of speech," explained the Cock. "Look at the Eastern sky. Do you not see the lovely Morn herself, in russet mantle clad, stepping along, her radiant face smiling from the folds of her hood upon the sleeping world? How gracefully she glides across the dewy hill, leaving light and beauty in her path!"

For a moment, the cock was silent, and then he said proudly:

"This is one of my most famous mornings," and burst forth with a triumphant "Cock-a-doodle-doo," that was echoed far and wide in the frosty air.

The scene changed. I was now in a court of the Palace of the Duke of Milan. A young gentleman, handsome, dignified, courtly in manner, and kindly of mien, entered, remarking to himself as he approached:

> "This is the hour that Madam Silvia

---

[203] *Hamlet* (I.1).

> Entreated me to call and know her mind;
> There's some great matter she'd employ me in.
> Madam, Madam!"[204]

"Who calls?" answered the Lady Sylvia, who appeared at the window with the rose of dawn suffusing her face and figure.

> "Your servant and your friend;
> One that attends your ladyship's commands."[205]

"Sir Eglamour, a thousand times good morrow," was Silvia's greeting.

"As many worthy lady to yourself"; and then Sir Eglamour added:

> "According to your ladyship's impose,
> I am thus early come to know what service
> It is your pleasure to command me in."[206]

What a fair and lovely lady! No wonder that "all the swains commend her," so "holy, fair and wise is she"; and I perfectly understood why Valentine, her lover, considered himself "as rich in having such a treasure as twenty seas if all their sand were pearl, the water nectar, and the rocks pure gold."

Silvia explained why she had sent for Sir Eglamour. Will he escort her to Mantua and to Valentine? Of course, Sir Eglamour will do so. Who would not serve fair Sylvia?

"And when and where shall he meet her?

This evening at Friar Patrick's cell. Silvia is going there for confession.

---

[204] *The Two Gentlemen of Verona* (IV.3).
[205] Same.
[206] Same.

Cock-A-Doodle-Doo

"I will not fail your ladyship" is the promise; and, bowing reverently and courteously, Sir Eglamour takes his leave with "Good-morrow, gentle lady,"

"Good-morrow, kind Sir Eglamour," smiles the grateful Silvia; and the lattice closes, shining golden in the morning light.

As Sir Eglamour walks away I know full well that "when the sun begins to gild the western sky," he will be waiting at Friar Patrick's little hermitage.

While I was musing over the delicate, charming, and distinguished Silvia, I was startled by the loud crowing of the little Cock at my side; and, at his bidding, another morning came into being.

I found myself in a very strange place. It took me several moments to identify it as Cymbeline's Palace in ancient Britain. Into the great hall Cymbeline's Queen stepped with her maids of honor and her physician, Cornelius. Turning to her ladies, the Queen commanded:

> "Whiles yet the dew's on ground gather those flowers
> Make haste: who has the note of them?"[207]

And the first lady replied: "I, Madam."

"Despatch," ordered the Queen.

The ladies departed, and the Queen addressed Dr. Cornelius: "Now, master doctor, have you brought those drugs?"

Cornelius handed her a little box.

> "My conscience bids me ask wherefore you have
> Commanded of me these most poisonous compounds,

---

[207] *Cymbeline* (I.5).

Shakespearian Fantasias

> Which are the movers of a languishing death;
> But, though slow, deadly?"[208]

Aside, Cornelius murmured that he will not trust this malicious woman with such drugs.

Those she has

> "Will stupefy and dull the sense awhile;
> Which first perchance she'll try on cats and dogs,
> Then afterward up higher."[209]

"Do you mark that?" the Cock asked me, looking very fierce and angry. "Do you mark *that*? This wicked Queen with her diabolical practice of trying brutal experiments on innocent animals and birds and causing such hideous suffering in our world — a world that humans consider so unimportant — really should belong to your *medical* (the Cock pronounced the word *medical* in a very sarcastic tone) age. Your century will have much to answer for — it is building up a nice Karma for the planet. Tell me," he continued, "why should our races be the prey for the cruelty of your so-called higher race. Humph! You are a stupid, materialistic lot anyway, and you don't know as much as you *think* you do. Why, if you only knew how often we get together and laugh at your lack of instinct (another name for *intuition*), your dull vision, your deaf ears, your blind eyes, and your failures to penetrate into *real* things, you would be quite ashamed of yourselves. Frankly, I do not think you are worth all the agony you cause to the animal world. Many a splendid, beautiful, and good animal, who should have been left to enjoy his little

---

[208] *Cymbeline* (I.5).
[209] Same.

Cock-A-Doodle-Doo

life, has been cruelly sacrificed for an utterly worthless, ignorant, stupid, and even wicked, human being. Frankly, you are not worth it."

"Frankly, I agree with you," I answered. "When it comes to the world of animals and birds, all of *whom* (I purposely use the pronoun *whom*) I firmly believe to have souls and brains — I think the world belongs just as much to them as to mankind. Indeed, I assure you, Mr. Chanticleer, my sympathies are entirely with my poor little abused and misunderstood dumb friends."

"Ah! but we are not dumb," replied the Cock, "we simply do not speak *your* language. We all have our own language and our own dialects."

"Now don't pay any attention to that wicked Queen," the Cock continued. "Cornelius did not give her any dangerous drugs. The vile creature intends to poison her step-daughter, the Lady Imogen, whom she hates because Imogen will not love her depraved son, Cloten. Ah! here come the ladies with their hands and baskets full of violets, cowslips, and primroses, which the Queen will make into various decoctions. Now I am going to call up one of my most beautiful mornings: Cock-a-doodle-doo! Here come musicians who are going to sing an *aubade* before Lady Imogen's door."

After a little tuning of lute and viol and a melody that sounded to me like one of John Dowland's airs, this song was heard:

> "Hark, hark! the lark at heaven's gate sings,
>   And Phoebus 'gins arise,
> His steeds to water at those springs
>   On chalic'd flowers that lies;
> And winking Marybuds begin

Shakespearian Fantasias

> To ope their golden eyes;
> With everything that pretty is,
> My lady sweet, arise;
> Arise, arise."[210]

"Perhaps you think that is only a song," said the Cock. "Words are living things: they create. Come out into the garden with me."

Oh, how sweet and fragrant this garden in the early dawn! All the flowers are wet with dew and the eastern sky is turning from rose to gold. In this shimmering mist a tiny speck is soaring higher and higher and pouring forth ecstatic melody. And through the soft pink clouds on the horizon appear the proud golden heads and flowing, breeze-tossed golden manes of the golden horses of the Sun-God, whose golden chariot rolls upwards over the clouds with radiant Phoebus standing in its curving prow guiding these horses with golden ribbons. Anything can happen in the world of dreams and so I am not surprised to see Phoebus drive his chariot right into the garden and let the horses drink deeply of the perfumed dew in the chalices of the roses and other flowers. The yellow marigolds, deeply in love with the Sun, begin to open their sleepy eyes in greeting to their beloved lord and wink and twinkle with the dew, which the bright face of Phoebus turns to flashing diamond drops.

"When everything so pretty is, what sweet lady would not arise to add a further grace to the morning?" the Cock commented; and then he added, very proudly, "This is one of my favorite mornings," and gave a long and jubilant crow, which other cocks of the country side took

---

[210] *Cymbeline* (II.3).

Cock-A-Doodle-Doo

up and returned, until there seemed to be a full orchestra of cocks, tooting their horns lustily from all directions in welcome of this perfect Shakespearian morning.

When the din had ceased my little feathered friend, after resting a moment, said: "Now let us hie to Verona."

No sooner said than done. Here we were, on the outskirts of the city, at the tiny cell of a monk.

"Ah! here comes Friar Lawrence himself," said the Cock, "with his basket, going to gather flowers and herbs, not for baleful use, like Cymbeline's wicked Queen, but with the kind purpose of healing. Ah! he speaks."

Friar Lawrence, talking to himself began:

> "The gray'ey'd morn smiles on the frowning night,
> Chequering the eastern clouds with streaks of light;
> And flecked darkness like a drunkard reels
> From forth day's path and Titan's fiery wheels:
> Now, ere the Sun advance his burning eye,
> The day to cheer and night's dank dew to dry,
> I must up-fill this osier cage of ours
> With baleful weeds and precious-juiced flowers.
> O, mickle is the powerful grace that lies
> In herbs, plants, stones and their true qualities:
> For naught so vile that on the earth doth live
> But to the earth some special good doth give.
> > Within the infant rind of this small flower
> > Poison hath residence and medicine power."[211]

"Look," exclaimed the Cock, "at that handsome young gallant dashing in with his 'Good-morrow, father.'"

"Benedicite!" Friar Lawrence replied.

It is so early that the Friar wonders why Romeo has

---

[211] *Romeo and Juliet* (II.3).

Shakespearian Fantasias

left his golden sleep; perhaps, indeed, he has not been in bed all night!

"Yes, that is true," Romeo acquiesces.

Oh, no, he was not with Rosaline: he has another and a greater love now — the fair daughter of rich Capulet — and he has sought the Friar now to perform, if he will, a secret marriage. Yes, Friar Lawrence will marry Romeo and Juliet, largely in the hope that the rancour of the Montagues and Capulets may thus be forever healed.

"*Romeo and Juliet* is one of my most important settings," explained the Cock. "So many things happen at my time of the day in this sad, poetic drama that I am kept very busy calling up the Sun. Now here is another of my gorgeous mornings. Here go three of my very loudest crows. Watch out now: Cock-a-doodle-doo-ooo!, Cock a-doodle-doo-ooo! Cock-a-doodle-doo-ooo! There! Now look," and the Cock, exhausted by his trumpeting, settled down in a little heap like a feathery muff and shut his eyes. I kept my eyes open, however, watching tensely.

Before I could see anything clearly in the pale light that was creeping over the dark curtain of night I perceived delicious perfume from a garden — a blending of lilies and roses, violets and carnations, gilliflowers and honeysuckle; and now I began to discover the "curious-knotted" beds so bright with all these lovely blossoms. Over the flowers there hung a balcony and on that balcony stood gallant, fascinating Romeo with his arms around Juliet, whose eyes outshone the stars. At this moment there fell through the air a rain of melody, a shower of delicate notes like the petals of a rose, notes so marvelous that they seemed to have color and perfume as

Cock-A-Doodle-Doo

well as sound. I listened in wonderment, for the cascade of silvery melodies was an aria from a tiny bird soaring far up into the vault of heaven.

"Tut! Tut! Cluck! Cluck! Cluck!" muttered the Cock, in a disgusted tone, "I don't want to look at, nor to listen to *that* bird. I can't bear larks and nightingales. I abominate their style of singing — absolutely antiquated, out-of-date, *demodé*, call it what you will — all pure Italian — all *fioriture, coloratura*, shakes, trills, turns, quaverings, and sprinklings of tiny notes — very trivial, very silly, very superficial, *I* think. Now, I am trained in another school — the declamatory style is the one *I* affect. I stand up and speak out — and with telling emphasis. I produce strong, carrying tones; all my registers are good; and my voice is well placed. If you like the Italian birds, for heaven's sake enjoy them; but don't ask *me* to waste my time on such sugary, sweety tunes. I despise the *melodic* style. Now I am going to take a nap until all this nonsense is over and done with. I must confess this is an enchanting dawn. I never produced a prettier morning; but I do wish that silly lark had not managed to thrust himself into the scene. He very nearly spoils the dawn for me!"

How lovely and how caressing the notes of Juliet's soft cooing voice:

> "Wilt thou be gone? it is not yet near day:
> It was the nightingale, and not the lark,
> That pierc'd the fearful hollow of thine ear;
> Nightly she sings on yon pomegranate tree:
> Believe me, love, it was the nightingale."[212]

---

[212] *Romeo and Juliet* (III.5).

Shakespearian Fantasias

"It was the lark," Romeo protests, "the herald of the morn,

> No nightingale: look, love, what envious streaks
> Do lace the severing clouds in yonder east:
> Night's candles are burnt out, and jocund day
> Stands tiptoe on the misty mountain tops.
> I must be gone and *live*, or stay and *die*."[213]

And Juliet protests:

> "Yon light is not daylight, I know it, I:
> It is some meteor that the sun exhales,
> To be to thee this night, a torch-bearer,
> And light thee on thy way to Mantua:
> Therefore stay yet, thou needs't not be gone."[214]

And Romeo answers:

> "Let me be ta'en, let me be put to death;
> I am content, so thou wilt have it so.
> I'll say yon gray is not the morning's eye,
> 'Tis but the pale reflex of Cynthia's brow;
> Nor that is not the lark whose notes do beat
> The vaulty heaven so high above our heads:
> I have more care to stay than will to go. —
> Come, death, and welcome! Juliet wills it so.
> How is't, my soul? Let's talk, — it is not day."[215]

"It is, it is," cries Juliet, "hie hence, be gone, away!

> It is the lark that sings so out of tune,
> Straining harsh discords and unpleasing sharps.
> Some say the lark makes sweet division;
> This doth not so, for she divideth us:
> Some say the lark and loathed toad change eyes;
> O, now I would they had chang'd voices too!

---

[213] *Romeo and Juliet* (III.5).
[214] Same.
[215] Same.

Cock-A-Doodle-Doo

> Since arm from arm that voice doth us affray,
> Hunting thee hence with hunts-up to the day.
> O, now be gone; more light and light it grows."[216]

Romeo sighs:

> "More light and light — more dark and dark our woes!"[217]

"Well, concert over?" asked the Cock, rising and stretching himself and shaking out his rumpled feathers.

"I am lost in the beauty of it all," I answer.

"Everything is all right but that silly lark," retorted the Cock.

"However," he added, philosophically, *"Chacun à son goût*, as my Gallic cousin is fond of remarking. We still have a big day in Verona and a terrible day it is, too. I must give *two* good rounds of crowing. Now *this* is music!"

This time there was quite an interval between the crowings. At the end of the second clarion call, there rose before me the hall of the Capulets.

"A great deal has happened," exclaimed the Cock. "It was arranged that Juliet should be married to her cousin, Paris, this morning, but Friar Lawrence gave her a drug to make her appear as if dead. There is a great bustle in the way of preparing for the wedding-day. I think myself it looks like pretty poor housekeeping to be getting ready at the last moment. Here comes lady Capulet and the Nurse."

"Hold, take these keys," said Lady Capulet, "and fetch more spices, Nurse."

"Spices were valuable in Shakespearian days,"

---

[216] *Romeo and Juliet* (III.5).
[217] Same.

explained the Cock, "they had to be kept under lock and key."

"They call for dates and quinces in the pantry," said the Nurse.

"I could eat those myself," the Cock murmured. "I wish I could get into that pantry! Oh, here's old Capulet. Foolish old thing and stupid old thing! No sympathy for anybody! Now he is playing the housewife! Listen to him."

"Come stir, stir, stir!" Capulet called, flying about the hall:

> "The second cock hath crow'd,
> The curfew bell hath rung, 'tis three o'clock:
> Look to the bak'd meats, good Angelica:
> Spare not for cost."[218]

"Hark!" exclaimed the cock. "Music! That is the bridegroom coming."

This excited Capulet who cried:

> "Nurse! — wife! — what ho! — what, Nurse, I say!
> Go waken Juliet, go and trim her up;
> I'll go and chat with Paris — hie, make haste,
> Make haste; the bridegroom he is come already:
> Make haste, I say."[219]

"Oh, dear Me! Dear me!" cried the Cock. "Here comes old Nursey. She has found Juliet lying on her bed — dead she thinks. She is weeping and wailing and you can hear Lady Capulet, too."

"For shame, bring Juliet forth; her lord is come," sternly calls Capulet; but Nurse and Lady Capulet bring the bad news and the hall is a scene of lamentation.

---

[218] *Romeo and Juliet* (IV.4).
[219] Same.

Cock-A-Doodle-Doo

Paris and Friar Lawrence now entered with the band of musicians:

"Come, is the bride ready to go to church?" asked Friar Lawrence.

O, how changed was Capulet's voice as he solemnly declared:

> "Ready to go, but never to return."[220]

Nurse, wringing her hands, wailed and sobbed:

> "O woe! O woeful, woeful, woeful day!
> Most lamentable day, most woeful day,
> That ever, ever I did yet behold!
> O day! O day! O day! O hateful day!
> Never was seen so black a day as this:
> O woeful day! O woeful day!"[221]

And Capulet ordered:

> "All things that we ordained festival
> Turn from their office to black funeral:
> Our instruments to melancholy bells;
> Our wedding cheer to a sad burial feast;
> Our solemn hymns to sullen dirges change;
> Our bridal flowers serve for a buried corse,
> And all things change them to the contrary."[222]

One of the Musicians observed:

> "Faith, we may put up our pipes and be gone";

but Peter, a serving-man, entreated:

> "Musicians, O, musicians, *Heart's ease, Heart's ease.*

---

[220] *Romeo and Juliet* (IV.5).
[221] Same.
[222] Same.

Shakespearian Fantasias

O, an you will let me live, play *Heart's ease*."[223]

"Why *Heart's ease?*" asked the First Musician.

"O, musicians," Peter answered, "because my heart itself plays *My Heart is full of woe*. O play me some merry dump to comfort me."

"I don't feel like hearing this music," I protested to the Cock. "Can't you show me something else to divert my mind from these star-crossed lovers?"

"Certainly," responded by little companion of the bright plumage. "Certainly."

Instantly the Cock began to crow in an extremely martial manner and kept on crowing until the hall of the Capulets melted away and there came slowly into view a small English army encamped in a narrow piece of ground between two woods with a view in the distance of the Plain of Agincourt, where the larger and more thoroughly equipped French army was lying. In the darkness a faint suggestion of the coming gray of twilit dawn was very subtly making itself felt. Great excitement and commotion were everywhere. I heard strange and unfamiliar Fifteenth Century noises of armorers with busy hammers rivetting those metal suits on knights and horses. And there were other sounds, too: steed threatening steed in high and boastful neighs; county cocks crowing far and wide; and clocks chiming out the third hour of drowsy morning. Fires burst forth here and there beside the tents and a royal figure walked from watch to watch and from tent to tent bidding all good-morrow with a modest smile, calling them brothers,

---

[223] *Romeo and Juliet* (IV.5).

Cock-A-Doodle-Doo

friends, and countrymen and with such cheerful semblance and sweet majesty that everyone beholding him plucked comfort from his looks. This "little touch of Harry in the night" thawed out cold fear and the soldiers began to prepare for the coming battle with hope and spirit. Yet Henry the Fifth seemed to be perfectly sensible of the terrible odds, for, as Gloster and Bedford entered, he gravely remarked:

> "Gloster, 'tis true that we are in great danger;
> The greater, therefore, should our courage be."[224]

Ah, here comes one of the officers in the King's army. Henry accosts him:

> "Good morrow, old Sir Thomas Erpingham:
> A good soft pillow for that good white head
> Were better than a churlish turf of France."[225]

The King bids them leave him to his meditations, but he is interrupted. Here come Pistol and Fluellen and the soldiers, Bates and Court and Williams, and the King accepts Williams's glove for a challenge. Again the King is alone; and he muses on the questionable advantage of being a king. Here comes Gloster again.

"Ay!" the King says solemnly, "I know thy errand. I will go with thee."

As they depart for battle I glance over into the French camp. I see a magnificent array of archers on horseback, men-at-arms, heralds, soldiers, officers, and noblemen — many, many thousands — far outnumbering the English army and far exceeding it in brilliant caparisonment. I

---

[224] *Henry V* (IV.1).
[225] Same.

recognize the Dauphin, Orlenas, Rambures, and other lords.

"The sun doth gild our armor; up, my lords," cries Orleans.

"Montez à cheval!" cries the Dauphin. "My horse, varlet, laquais, ha!"

How the horses neigh and champ and stamp and caracole!

"To horse! To horse!"

The French have much to do today. Well perhaps not so much either, they think. Those "ragged island carrions" ill become the brilliant field of Agincourt this lovely morning! English shall soon crouch down and yield! Then let the trumpets sound the tucket sonance and the note to mount! Come, come away! The day is advancing! The sun is already high!

"Hurrah!" screamed the Cock. "O how I love this! Three cheers for both armies! Let me sound *my* tucket with *my* trumpet: Cock-a-doodle-doo! Cock-a-doodle-doo! Cock-a-doodle-doo!"

"I hate battles and everything connected with war," I said, "please draw veil over the field of Agincourt."

"All right," agreed the Cock, "but you must come back for a moment to the English camp. See, here is beloved King Henry, Falstaff's erstwhile scapegrace companion — one of the minions of the moon — addressing his soldiers"; and across the centuries I hear Harry's clear voice solemnly chanting to his soldiers:

> "This day is call'd the feast of Crispian:
> He that outlives this day, and comes safe home,
> Will stand a tiptoe when this day is nam'd,

Cock-A-Doodle-Doo

> And rouse him at the name of Crispian.
> He that shall live this day, and see old age,
> Will yearly on the vigil feast his neighbors,
> And say, 'Tomorrow is Saint Crispian':
> Then will he strip his sleeve and show his scars,
> And say, 'These wounds I had on Crispin's day.'"[226]

Now the tuckets sound again in the trumpets, blare, and my friend the Cock, perfectly delirious with delight, joins in with his shrill-sounding horn.

Another change of scene!

This time it is an orchard with a view of Rome in the distance. The gray lines that fret the clouds are messengers of morning. The air is dark and damp and very raw and chilly in the dawn of this March day.

"I hope you know that this is Brutus's orchard," explained the Cock. "See him in that group of conspirators, planning Caesar's death? That is Casca speaking":

> "The morning comes upon's: we'll leave you, Brutus:
> And friends, disperse yourselves: but all remember
> What you have said, and show yourselves true
>   Romans."[227]

"Good gentlemen, look fresh and merrily," replied Brutus.

> "Let not our looks put on our purposes;
> But bear it as our Rroman actors do,
> With untir'd spirits and formal constancy;
> And so, good-morrow to you, every one."[228]

---

[226] *Henry V* (IV.3).
[227] *Julius Caesar* (II.1).
[228] Same.

Shakespearian Fantasias

They go; but Brutus was not alone for long, for his noble wife, Portia, joined him, with a tender "Brutus, my lord!"

"Portia, what mean you?" Brutus asked.

> "Wherefore rise you now?
> It is not for your health thus to commit
> Your weak condition to the raw, cold morning."[229]

"Nor for yours, neither," Portia returned, and begged Brutus to tell her what disturbs him so greatly. She even knelt. Is she not his wife; should she not share his secrets?

Brutus, with tender love, assured her

> "You are my true and honorable wife:
> As dear to me as are the ruddy drops
> That visit my sad heart."[230]

If this were true, then Portia should know all.

"I grant I am a woman," she protested; "but withal

> A woman well-reputed — Cato's daughter.
> Think you I am no stronger than my sex,
> Being so father'd and so husbanded?"[231]

"O ye gods, render me worthy of this noble wife!" exclaimed Brutus; and then as a knocking at the gate was heard he sent Portia in. As Portia moved away with her graceful, gliding step, the knocking grew louder and louder. Brutus called to his boy:

"Lucius, who's that knocks?"

And the Cock, turning to me asks, "Doesn't that knocking remind you of another and a greater

---

[229] *Julius Caesar* (II.1).
[230] Same.
[231] Same.

Cock-A-Doodle-Doo

Shakespearian morning?"

Before I can reply, Brutus's orchard and the Roman building in the distance have vanished and in their place is the dark courtyard of the grim Castle of Inverness. In the misty gray of approaching dawn that is struggling with the darkness I see a stairway leading to apartments on the left.

At their base a trembling man is standing, who every now and then throws a frightened glance at the windows above looking from the room where the murdered Duncan is now lying and where Lady Macbeth is now taking the daggers to place them by the sleeping grooms.

Macbeth for the moment is deeply repentant of his horrid deed. While he is standing here in the cold, dark, and gruesome courtyard, the silence of the sleeping Castle is suddenly broken by a loud knocking at the gate and the sound, with its reverberating echo from the stone walls, is perfectly awful. Macbeth feels it even more than I do. Half indignantly he asks, looking in the direction of the gate: "Whence is that knocking?" and then exclaims: "How is't with me, when every noise appalls me?

> What hands are here? Ha! they pluck out mine eyes!
> Will all great Neptune's ocean wash this blood
> Clean from my hand? No; this my hand will rather
> The multitudinous seas incarnadine,
> Making the green one red."[232]

Lady Macbeth returns, her heart white with horror.

"My hands are of your color, but I shame

---

[232] *Macbeth* (II.2).

Shakespearian Fantasias

> To wear a heart so white,"[233]

she remarks to her husband; and then she whispers in terror:

> "I hear a knocking
> At the south entry: retire we to our chamber.
> A little water clears us of this deed:
> Hark! more knocking;
> Get on your nightgown, lest occasion call us,
> And show us to be watchers — be not lost
> So poorly in your thoughts."[234]

But Macbeth is too appalled by his deed even to run to cover. He stands transfixed and, for the moment, penitent:

> "To know my deed, 'twere best not know myself,"[235]

And then, looking in the direction of the knocking:

"Wake Duncan with thy knocking! I would thou couldst!" he sighs.

The drunken Porter reels in and opens the gate to Macduff and Lennox.

"Faith, sir, we were carousing till the second cock," he explains.

"You see he heard me," said the Cock with a wink of his bright, beady eyes. Macbeth comes in to bid Macduff and Lennox good-morrow; Macduff goes up the stairway to wake Duncan for his proposed journey; and Lennox remarks:

> "The night has been unruly: where we lay

---

[233] *Macbeth* (II.2).
[234] Same.
[235] Same.

Cock-A-Doodle-Doo

> Our chimneys were blown down: and, as they say,
> Lamentings heard i' the air; strange screams of death,
> The obscure bird clamor'd the whole night long,
> Some say the earth was feverous, and did shake."[236]

"'Twas a rough night," Macbeth observes quietly.

Here comes Macduff rushing in with the cry that Duncan has been murdered. The whole castle is in an uproar: the alarm bell is rung. Lady Macbeth comes in, as unconcernedly as possible, to know

> "What's the business,
> That such a hideous trumpet calls to parley
> The sleepers of the house?"[237]

In the hubbub and excitement, and more particularly at Macbeth's description of the murdered Duncan, Lady Macbeth's nerves give way and she faints. She is carried out. All leave in terror. The sombre courtyard of Inverness is alone: grim, ghost-haunted, and cold in the early dawn.

"Terrible morning!" exclaims the Cock. "I never did like having to be in this scene. Let's get away! Cock-a-doodle-doo!"

A gray Scotch mist rolls in and grows thicker and darker until it becomes a heavy fog and this fog deepens and deepens. For a few moments I am lost in a blanket of nothingness and then the fog grows gradually lighter and thinner, turns to mist again, and lifts like the curtain in a theatre.

I am now in the heart of a park-like forest, full of noble

---

[236] *Macbeth* (II.3).
[237] Same.

Shakespearian Fantasias

and ancient trees and long stretches of emerald sward. It is a radiantly beautiful summer night.

"A wood near Athens!" I joyfully exclaim.

"Oh no!" cries the Cock, "Epping Forest near London. And full of English people and English fairies on this night that we shall soon see break into morning, at least as soon as I decide to call the Sun to rise. Theseus is an English Duke and Hippolyta and Egeus and Lysander and Demetrius and Hermia and Helena are true Elizabethans. Not a bit of Greek about *them*. And I hope you understand that Nick Bottom the weaver, Francis Flute the bellows-mender, Peter quince the carpenter, and the rest are not really Athenian mechanics, but are "hempen homespuns," of London town. This is the most English of plays," the Cock went on, "and I am very proud to say that I am mentioned in it."

"I'm sorry, but I don't remember you," I retorted, a little puzzled.

"Act Two, Scene Two," the Cock promptly answered. "Yes, indeed: 'Meet me before the first cock crow' is the line. Cock-a-doodle-doo!"

Ah, here comes Puck with the little purple pansy "whose juice on sleeping eyelids laid" can work a spell of love. Oberon will try it on Titania and Puck must have some of it to anoint the eyes of a disdainful youth:

> "But do it," commands Oberon, "when the next
>   thing he espies
> May be the lady: thou shalt know the man
> By the Athenian garments he hath on.
> Effect it with some care, that he may prove
> More fond on her than she upon her love:

Cock-A-Doodle-Doo

And look thou meet me ere the first cock crow."[238]

Puck answers:

"Fear not, my lord, your servant shall do so."[239]

"That can't be done," laughed the Cock, "for I am going to crow now. Cock-a-doodle-doo! It is so very nearly morning that I will only be a few minutes before the time; but I do want to get ahead of that mischievous Puck, who is always playing tricks on everybody. Now I have played one on him. He cannot get through all he has to do tonight before the first cock crow, or even before the second cock crow; for I've already crowed once and here goes my number two — Cock-a-doodle-doo!"

Now beautiful and distressed Helena runs in, pursued by Demetrius and Lysander, and then beautiful and distressed Hermia joins them. All are at cross-purposes, for Puck has squeezed the purple flower on the wrong eyes. Puck only laughs mockingly: "Lord, what fools these mortals be!"

Oberon appears and chides Puck. Yes, Puck did make a mistake, but it is great sport.

"Well, never mind, but, Robin, you must set everything right. Lead the lovers astray, put them to sleep and crush the pansy juice into the proper eyes this time. Meanwhile, I will release my Titania from monster's view."

Puck warns:

"My fairly lord, this must be done with haste,
For night's swift dragons cut the clouds full fast:

---

[238] *A Midsummer Night's Dream* (II.1).
[239] Same.

Shakespearian Fantasias

And yonder shines Aurora's harbinger."[240]

But Oberon replies:

> "I wish the morning's love have oft made sport,
> And, like a forester, the groves may tread
> Even till the eastern gate, all fiery-red,
> Opening on Neptune's with fair blessed beans,
> Turns into yellow gold his salt-green streams."[241]

Not very far away we see Titainia winding her graceful, snow-white arms around Bottom and decorating his long, hairy, upright ears with musk roses, while Bottom, insensible to all things that are delicate, calls for oats and hay and a handful of dried peas. Sleep comes suddenly upon them.

Oberon gazes lovingly upon the dainty little Queen; and, touching her eyes with an herb, he bids her wake.

"My Oberon!" Titania exclaims, "what visions I have seen! Methought I was enamoured of an ass!"

"There lies your love," laughs Oberon; and to Puck he commands:

"Robin, take off his head." Then, calling for music, Oberon again addresses Titania:

> "Come, my queen, take hands with me,
> And rock the ground whereon these sleepers be.
> Now thou and I are new in amity,
> And will tomorrow midnight solemnly
> Dance in Duke Theseus's house triumphantly,
> And bless it to all fair posterity:
> There shall the pairs of faithful lovers be
> Wedded, with Theseus, all in jollity."[242]

---

[240] *A Midsummer Night's Dream* (III.2).
[241] *A Midsummer Night's Dream* (III.2).
[242] *A Midsummer Night's Dream* (IV.1).

Cock-A-Doodle-Doo

Puck breaks in with

> "Fairy King, attend and mark;
> I do hear the morning lark."[243]

Oberon taking the hint, murmurs:

> "Then, my queen, in silence sad,
> Trip we after the night's shade:
> We the globe can compass soon,
> Swifter than the wand'ring moon."[244]

"Come, my lord," Titania acquiesces, "and in our flight,

> Tell me how it came this night
> That I sleeping here was found
> With these mortals on the ground."[245]

"I'm going to drown out that morning lark," the Cock clucked. "Here goes!" and my little feathered friend gave a quick succession of very loud crows; but his shrill trumpet was soon drowned in its turn by the louder and richer horns of approaching huntsmen and the bell-like baying of a pack of hounds, whose long ears swept away the morning dew as they bounded towards us.

"Cock-a-doodle-doo!" again trumpeted the Cock, his gold and red enamelled feathers glistening in the morning sunlight. "Here comes Duke Theseus with his party. I've waked up everybody now as well as the Sun; and so I am going. No more need for me! Good-bye!"

"Oh, stay!" I cried, "I want to ask you several things."

But the Cock had vanished; and instead of an answer, I heard a far-away and very sweet voice chanting with an

---

[243] *A Midsummer Night's Dream* (IV.1).
[244] Same.
[245] Same.

Shakespearian Fantasias

Elizabethan accent:

> "Full many a glorious morning have I seen
> Flatter the mountain-tops with sovereign eye,
> Kissing with golden face the meadows green,
> Gilding pale streams with heavenly alchemy."[246]

---

[246] *A Midsummer Night's Dream* (IV.1).

Appendices

Appendix I:

"Was Edward de Vere Shakespeare?"
By Esther Singleton
Published posthumously in *The Shakespeare Fellowship Newsletter* (American), Vol. 1/4 (June/July 1940): 9-10.

Was Edward de Vere Shakespeare? I believe he was. You who read this, I beg you not to condemn me and the theory but to read further on.

A week ago I still believed that William Shaksper of Stratford-upon-Avon was the author of the great plays that have borne his name for three hundred years. Heretofore, any suggestion calling this into question incurred my antagonism, and my enmity to the idea bristled up instantly, "like quills upon the fretful porcupine." In fact, so intolerant was I of the barest hint of any other than the Stratford belief that to relinquish such a fixed idea, with all the time-honored atmosphere that has grown around the Warwickshire lore, was not easy.

However, a book fell into my hands. *"Shakespeare" Identified*, by J. Thomas Looney, published in 1920. I opened it with prejudice and deep contempt and antagonism. I had no intention to surrender the William Shaksper of Stratford for any theory. Long ago I had rejected Bacon and every other new candidate brought forward. But I read on and on, much impressed with the modesty of the discoverer of the new author, much enthralled by his careful and original process of discovery, the fine marshaling of facts and logical deductions, the painstaking examination of the evidence, and

Appendices

the skill, honesty, and charm of the presentation of the theory.

Amazed, fascinated, and with mind clarified, I rose from a study of the book. I read it again, then I read it for the third time (a big book, 458 pages). And I now pronounce myself a believer in the theory that Edward de Vere, Earl of Oxford, was the author of the great Shakespearean plays.

I wish I believed in everything with the same conviction. Moreover, I feel I have been enriched by the acquaintance with this great personality with whom I have been living now for a week! I cannot get him out of my mind. He passes between everything I try to do. I can turn to no duty until I record my belief and pay tribute, small and insignificant as it is, to this mighty genius.

I cannot explain the effect that this discovery has had upon me. All the plays that I know so well, that I have read and reread since childhood until they have become bone of my bone and flesh of my flesh, are now more wonderful. Some things that have been obscure have become as clear as glass; more true in their philosophy; more brilliant in their wit; more sincere in their scholarship more charming in their tenderness; more subtle in their delicacy; more penetrating in their wisdom; and truer to life when it is known that their author, instead of being of a middle class man of mean associations and little or no education, rather sordid in money matters, and with no connection with people of culture, was a man of aristocratic lineage, a courtier himself, a man accomplished in all the arts, graces, sports, and pastimes of the age—a gifted genius with whom the "time is out of joint." The plays themselves become autobiographical.

And at last, thanks to Mr. Looney, we can find our Shakespeare, the dramatist, in such characters as Hamlet (biographical throughout), Biron in Love's Labour's Lost, and Bertram in *All's Well* (another biography).

Appendices

I used to take refuge in "you can't limit genius," and felt that by some supernatural means the superior Shakespeare had existed, disregarding the lack of correspondence between the plays and the scanty records of their ostensible author's life. Like Mr. Podsnap,[247] with a wave of the hand, I swept all this behind my back. I read the plays as works apart, dissociating them from their author. But now—it is all so clear, so plain, so reasonable, and so delightful.

I ask myself, how could a man like Shaksper of Stratford portray with such intimacy elegant men and women, particularly the Queen herself. Take the Duke in *Twelfth Night*; Benedick in *Much Ado*; Bassanio, Antonio, Romeo, Mercutio, Paris. The more you look at it the simpler it becomes—the life of the Elizabethan bloods, the high-spirited, hotheaded, witty-tongued guests, to parry and thrust with words as with swords—could the butcher boy of Stratford ever do that?

In the historical plays, the sympathy with the Lancastrian cause is most marked. Shakespeare must have been of a family of Lancastrian leanings.

The large number of plays with Italian settings or derived from Italian sources. Shakespeare must have known Italy—everything bespeaks an Italian enthusiast. Also one highly educated in music. His attitude towards money shows that he abhorred money as such. It is the arch-villain, such as Iago, the time-serving politician, such as Polonius, the cruel Shylock, who are the moneylenders. Antonio, who gives freely to his friend, and Bassanio, the spendthrift, are of the dramatist's chosen ilk.

But William Shaksper, the Stratford Shaksper, was a man who, after he had become prosperous, prosecuted others for

---

[247] A character in Charles Dickens's *Our Mutual Friend* who has a high opinion of himself and refuses to face unpleasant facts.

petty sums!

Sir Sidney Lee, a believer in the Stratford theory, says: "His literary attainments and successes were chiefly valued as serving the prosaic end of providing permanently for himself and his daughters." Compare that statement with what the Bard himself says:

> How quickly nature falls into revolt
> When gold becomes her object!
> For this the foolish over-careful fathers
> Have broke their sleep with thoughts, their
> Brains with care,
> Their bones with industry;
> For this they have engrossed and pil'd up
> The canker'd heaps of strange-achieved gold.
> - *2 Henry IV*, IV.5.66

A close inspection of Shakespeare's work reveals a more intimate personal connection with aristocracy than would be furnished by mere family tradition. Kings and queens, earls and countesses, knights and ladies move on and off his stage "as to the manner born." They are no mere tinsled models representing mechanically the class to which they belong, but living men and women. It is rather his ordinary "citizens" that are the automata walking woodenly onto the stage to speak for their class.

The suggestion of an aristocratic author for the plays is, therefore, the simple common sense of the situation, and is no more in opposition to modern democratic tendencies than the belief that William Shaksper was indebted to aristocratic patrons and participated in the enclosure of common lands. "We feel entitled, therefore" as Mr. Looney states, "to claim for Shakespeare high social rank and even a close proximity to Royalty itself."

Appendix 2:

Esther Singleton
"A Great Courtier" [Review of *The Seventeenth Earl of Oxford* by Bernard M. Ward]
Saturday Review, July 21, 1928, p. 1049-51.

Edward de Vere, Seventeenth Earl of Oxford, has been for centuries the least known and the most cruelly misjudged of all the great Elizabethans. The general impression has been that Edward de Vere was an eccentric personage of disgraceful character and boorish manners, atrociously rude to Sir Philip Sidney on the occasion of the famous Tennis Court quarrel and at odds with his father-in-law, Lord Burleigh. Indeed Froude described him as 'Burleigh's ill-conditioned son-in-law.

So far back as 1872, Dr. A. B. Grosart, in a preface to a small collection of Lord Oxford's poems, regretfully remarked: "An unlifted shadow somehow lies across his memory." This "shadow" has happily now been lifted by B. M. Ward, a new English historian, who, after five years of research among unpublished manuscript records, has produced a scholarly and fascinating biography of the man who was "second only to the Earl of Leicester as chief favorite of the Queen."

Every statement in this biography is based on recorded facts, the sources of which are documents in the British Museum, the Public Record Office, the Bodleian Library, and the unique collection of manuscripts at Hatfield House, from which treasury, by permission of the Marquess of Salisbury (a descendant of Lord Burleigh), many important letters are here printed for the first time. Among other matters of importance Burleigh's own letters prove the falsity of the

Appendices

long supposed enmity between him and Edward de Vere, Indeed, in one letter Burleigh says of Lord Oxford: "I do honor him so dearly from my heart as I do my own son. I take comfort in his wit and knowledge grown by good observation."

The frontispiece-portrait (from the Duke of Portland's estate, Welbeck Abbey), painted in Paris when Edward de Vere was twenty-five, shows a proud, handsome, aristocratic, and distinguished young man with a clear, honorable, high-minded, and intellectual countenance, large, intelligent, and observant eyes and a mobile, sensitive mouth, sweet and tender in expression. He is dressed in the height of taste and fashion and wears his clothes with elegance. It is easy to understand how he became a favorite with Queen Elizabeth.

A dashing and fascinating person, this Edward de Vere, excelling in all the accomplishments of the day—a superlative dancer, a skilled musician, a marvellous horseman, a winner of tournaments, a brilliant linguist, a writer of polished verse, a splendid actor, and an *elegant* in dress and manners. Therefore, it is not surprising that he captured the hearts of the belles and beauties in his large circle of relatives and friends.

Oxford was born to the purple. His father was Lord Great Chamberlain and his mother a Maid of Honor to Queen Elizabeth. At their death the young Earl (representing an Earldom of six hundred years) was made a Royal Ward and for eight years he lived at Cecil House, under the guardianship of Lord Burleigh. His position was strange: by birth and training a scion of the old aristocracy, by circumstance an associate of the self-made leaders of the new order of things—Burleigh and Bacon—two warring factions presided over by the enigmatic Queen Elizabeth. Oxford was, therefore, caught into all the entanglements of this great and

Appendices

formative age of intrigue and performance. The thread of his life—now dark, now golden—is woven through the tapestry of the period, both as a man of action and as a man of letters. As a man of action he saw service under the Earl of Sussex on the Scotch Border; he attempted to rescue the Duke of Norfolk from the Tower; he was a promoter of Frobisher's adventures for the discovery of the "North West Passage"; he fitted out a ship against the Spanish Armada in 1588 and took part in the fighting; he bore the Golden Canopy over Queen Elizabeth at the St. Paul's Thanksgiving in 1588; and he served as Privy Councellor to King James I. Literature was the passion of his life. Tutored by his uncle, Arthur Golding (whose translations from Ovid were prolifically used by Shakespeare), he received a degree at Cambridge University at the early age of fourteen, became Master of Arts at Oxford at the age of fifteen, and at the age of seventeen was admitted to Gray's Inn. In the midst of dancing, feasting, and all court revelries, he found time for writing.

His first essay seems to have been a learned and graceful preface in Latin prose to a Latin translation from the Italian of Castiglione's *Il Cortegiano*; of which six years later Gabriel Harvey wrote to Oxford: "Let that courtly epistle, more polished even than the writings of Castiglione himself, witness how greatly thou dost excel in letters." Thenceforward Oxford is found publishing at his own expense many productions of his contemporaries, writing serious verse, supporting companies of actors, leasing the Blackfriars Theatre, providing the Queen with dramatic entertainments, acting in plays, and, in short, taking so large a part in the intellectual life of the period that it is safe to say he was one of the leading spirits of the magnificent period of literary achievements, particularly of the drama. There are many contemporary eulogies of Oxford as a playwright. For

Appendices

example, Francis Meres said in *Palladis Tamia* (1598): "The best for Comedy among us be Edward Earl of Oxford"; and Lord Lumley in *The Art of English Poesie* (1589) wrote:

> And in her Majesty's time that now is are sprung up another crew of courtly makers (i. e. poets Nobleman and gentlemen of Her Majesty's own servants) who have written excellently well as it would appear if their doings could be found out and made public with the rest, of which number is first, that noble gentleman Edward, Earl of Oxford.

From 1589 to 1604 Lord Oxford lived in retirement, still drawing his extraordinarily large annuity for some unspecified service to the Queen. He had now married for a second time, Elizabeth Trentham, Maid of Honor to the Queen, and was engaged in literary pursuits.

On ringing down the curtain Mr. Ward concludes with an epitaph preserved among the Harleian Manuscripts: "Edward de Vere, only son of John, born the 12th day of April 1550, Earl of Oxenford, High Chamberlain, Lord Bolbec, Sandford and Badlesmere, Steward of the Forest in Essex, and of the Privy Council to the King's Majesty that now is of whom I will only speak what all men's voices confirm: he was a man in mind and body absolutely accomplished with honorable endowment." The format is entirely praiseworthy; and the book, notwithstanding its illustrations and maps, is light in weight and pleasant to handle. The binding is dark old rose with the de Vere arms in gold and the moto *Nero nihil Verius*. Happily the truth regarding this most distinguished member of a most distinguished race has at last triumphed over calumny and has been put forward in a book that will rank high both as a biography and as a picture of the Elizabethan period.

Appendix 3:

"Introduction" by Eva Turner Clark to the 2nd edition (1931) of *The Shakespeare Garden* by Esther Singleton. New York: W. F. Payson.

INTRODUCTION

It was my privilege to be counted among Esther Singleton's friends. I knew her love of beauty, whether in Nature or the Arts. I knew the fertile resources of her mind. I knew her industry in searching out facts to support whatever new theme she was engaged upon, and the speed and accuracy with which she wrote in putting her facts together. Of the many books she wrote, and they would fill a very long library shelf, there was not one I can think of that gave her greater satisfaction than *The Shakespeare Garden*. She loved the way Shakespeare spoke of flowers, expressing his knowledge of them with such fine felicity.

Miss Singleton's acquaintance with Shakespeare's plays was unusual for this hurried age. She could repeat, word for word, nearly all of the comedies; she knew almost equally well the greatest of the tragedies. A quotation from the plays she would recognize at once, she could tell what play it was taken from, and could generally cap it with the lines that followed.

About two years after *The Shakespeare Garden* was published, Miss Singleton said to me abruptly one day, "I don't know whether Shakespeare wrote Shakespeare!" "Bacon?" I queried. "No," she answered, "I've just read a book called *"Shakespeare" Identified as the Seventeenth Earl of Oxford*, and it has shaken my faith in the Stratford

Appendices

man. I don't know what to think."[248] The result of this conversation, which was much longer than outlined, was that I secured a copy of that interesting book. Not only was my orthodox belief in the authorship of the Shakespeare plays shaken by it, but I became so interested in the new theory that I began a study of it on my own account. This study led me to the discovery of a key which has, to my satisfaction, more than confirmed the conclusions reached by the author of *"Shakespeare" identified*, the result of this study having been recently published under the title, *Hidden Allusions in Shakespeare's Plays, A Study of the Oxford Theory Based on the Records of Early Court Revels and Personalities of the Times*. During the progress of my research and the writing of my book, I was continually encouraged by the sympathetic understanding of Miss Singleton, who was herself too busy with her usual program of writing to undertake the research herself, yet she was always eager to hear of any new discovery I made in connection with the plays.

In reading *The Shakespeare Garden*, it will be illuminating to consider this book from Miss Singleton's later viewpoint, to remember that "Shakespeare," in the person of Edward de Vere, was, from the age of twelve, the ward of Lord Burleigh, and that he lived with Lord Burleigh in his great mansion in the Strand in London and at the great country estate of Theobalds in Hertfordshire. Both of these places possessed wonderful gardens under the care of the famous Gerard,[249] as described by Miss Singleton in the pages that follow. After the young Earl's marriage to Lord

---

[248] *The Shakespeare Garden* was published in 1922, which would place Singleton's reading of Looney's *"Shakespeare" Identified* in 1924.

[249] John Gerard (c. 1545-1612), author of the 1,484-page illustrated *Herball, Generall Historie of Plants* (1597). Gerard dedicated the book to Edward de Vere, Earl of Oxford.

Appendices

Burleigh's daughter, he made his home at Oxford Court, near London Stone, and there he had his own garden on the west side of the house.

It was at Castle Hedingham, the Earl's family seat, dating from Norman times, that he first learned to love flowers. Afterwards he was to become acquainted with all of the most beautiful gardens in the kingdom, not only those of Lord Burleigh, but, as one of the Queen's favorites who accompanied her on her various Progresses about the country from year to year, he saw the gardens of other great noblemen, gardens with lakes, fountains, cascades, gardens with unusual planting, gardens with rare specimens of plants, all arranged with the special design of pleasing the Queen. Simpler gardens were familiar to him, as well, for he had seen them in his childhood in Essex, and there must have been many in and about London in Elizabeth's day.

It was through the eyes of Edward de Vere that Esther Singleton visualized the gardens of Shakespeare's plays in her last years. She felt that the mist was clearing away and that she could see the flowers of those gardens as the author saw them.

EVA TURNER CLARK

New York, N.Y.,
January 19th, 1931

From the dust jacket: "A new edition of this unique and fascinating garden book which has long been out of print. The illuminating introduction by Mrs. Clark, attributing the Shakespearian Plays to Edward de Vere, 17th Earl of Oxford—a conviction to which Esther Singleton was converted after the publication of *The Shakespeare Garden*—makes of this book a unique literary item in that it is the first reprint of a work in the Shakespearian field newly harmonized with the Oxford theory."

Appendix 4:
Other Writings about Esther Singleton

Col. Bernard R. Ward
"An Introduction to Shakespeare"
Shakespeare Pictorial, February 1930, p. 20.

It was in the year 1806 that Charles Lamb and his sister and life-long companion Mary set to work to turn the plays of Shakespeare into tales for young readers. . . . the famous *Tales from Shakespeare* have been reprinted many times. To take the 20th century alone, there have been no less than fourteen reprints of the "Everyman" edition, which was first brought out in 1906.

The original preface commenced by stating that the *Tales* were meant to be submitted to the young reader as an introduction to the study of Shakespeare, for which purpose his words are used "whenever it seemed possible to bring them in," and it ended with the following words, "What these Tales shall have been to the *young* readers, that and much more it is the writers' wish that the true Plays of Shakespeare may prove to them in older years—enrichers of the fancy, strengtheners of virtue, a withdrawing from all selfish and mercenary thoughts, a lesson of all sweet and honourable thoughts and actions, to teach, courtesy, benignity, generosity, humanity: for of examples teaching these virtues, his pages are full."

It was thus that Charles and Mary Lamb introduced Shakespeare to young readers in the opening decade of the Nineteenth Century and their introduction still served throughout the third decade of the Twentieth Century, but historical research and literary criticism have made that same decade memorable in the history of Shakespeare study. It is

Appendices

therefore fitting that a new approach to the study of the Plays should be available for young readers, and indeed for all readers now that we are entering upon the fourth decade of the century.

Miss Esther Singleton—a member of the Shakespeare Fellowship, and a well-known American writer—has tackled afresh the problem that occupied the thoughts and energies of the Lambs throughout the summer of 1806 in Mitre Court buildings; and the Fellowship and Shakespeare lovers in general may congratulate themselves that the present age has produced a writer capable of interpreting the romance, the courtesy, and the humanity of Shakespeare in a manner not unworthy to be compared with the work of Charles and Mary Lamb in charm and imaginative sympathy.

Shakespearian Fantasias—Adventures in the Fourth
Dimension
by
Esther Singleton
1929

* * * * *

Col. Bernard M. Ward
"A Poetical Alice in Wonderland"
Shakespeare Pictorial, March 1930, p. 16.

For a thorough appreciation of Shakespeare it is of course essential to see him on the Stage. The reading of the plays—especially where a number of characters are involved—makes understanding and appreciation a matter of some effort and concentration. Charles and Mary Lamb aimed at making the approach to Shakespeare easy for young readers. Miss Singleton has attained this object for readers of all ages.

Appendices

A profound knowledge and love of Shakespeare, combined with creative imagination, make the best of these Fantasias a sheer delight, and bring back to us as we read them all the romance of the Elizabethan age.

An interesting feature of this book is the cover, which is "thick inlaid with patines of bright gold" on a background of daffofil yellow, with black decorations, modernistic in design, and linking the twentieth century with the sixteenth.

The story is in every case easy to follow, and the gap between the Elizabethan age and our own is bridged over in the happiest manner by the power of imaginative description.
. . .

A point that will specially interest members of the Fellowship is that the Earl of Oxford is introduced in the characters of Berowne in "The Merry Mad-Cap Lord," Jaques in "Under the Greenwood Tree," and Benedick in "Saucy Beatrice"; also that his acknowledged verses, such as the characteristic poem, "On Women," which gave Mr. Looney the clue ten years ago by which he made his famous identification, are quoted alongside the words of Shakespeare himself, thus showing that Miss Singleton has no doubt as to the truth of Mr. Looney's hypothesis.

Quite apart, however, from this unobtrusive confession of faith in the Oxford theory, there is an unexpected charm in these delightful Fantasias which will beguile even the most prejudiced 20 century novel reader into the discovery that Shakespeare is an author whose reputation for dullness and superiority is as far from the truth as such popular opinions are apt to be. It may also show that unorthodox views on the subject of authorship, when held by a writer of originality and genius, are not inconsistent with the deepest admiration for the romantic atmosphere and unapproachable music of the greatest of English poets.

Appendices

Shakespearian Fantasias by Esther Singleton. Price 2.50 dollars. Privately printed.

Orders should be addressed to the Author, at 53, East 87th Street, New York.

* * * * *

Claire McGlinchee
"Esther Singleton" [Letter]
New York Times, August 31, 1930, p. X7.

The passing, in early July, of Esther Singleton, writer and authority on music, literature and art, took from the world a brilliant figure in letters and took from her friends one of those rare spirits who are a constant uplift.

Miss Singleton realized as few do the necessity for close relationship between the arts . . .

Like her teacher, Sidney Lanier, and like that great stylist, Newman, Miss Singleton coupled her love of music and literature. The enthusiasm that she felt as a young girl for the wizardry of Seidl's Wagner fired her accounts of it. Her whimsical imagination shows best through the pages of the *Shakesperian Fantasias*, fourth dimensional studies of the comedies, in which the author, as the twentieth century meets Shakespeare's characters on their own ground and carries her readers through the plays in intimate and delightful fashion.

* * * * *

Appendices

Col. Bernard R. Ward
"Miss Esther Singleton"
Shakespeare Pictorial, September 1930, p. 16.

I regret to have to announce the death on the 2nd July at Stonington, Connecticut, of one of our most distinguished members, Miss Esther Singleton, author, editor, music and art critic, whose latest book was reviewed in this column last March. Members of the Fellowship will be interested to read the following sentences from a letter she wrote me from New York on the 6th May last year: 'I have just completed my *Shakespearian Fantasias*. This is the best work that I have ever done, and the most original . . . In two of the stories I have put in a de Vere touch, which is my way of acknowledging our glorious Edward de Vere." Shakespeare and Wagner were Miss Singleton's two great interests. One of our members characterised her latest book as a poetical Alice in Wonderland, and I know no better title for this little master-piece.

* * * * *

"The Oxford-Shakespeare Book that Charmed Mr. Folger:
Esther Singleton's *Shakespeareian Fantasias*"
Shakespeare Fellowship Quarterly, Vol. VII/1 (Jan. 1946):
14.

One of the first American authors to read and grasp the full significance of J. Thomas Looney's identification of Edward de Vere as the long-sought "Shakespeare" was the late Esther Singleton.

A discerning admirer of the Poet from early youth, many of Miss Singleton's books reflect her familiarity with the

Appendices

plays and poems, and her clairvoyant feeling for their atmosphere and characterizations. Her *Shakespeare Garden*, a truly captivating study of the plants, herbs and flowers that add life and perfume to so many of his scenes, has become the unique classic of its kind, inspiring the creation of many "Shakespeare Gardens," wherever it has been read.

Under the influence of *"Shakespeare" Identified* Miss Singleton published in 1929 another volume which she called *Shakespearian Fantasias: Adventures in the Fourth Dimension*. It consists of eleven stories, founded upon the leading characters of Shakespeare's best known comedies, with the merry mad-cap Earl of Oxford introduced as the Berowne of *Love's Labour's Lost*, the melancholy Jaques of *As You Like It* and the Benedick of *Much Ado About Nothing*. There is a sparkle and a diverting charm about these tales that make them as welcome as a spring morning.

Mr. Henry Clay Folger of the Folger Shakespeare Library found them so much to his taste that he purchased twenty or more copies of the book to present to his friends. He was also negotiating with Miss Singleton for the purchase of the original manuscript of *Shakespearian Fantasias* at the time of his death. By a sad coincidence, Miss Singleton herself passed away only two weeks later. Her heirs later presented the manuscript to the Folger Library in her memory.

The book was never adequately publicized owing to its author's sudden demise, and all unsold copies were finally shipped to Miss Singleton's sister, Mrs. FitzRoy Carrington, in England. There they were held in storage for many years, the advent of the war among other conditions, preventing their distribution.

Recently, however, The Fellowship has secured a consignment of the *Shakespeareian Fantasias* which they

Appendices

now offer for sale at $2.75 per copy, postpaid.

Consisting of 270 pages, and printed by the Plimpton Press, the volume is bound in strikingly designed covers of daffodil yellow, with black and gold decorations—altogether an example of artistic book-making rarely seen today. Orders may be placed with The Secretary, The Shakespeare Fellowship, 17 East 48th Street, New York 17, N.Y.

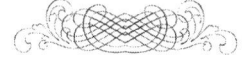

Made in the USA
San Bernardino, CA
14 April 2020